THE 39 CUPCAKES

MOVIE CLUB MYSTERIES, BOOK 4

ZARA KEANE

D1453090

BEAVERSTONE PRESS LLC

THE 39 CUPCAKES
(Movie Club Mysteries, Book 4)

Clues. Chaos. Cupcakes.

Ex-cop-turned-P.I. Maggie Doyle is stuck chaperoning a group of bratty summer camp kids to an archaeological dig on Whisper Island. After a day of fart jokes, fidget spinners, and fist fights, Maggie's regretting volunteering—and then one of her feral charges discovers a skeleton.

At first it looks like a cold case, but the situation takes a sinister turn when a member of the excavation team winds up dead. Maggie is determined to get to the bottom of the mystery before more bodies stack up. With her police officer boyfriend on vacation, his nitwitted fellow officer is what passes for law and order on the island. Now if only she can dodge the bumbling Sergeant O'Shea…

Join my mailing list and get news, giveaways, and a FREE Movie Club Mystery story!
http://zarakeane.com/newsletter2

NOTE ON GAELIC TERMS

Certain Gaelic terms appear in this book. I have tried to use them sparingly and in contexts that should make their meaning clear to international readers. However, a couple of words require clarification.

The official name for the Irish police force is *An Garda Síochána* ("the Guardian of the Peace"). Police are *Gardaí* (plural) and *Garda* (singular). Irish police are commonly referred to as "the guards".

The official rank of a police officer such as Sergeant Reynolds is Garda Sergeant Reynolds. As the Irish frequently shorten this to Sergeant, I've chosen to use this version for all but the initial introduction to the character.

The official name for the Whisper Island police station would be Whisper Island Garda Station, but Maggie, being American, rarely thinks of it as such.

The Irish police do not, as a rule, carry firearms. Permission to carry a gun is reserved to detectives and specialist units, such as the Emergency Response Unit. The police on Whisper Island would not have been issued with firearms.

Although this book follows American spelling conventions, I've chosen to use the common Irish spelling for proper names such as Carraig Harbour and the Whisper Island Medical Centre. An exception is the Movie Theater Café, which was named by Maggie's American mother.

1

After two hours of fights, fidget spinners, and fart jokes, I was ready to hurl myself at an OB-GYN and beg to have my tubes tied. Against my better judgment, I'd answered my cousin Julie's plea to chaperone thirty summer camp kids on an educational tour of Whisper Island. So far, the only educational part had been me learning Gaelic swear words.

I staggered down the aisle of the rocking bus and pulled two eight-year-old boys apart. "For the last time, that's enough," I snarled. "And don't even think of having a go at me, Tommy Greer, because I'll kick your butt."

The fair-haired boy jutted his chin belligerently. "Adults can't beat up kids, and you're supposed to be looking after us today."

"That's right," interjected Derrick, his dark-haired opponent. "You've gotta be *nice* to us."

"I'd rather you be nice to *each other*. Now get back in your seats, and stay there."

The boys grumbled but obeyed. Tommy Greer shot me a stinker of a look and stuck his tongue out at me. I resisted the urge to flip him the bird.

Muttering under my breath about the perils of being obliged to behave like an adult, I returned to my seat at the back of the bus. When I reclaimed my place, Lenny Logan, my friend and sometimes assistant for my private investigation business, offered me his hip flask. "Want some? You look like you need it."

"I'm pretty sure we're not supposed to drink your grandfather's poteen while we're playing chaperone."

He grinned. "It's not poteen. Right, Günter?"

My cousin's boyfriend held up an identical hip flask. "No alcohol, Maggie. But you'll like it."

Günter was a tall, blond German. His relationship with Julie was in its infancy, but I had high hopes for them.

I reached for Lenny's flask, unscrewed the top, and took a cautious sniff. And inhaled the scent of strong, black coffee. "Man, if I weren't already spoken for, I'd kiss you guys." I took a long drink and let the rich brew work its magic on my mood.

"We filled up at the Movie Theater Café before the bus left," Günter supplied. "Julie roped me into helping out at the summer camp's theater practice last week, so I knew what we were facing."

I raised an eyebrow. "Dude, you must be in love. I

can't imagine subjecting myself to this crowd for the second time."

Günter laughed and took a swig from his flask.

"Even if Julie hadn't called Tommy by his full name, I'd have guessed he was Paul and Melanie Greer's kid." I shook my head. "Looks, behavior—they all fit. Can you imagine dealing with a kid like him in a classroom every day? Julie deserves danger pay."

"Were we this obnoxious when we were eight or nine?" Lenny tugged on his scraggly goatee. "No, don't answer that. We probably were."

I took another drink from the flask and returned it to my friend. "Cool flasks. Where did you guys get them?"

"A gift from my brother," Günter said. "They're perfect for keeping coffee hot and water cold."

"That's the first time I've heard you mention your family. I was beginning to think you'd arrived on the shores of Whisper Island with no past."

"Günter, Man of Mystery," Lenny added.

Günter laughed, but was quick to divert our attention from his past by pointing out the window. "Look. We're almost there."

"There" was an archaeological site that a group affiliated with Trinity College was excavating. I was vague on the specifics of what they were working on. As some members of the team were renting cottages in my complex for the duration of the dig, Julie had badgered me to wrangle a tour for her summer camp kids. Ellen Taylor, the team's assistant leader, had kindly agreed. Due to a distinct lack of clients at Movie Reel Investigations, my recently launched private investigation business, I let my cousin rope me into acting as chaperone today.

The bus rattled up the hill toward the site and shuddered to a halt before a wooden fence. Julie stood up from her seat at the front of the bus and held her megaphone to her mouth. "Listen up, everyone. I want you to be on your best behavior—"

Tommy Greer let out a loud fart, reducing his fellow campers to fits of giggles.

"—*and* I want you to stick to your assigned groups. Like at the caves this morning, the five chaperones will each be responsible for six kids. Everyone in a red cap is with me. Green is with Mr. Tate." Julie indicated the handsome gym teacher who was sitting beside her. "Mr. Hauptmann will be in charge of the blue group, and Mr. Logan will have purple."

"Lucky me," muttered Lenny. "That means I'm stuck with Princess Puke again."

"It was travel sickness," I whispered, convincing neither of us. "I'm sure Fiona is fine after taking anti-nausea medicine."

"And last but not least," Julie shouted through the megaphone, "yellow is with my cousin, Ms. Doyle."

I gave an unenthusiastic thumbs-up at the scowling group of yellow-capped kids I was destined to hang out with for the next few hours. As the group included Tommy Greer, the son of my obnoxious former boyfriend and his equally odious wife, I doubted I'd have fun.

"I also want to remind you of what I said when we got on the bus this morning," my cousin continued. "Taking photographs at the caves was fine, but cameras—including phones with cameras—are not allowed at the excavation site. The team has an official photographer, and she's promised to take a few photos of us together."

Günter took a final swig from his hip flask and got to his feet. "Contemplating the fun before us, I regret not taking up Lenny's offer to spike this with poteen."

I laughed. "You and me both."

I followed Günter and Lenny down the aisle. The kids disembarked and gathered beside the bus in their color-coordinated groups.

Oisin Tate, the elementary school's gym teacher, cast me a sympathetic look when I trudged over to the yellow group. "Chin up, Maggie. It's only for another few hours."

"Easy for you to say. You've scored the best-behaved kids."

It was true. All the kids kitted out in green T-shirts and caps were quiet and obedient and didn't ask to go to the restroom twenty million times. I eyed Oisin with suspicion. If I were a betting woman, I'd say he'd persuaded his father, the school principal and the director of the Smuggler's Cove Bandits, to assign the easiest kids to him.

I shifted my focus to my group and swallowed a

sigh. Alfie Ahearn was mooning his yellow-capped comrades, while his partner in crime, Tommy Greer, took photos with his digital camera. A kid named Joey Dillon pummeled another boy. During this morning's visit to the caves, Joey had disgraced himself by carving his initials onto a stalagmite, and cussing when I'd told him to stop.

I marched up to the boys and pulled them apart. "Cut that out. If you behave like wild animals, you won't be allowed onto the excavation site. And as for you—" I turned to Tommy Greer, "—I'm deleting those photos and confiscating your camera for the rest of the trip. You heard what Ms. O'Brien said: no cameras are allowed at the excavation site."

Once I'd dealt with the butt photos and stashed Tommy's camera in my backpack, I addressed the group. "I want you all to be on your best behavior. Getting the chance to see archaeologists at work is a treat most kids never get."

A dark-haired girl with thick glasses and an indecipherable name tag rolled her eyes. "*Puh-lease*. It's not like we want to be here."

"Yeah," Alfie piped up. "Who wants to look at broken bits of pottery, anyway? It's *boring*."

I bit back a sharp retort and forced myself to count to ten before responding. "Okay, here's the deal. This day trip is supposed to end with an ice cream sundae at my aunt's café. If you don't behave, none of you is getting one."

Tommy sneered. "I'll just get one at home. We have a restaurant at the hotel, remember?"

"Once I finish telling your parents what a brat you've been today, I doubt you'll be seeing ice cream this side of next week."

That shut him up. Six sullen faces stared up at me from beneath the brims of their yellow baseball caps. The pudgy girl with the thick glasses and the unpronounceable name broke the silence. "So if we're going to look at holes in the ground, what are we supposed to be looking *at*?"

"Well, uh, Kao-im-ee—" I stumbled over the name written on the girl's name tag. From the kids' raucous laughter, I'd gotten it wrong.

"C-A-O-I-M-H-E spells Qweeva."

Of course it did. Made total sense…if you'd imbibed a hip flask filled with Lenny's grandfather's moonshine. "Wait a sec…I thought Gaelic 'B-H' was pronounced like a 'V.'"

The children regarded me with disdain.

"So's 'M-H,'" Oisin Tate supplied. "Sometimes, and depending on the dialect."

"Well, that's totally straightforward," I said, deadpan.

Oisin regarded me smugly. "Time for you to sign up for Julie's and my beginners Irish class."

He had a point. During my almost seven months in Ireland, I'd learned how to pronounce a few Gaelic words and place names, but people's names still tripped me up. And while I could get by just fine with English, learning a bit of the old lingo wouldn't hurt.

"Okay, *Qweeva*, to get back to your question. I'm no expert. I understand the site dates to the Middle Ages, and the excavation team will be able to give us more specifics."

As if on cue, Ellen Taylor, the team's assistant leader and the person I'd asked to arrange this visit, strode down the hill to meet us. Her ash-blond hair was dragged back from her forehead in a severe bun, and she wore no makeup. Even in her muddy work clothes, she was a striking-looking woman. She peeled off a glove and held out a hand to me. "Hi, Maggie."

"Hey, Ellen." The woman had a firm handshake. "Thanks so much for letting us visit the site."

Her smile was brief but genuine. "We're always happy to encourage children to take an interest in the past."

Tommy Greer snorted. "Booo-ring."

I glared at the kid. "Remember what I said about ice cream?"

The boy regarded me with a sullen expression, but shut up.

After I'd introduced Ellen to the other summer camp chaperones, the archaeologist led us up the hill to where she and her team had divided the excavation site into various plots, each roughly fifteen feet square.

Ellen's boss, Professor Dean Frobisher, stood next to the open door of a shed filled with equipment. The professor was a grizzly-haired man in his fifties who bore the weather-beaten look of a guy who'd spent most of his life outdoors. Brow furrowed in concentration, he was pouring over a map and barely acknowledged our arrival. Beside him stood the man who'd rented the cottage two doors down from mine, a tall and handsome fifty-something guy named Richard Carstairs. If George Clooney had had a beard and a messy ponytail, the archaeologist could have been his mirror image. Richard and I were on first-name terms. He nodded to me and smiled before returning his attention to the chart.

A petite brown-haired girl in her mid-twenties hurried over to join Ellen. I squinted at the newcomer. I was pretty sure she was among the new residents of Shamrock Cottages, which meant she must be an important team member. All the student helpers had been given rooms at Mamie Byrne's B&B in Smuggler's Cove.

Ellen, who'd volunteered to take on the role of tour guide, cleared her throat. "Hello, everyone. I'm Dr. Ellen Taylor, and this is my assistant, the soon-to-be Dr. Susie O'Malley."

The brown-haired girl blushed and gave us a tentative wave.

"We're part of a team of archaeologists and trainee archaeologists from Trinity College, Dublin. We're excavating this site with the cooperation of the Whisper Island Historical Society, and a few of their members have volunteered to help on the dig."

Ellen indicated one of the cordoned-off plots

where a man and a woman I recognized from my aunt's café were hard at work. They were under the supervision of a young archaeologist named Ben, a hipster type who was sharing a cottage with Richard Carstairs. From Ellen's tone when she mentioned the Historical Society volunteers, I picked up the vibe that she wasn't thrilled at the prospect of working alongside amateurs.

"The entire team and I wish a warm welcome to all the Smuggler's Cove Bandits," she continued. "We don't have pirate loot to show you today, but what archaeologists do is a little like digging for treasure. Sometimes, our treasures are broken pieces that only we get excited about. A single shard of pottery can offer clues as to how our ancestors lived. Other times, we uncover genuine treasure in the form of jewelry, chalices, and other valuables."

Joey Dillon yawned loudly, triggering a wave of giggles.

Julie shushed the children and turned to Ellen. "What are you hoping to find on this excavation?"

The woman's face lit up. "As some of you might know, a team of archaeologists excavated the remains of a monastic settlement on Whisper Island in 2000. They were able to date the founding of the settlement to the early seventh century, with additions having been constructed onto the main building up to the late ninth century. During that excavation, several objects of Viking origin were discovered. We know the Vikings were active in raids all along the Irish coast during this period, but my team is working on the theory that they formed a settlement on Whisper Island."

"And you think that settlement was here?" Julie gestured to the neatly divided plots where archaeologists were sifting through dirt.

"Yes. The monastery was found up there." Ellen pointed to the top of the hill, where the rugged outline of grass-covered stones was visible. "We're hoping to find the remains of a Viking domestic settlement in this spot."

"Why do you think the settlement is here?" I asked.

Ellen's silent sidekick, the not-yet-Dr. Susie, developed a voice. "Five years ago, a farmer plowing the hill unearthed a piece of Viking earthenware that dates to the ninth century."

Oisin frowned. "Is that proof of a settlement? The Viking raiders must have brought utensils with them on their longships."

"True," Ellen conceded. "However, it's indicative that there *could* have been a settlement here, however briefly."

"So you're digging up the place, and you don't know if there's any point?" Caoimhe demanded. "Isn't that kind of stupid?"

Ellen's jaw tightened, but before she could respond, Susie jumped in. "Before archaeologists decide to dig, we do a lot of research. In the case of this site, we took aerial photographs and examined the landscape for telltale humps and bumps that indicate a settlement. Once we'd identified a possible settlement, we used magnetism and radar to back up our hunch."

"How do those work?" Caoimhe, despite herself, was showing interest.

Ellen picked up the mantle. "Magnetism involves bouncing magnetic rays into the ground and measuring the response. Stones have a different response to earth, for example, and may indicate the presence of a wall."

"And magnetism is great at identifying areas that have been affected by fire," Susie added. "It's ideal for finding hearths within an old house, or a cremation site."

"What about radar?" I asked. "I assume that works on a similar principle as magnetism. What can it show that magnetism can't?"

"It's not so much about showing stuff that magnetism can't find, but about backing up the evidence magnetism has shown us. Bouncing radar waves into the ground is an excellent way to discover buried walls, for example." Ellen addressed the group at large. "As you can tell, deciding where to dig is educated guesswork. Technology and experience can give us a good idea that we're on the right track. Unfortunately, the only way to be sure is to excavate a site."

"You mean dig it up?" Tommy Greer asked. "Can we help?"

Ellen beamed. "Yes, you can—with supervision, of course. Each of your groups will be assigned to one of my team members, and he or she will talk you through what work they're doing on their unit. If you're very good, you'll even be allowed to have a go."

Ellen nodded to her assistant, and an unspoken message was conveyed. Susie smiled at my yellow-capped group. "You're with me."

While Ellen paired each of the other groups with an archaeologist, we trooped after Susie. She led us to a cordoned-off unit at the end of the site, where a guy of around Susie's age was sifting dirt into a container. He glanced up when we approached, and his face lit up at the sight of Susie. "Everyone, this is Alan Doherty. He's studying for his Ph.D. under Professor Frobisher. Have you found anything interesting, Alan?"

"Not so far, but the day is young." His smile, while briefly directed at all of us, was meant for Susie.

If the woman's blush and awkward stance were indications, she was aware of Alan's admiration and it made her uncomfortable. I couldn't tell if she was merely shy about a boyfriend openly admiring her in public, or if the guy gave her the creeps.

Over the next twenty minutes, Alan and Susie explained how they were digging in layers. Once they'd reached a ten-centimeter depth, they sifted the excavated dirt through a wire mesh, as we'd seen Alan doing when we'd arrived. Susie and Alan allowed each child in turn to have a go with a shovel, or to sift some of the dirt. Like all kids, they were thrilled to handle dirt, but the only treasure they found was an old twenty pence coin dating from the time before Ireland adopted the euro as its currency. I was so intent on watching the archaeologists work that I failed to notice Tommy slip away from our group. An incensed shout from further down the site alerted me that something was wrong. I whipped around and saw Tommy shoveling dirt in the unoccupied unit two down from Susie and Alan's.

"Tommy," I shouted. "Get out of there right this minute."

The boy ignored me and continued to destroy the neatly gridded unit. I ran over and climbed in, intending to haul him out. Before I could do so, the boy let out a cry and leaped back, almost knocking me over.

"What's wrong, Tommy?"

The boy blanched under his tan and pointed at the spot he'd been digging, his eyes wide with terror. "Look," he said in a choked voice. "It's totally gross."

I eyed him with suspicion and followed his gaze. And tasted bile. Nestled at the center of the hole Tommy had dug was the bony outline of a human skull.

2

My heart hammered in my chest. I'd seen dead bodies before—quite a few since I'd moved to Whisper Island—but this was my first encounter with a skeleton. I took a deep breath, and my detective's instincts overrode my repugnance. Ignoring Tommy's snot-filled wails, I kneeled to take a closer look at the skull.

A round hole in the temple indicated death by firearm. I shone my flashlight at the hole to take a closer look. Metal fragments were visible around the contours. Once the skull was fully exposed, I'd expect to see a more dramatic exit wound at the back, or a musket ball still in the skull. Definitely not a Viking, but whoever this was had been killed by musket fire. I cast my mind back to my amateur military historian father's lectures on historical weapons. If I recalled correctly, use of muskets died out during the nineteenth century. Relief spread through my body. At least we weren't dealing with a modern-day murder.

I cast the beam of the flashlight over the rest of the skull. When I peered into its gaping mouth, I sucked in a breath. Although one side was packed with dirt, Tommy's digging efforts had dislodged most of the debris from the left side of the mouth, revealing a feature that shouldn't be present in an old skeleton.

I leaped to my feet and reached for the box of utensils beside the pit. After I'd located a brush like the one Susie and Alan had shown us how to use, I hunkered down beside Tommy's ghoulish discovery. With deft, gentle strokes, I brushed the remaining dirt from the left side of the mouth. Once I was satisfied that it was as clean as it was going to get under the circumstances, I slipped my mini flashlight from my pocket and shone the light onto my handiwork. *Bingo.* My hunch had been correct, even if it made no sense. Why would a contemporary murder victim be killed with a historical weapon?

I stood and brushed dirt from the front of my jeans. A crowd had gathered at the edge of the pit, staring down at the skull with matching expressions of horror.

Professor Frobisher, the excavation team's leader, pushed his way to the front of the crowd. He was purple in the face and shot me a look of pure venom. "Are you insane?" he snarled. "You can't go around interfering with the units. This is an excavation site."

I stared him down. "This is also a crime scene."

"Don't be so quick to jump to conclusions, Ms. Doyle. For all you know, you and that infernal brat have just tampered with an important archaeological find."

"Susie just told our group that the Vikings favored cremations," Caoimhe said, jutting her chin. "That can't be a Viking."

Touché. I was beginning to warm to the kid.

The professor's complexion turned even redder. "It's unlikely to be a Viking. The skeleton could come from the monastic community, or come from a later period than what we're looking for. It's not uncommon to make finds from other periods during a dig. We know there was a religious community in this area up to the seventeenth century."

I rolled my eyes. "Dude, unless the monks had orthodontics, that skeleton's not been dead that long. Add in the hole through the forehead, and we can conclude that this is a case for the police."

Professor Frobisher recoiled, but Ellen Taylor pushed past him and climbed into the pit with me. She examined the skull, then looked up at her boss. "Maggie's right. The skull has a retainer on the inside of the bottom four teeth. And this does look like a musket ball hole."

The professor's face underwent a series of spasmodic movements. "Impossible," he spluttered. "Not on my dig."

Ellen exchanged an exasperated glance with me.

"I took a postgrad course in forensic archaeology. I might not practice as a forensic archaeologist, but I know what I'm looking at. We have to call the police."

Her boss ran a hand through his wild gray curls. "They'll close down the dig. All our work—"

I let Ellen deal with his tirade and hit speed dial. Before the call connected, Susie and Alan appeared at the edge of the pit. Susie's hand flew to her mouth. "Oh my goodness."

Alan swayed from side to side. "I think I'm going to be sick."

I wasn't in the mood to play nursemaid. "Puke somewhere else. Forensics will want as little touched as possible."

The grad student's eyes rolled back in his head, and he pitched forward into the pit. Ellen and I scrambled to break his fall and prevent him from landing on the skull, but the man's weight knocked us sideways. I landed with a thud and found myself face to skull with Tommy's gruesome discovery. In the tumult, I dropped my phone. Naturally, my sort-of boyfriend chose that moment to answer.

The green button glowed on my phone, but I hadn't hit speaker, and I couldn't hear what he was saying. Alan moaned on top of me. *For heaven's sake.* I pushed the Ph.D. student off me and rolled him as far from the skull as I could manage. Once I was sure he wouldn't suffocate in the dirt—I was nice that way—I groped for the phone.

"Hey, Liam," I said in a breathless voice.

"Uh, hi. What's going on, Maggie? What's with all the groaning in the background?"

"Some dude named Alan. He's fine. I shoved him into the recovery position."

Reynolds made a choking sound on the other end of the line that might have been laughter.

"Listen, I need you to get to the excavation site on St. Finbar's Hill as soon as you can. And call forensics."

"I thought you said Alan was fine," Reynolds said in confusion.

"Forensics isn't meant for him."

"Oh, no," he groaned. "Please tell me you're pulling my leg. Today is my last day of work before my daughter arrives."

"No joke, I'm afraid. The good news is that I didn't find a dead body."

"That's great," he said gloomily. "Now hit me with the bad."

"Tommy Greer dug up a skull on the excavation site."

"And you don't think it's from an ancient burial?"

"Not unless the skull's owner was a time traveler. He had a retainer on his lower teeth. And from the size and shape of the hole in his forehead, I doubt we're talking an accidental death."

Liam sighed. "Of course he was murdered. *You're* in the vicinity."

"A low blow. Before today, I hadn't found a dead body in six weeks. And this is *just* a head."

In the background, Alan let out a yowl. With eyes filled with terror, he held up a skeletal hand and threw it in my direction. It landed in my lap. *Seriously, this day…*

"Well," I conceded, "we have a head *and* a hand."

"That's…not reassuring," Liam said dryly. "Okay, give me thirty minutes, and I'll be with you. I have no idea how long it'll take forensics to get to Whisper Island. I'll call them right away."

After I'd disconnected, I returned my phone to my pocket and climbed out of the pit. Alan had been hauled back to the surface by members of the excavation team and was sitting, white-faced, with his head in his hands. Ellen sat beside him, equally pale but otherwise composed.

"Are the police on their way?" The question was directed at me by Clodagh Burke, a volunteer from the Whisper Island Historical Society. It had taken me a while to put a name to her face, but I now recognized her as the owner of a craft store in Smuggler's Cove.

"Yes. Sergeant Reynolds is on his way."

Richard Carstairs, the George Clooney lookalike who was staying at Shamrock Cottages, ambled over to the pit. "I thought Liam was on his holidays. I had a drink with him on my deck last night."

"He's on duty until tomorrow," I said. "He'll be here soon."

"How long is 'soon?'" Oisin demanded, folding

his beefy arms across his muscular chest. "We need to get the kids home."

"We're not going anywhere until Sergeant Reynolds arrives," Julie said firmly. "I'll phone your father and tell him to inform the parents that we'll be late."

"Wow, Maggie." Lenny bounced over to my side, a delighted expression on his bony face. "Remind me to stick close to you. Exciting stuff always goes down when you're around."

Günter cast me a sympathetic look. "I think Maggie would prefer to live a less exciting life."

"Very true." I picked up a movement from the side of my eye. Tommy Greer had snuck to the far side of the pit and was snapping pictures of the skull. "Hey," I yelled. "That's the camera I confiscated from you earlier. Did you take that out of my backpack?"

The boy shrugged. "It belongs to me."

I put my hands on my hips. "If you're capable of misbehaving, you've recovered fast from the trauma of finding a skull."

The boy squinted at me from beneath the brim of his yellow baseball cap. "I was grossed out at first. Now that I've had time to get used to the idea, it's actually kinda cool."

A few of the kids sniggered.

I sighed. "Cool or not, no more photos, Tommy, or I'll take the camera off you again. The excavation team specifically requested that we honor their no-photos policy, and your antics have caused enough chaos for one day."

"Okay," he grumbled, "but this has been the most interesting thing to happen all day."

"'Interesting' isn't the word I'd have chosen for discovering a skull," I said dryly, "but whatever."

An approaching siren floated on the breeze.

"That'll be the sarge." Lenny bounced on the spot with excitement. "He's going to be delighted you've found another corpse."

"Skeleton," I corrected. "And Tommy and Alan found the skull and the hand. I just happened to be nearby."

A minute later, a squad car bumped over the rocky terrain and parked beside the entrance to the excavation site. Reynolds leaped out of the driver's side and sprinted up the hill. A sizzle of awareness coursed through my body. He was tall and muscular with close-cropped dark blond hair. His face was saved from classical good looks by a nose that had been broken more than once. To me, Reynolds was perfection, although I hated admitting how strongly I felt about him, even to myself.

When he reached the excavation site, our eyes met for a brief moment, and his teasing half smile turned the sizzle of awareness into a jolt of desire. Thank goodness he was the one to come out to the site. Apart from my attraction to him, Sergeant Reynolds was an excellent police officer. I trusted him not to screw up this investigation.

He dragged his gaze away from me and addressed the crowd. "I'm Sergeant Liam Reynolds of Whisper Island Garda Station." He nodded at the excavation team. "I know some of you from Shamrock Cottages."

Professor Frobisher broke away from the throng of children, chaperones, and excavation team members, and shook Reynolds's hand. "Thanks for coming, Liam. I hope it's a mistake and we're dealing with a skeleton that's hundreds of years old."

Reynolds's jaw tightened. "I hope so, too, but Maggie's rarely wrong about these matters."

"I know amalgam fillings when I see them," Ellen Taylor interjected, "and the retainer is obviously modern."

Reynolds turned his attention on her. "How certain are you?"

"I have a qualification in forensic archaeology, although I ultimately chose to focus on regular excavations." Ellen gave a wry smile. "Despite what we see on TV, there's not much call for working forensic archaeologists, however interesting a field it is to research."

"There's a catch," I added. "I didn't want to hit you with it while we were on the phone."

He turned to me, and his wry smile turned my knees to jelly. "Of course there's a catch. No murder investigation involving Maggie Doyle can be straightforward."

Professor Frobisher stared at me, aghast. "Does she often get involved with murders?"

"Occasionally," I said at the same time Reynolds answered, "Regularly."

Reynolds looked at me. "You mentioned a catch. What is it?"

"I'm pretty sure the head wound was caused by a musket ball. It's the right shape, and there are metal fragments embedded around the edges of the wound."

The police officer's eyebrows shot up. "Death by musket fire? Muskets were no longer in use by the time orthodontics was invented."

Ellen Taylor cleared her throat. "Actually, orthodontic treatments have been around for centuries. However, this type of retainer wasn't in use before the Seventies."

"To sum up," I said in a matter-of-fact tone, "we're dealing with a skull whose owner had modern orthodontic treatment, but who was probably killed by a weapon that fell out of popularity in the nineteenth century. Makes total sense, right?"

"Not much about this scenario makes sense." Reynolds looked up at the dark clouds. "I want to get a look at the skeleton in situ before it rains, and I'd like to speak to Tommy first. His dad should be here any minute. I called him on my way out here."

As if on cue, a sleek BMW pulled up beside the squad car. Paul Greer, Tommy's father and my first boyfriend, hopped out. He ignored all of us and made a beeline for his son. "Are you okay, Tommy?"

The boy, having been perfectly composed throughout his picture-taking frenzy, burst into tears and threw himself into his father's arms. If I were a nicer person, I'd have put his current histrionics down to him being a kid who'd just had a traumatic experience. As it was, I suspected Tommy was going to milk the situation for his own benefit.

Reynolds approached the Greers. "Thanks for coming out here, Paul. With your permission, I'd like to ask Tommy a few questions."

Paul straightened. "Of course. You okay with that, Tommy?"

The boy blew his nose and nodded. "There's not much to tell. I was bored during the tour and checked out one of the other pits."

"What made you choose that particular pit?" Reynolds asked. "Did you spot something in there that interested you?"

Tommy shook his head. "No one was digging in it, so I thought I'd have a go. I'd only just started when my spade struck…it." The boy shuddered and turned a ghastly shade of white, making me feel bad for judging him. "But," he said, recovering himself, "it was pretty awesome. All the kids at school will be green with envy when I tell them I found a real-life skull."

More like a real dead skull, but whatever.

"Thanks, Tommy. I might need to ask you more

questions later." Reynolds looked at Paul. "I'll give you a call to arrange another chat if it's necessary."

Paul's mouth was tight. "Okay. Can I take him home now?"

"Sure." Reynolds turned to Julie. "There's no need for you and the kids to stay. If I need to ask any of you questions, I'll be in touch."

Relief flooded Julie's face. "Thanks. We'll round them up now and get going."

The professor and Ellen led him to the edge of the pit. Before he climbed in, Reynolds sought me out. "You got up close and personal with the skull, Maggie. Want to take another look?"

I glanced back at Julie.

"Go on," my cousin said. "Call me later."

"Will do."

"How will you get home?" Lenny asked me over his shoulder. "Need a lift?"

"I'm not sure how I'll get back. I'll figure something out."

"If you're stuck, give me a call," he said. "My only plan tonight is to hang out with Granddad and watch old *Magnum, P.I.* episodes."

I suppressed a smile. "Thanks, Lenny. I will."

After my friend left to catch up with the rest of the Smuggler's Cove Bandits, I raced back to the pit. My heart soared at the opportunity to be included in the investigation, even if my contribution was to be peripheral. When I reached the edge of the pit, I took one of the pairs of disposable rubber gloves that

Reynolds was handing around and put them on before stepping down into the partially excavated unit. "Given that my hair and fingerprints are likely to be all over the place, I'm not sure how much good the gloves will do."

"Yours and countless others." Reynolds sighed. "To be realistic, it's unlikely that you or anyone here today had anything to do with the skeleton ending up in the ground. We have no idea how old it is, except to say that it predates the excavation."

"How long does it take for a body to…" I eyed the children still edging toward the pit and modified my language, "…become a skeleton?"

"That depends on many factors." Ellen Taylor hunkered down and examined the skull. "In this sort of soil, and at the depth the skull was found, I'd say it's been here at least ten years. Probably longer. Possibly a lot longer."

"Can't you be more specific?" Reynolds asked. "I'm going to need to wade through old missing persons reports. Having a rough idea of how far back I need to look would be good."

Dr. Taylor took another look at the skull and the hand Alan had unearthed. "Amalgam fillings have been in use for at least one hundred and fifty years, but these are too modern to be that old. Also, the condition of the teeth indicates excellent dental care, and probably orthodontic work at some point in his or her youth." She shook her head. "Without testing equipment, I can't be more specific, and I lack field experience for this sort of analysis. However, my gut tells me you should look at files that are between ten and twenty years old."

"Thanks, Dr. Taylor." Reynolds rubbed his stubbled jaw. He was usually clean-shaven on workdays, but he'd been putting in long hours getting all his paperwork done before his vacation. "I'll take a few photos. When forensics gets here, they'll take formal photographs. For the moment, we need to cover the site." Reynolds held up a palm and caught a drop of rain. "Preferably before it turns into a deluge."

"We're used to rain on digs," Professor Frobisher said. "We came prepared."

Within a few minutes, the professor, Richard, and Ben, the young archaeologist who shared a cottage with Richard, had erected a tarpaulin over the pit to shield it from the elements.

Professor Frobisher stood back and admired their handiwork. "That should do the trick."

"Thanks for your help," Reynolds said to the excavation's team leader. "I suggest that you and your team pack up and go home. I can't reopen the dig until the forensics team arrives, and it's looking like that won't be before tomorrow morning."

A muscle flexed in the professor's cheek. "We're on a tight schedule, Sergeant. A delay is inconvenient."

"Murder is also inconvenient," Reynolds responded mildly. "Like I said, you'll be informed when the site reopens."

The older man's nostrils flared. For a moment, I thought he'd argue the point. "Fair enough," he said eventually. "Let us know as soon as we can get back to work."

"I, or one of the other guys at the station, will keep you informed."

Muttering under his breath, Professor Frobisher stalked off to help his team pack.

3

I stared after the professor's retreating back. "He's not happy," I remarked.

"You can't blame him." Reynolds stretched his neck from side to side. "A dig like this is expensive to fund. He's not going to get back the days he loses to the police investigation."

"Can forensics really not get here until the morning?"

He grimaced and inclined his head. "They want their one and only forensic anthropologist to join them, and he's working a case in Donegal."

I pulled my raincoat out of my backpack and put it on. "What will you do with the site until then?"

"I'll post a police guard here overnight."

I raised an eyebrow. "I thought you were short-staffed until the new police officer arrives."

"We are." Liam's smile was tinged with irony. "The police guard will be me."

I stared at him. "Liam, you can't. You're supposed to collect Hannah from Shannon Airport tomorrow morning."

He rubbed the back of his neck. "I know. I'll hand over to O'Shea first thing and drive straight there."

"After no sleep?"

He shrugged. "It's not far."

"How many times have you heard a driver use that excuse after a traffic accident?" I demanded. "On no sleep, you're in no condition to drive. Why don't I collect you tomorrow and drive you to the airport? I'm not working at the café until the afternoon."

"That's very kind of you, Maggie, but I'll find a solution."

I burst out laughing. "Are you worried about traveling in my car?"

He grinned. "Your car is a wreck. I'm amazed it passed the NCT."

He wasn't entirely incorrect. My latest vehicle was Lenny's grandfather's castoff and had been abandoned in a shed until his grandsons had resurrected it for me a few weeks ago. Since moving to Whisper Island, I hadn't had much luck with cars. The Yaris was my third, and I hoped it would last me longer than its predecessors. "The car moves, and the brakes work. That's a win-win in my book."

"Your standards are not high," he said dryly.

"Seriously, I don't mind giving you a ride to the airport. What time does Hannah's flight land?"

Reynolds shifted uncomfortably. "Ten."

"I could pick you up in plenty of time. I'm going to meet her sooner or later, anyway."

A furtive expression crossed over his face. "About that…"

"Yeah?" I prompted.

"I haven't actually mentioned to her that I'm seeing someone."

This revelation shouldn't have hurt as much as it did. I swallowed past the sudden lump in my throat. "Oh."

"Yeah." He averted his gaze. "I wanted to talk to her about it, you know? Ease her into the idea of me having a girlfriend."

I found my voice. "Doesn't her mother have a partner?"

"Yes, and Hannah's aware he exists. So far, he's never met her."

I slow-blinked. "Wait a sec…how long has your ex been seeing this guy?"

"Eighteen months. Robyn wants to keep her relationship with him separate from her life with Hannah." Easy to do when her daughter was in boarding school during the week. Not so easy when Hannah would be living with Liam 24/7 for three weeks—and me next door.

"Surely your ex doesn't expect you to compartmentalize your life in the same way she does?"

"I don't think she expects that of me. All I'm saying is that her keeping her relationship separate from her life with Hannah means that Hannah hasn't yet had to deal with meeting one of her parent's partners."

"*Had to deal with…*" I winced. "That's a bit harsh."

"I didn't mean—" He stopped himself and sighed. "Look, the divorce was tough on Hannah, and this is her first visit to Whisper Island. I want to take things one step at a time."

His defensiveness knocked me off my guard. I'd expected him to comfort me, to reassure me that he just wanted to talk to his child first.

"I understand Hannah might not warm to the idea at first, but I won't have our relationship kept a dirty little secret. That's degrading to both of us."

"I have no intention of keeping it a secret, Maggie. It's just that we're pretty new, and…"

My heart twisted. "And you'd like to be more certain before you introduce me to your daughter." The words came out dully, along with the crashing realization that I'd taken Reynolds's feelings for me for granted. All these months, I'd assumed *I* was the one who had to decide if I was ready for a relationship with him after the breakup of my marriage. It had never occurred to me that he might be unsure about how to proceed with me.

The arrogance of my assumption chastened me. I was hardly Ms. Confidence when it came to the opposite sex, but Reynolds had made no secret of his attraction to me. Although I'd had the odd crisis of self-confidence, it had never crossed my mind that he might want to keep our relationship casual.

Reynolds closed the space between us and cupped my chin in his hands. "I am sure about us, Maggie. I didn't mean to hurt your feelings. I'd planned to talk to Hannah about our relationship tomorrow evening. I don't want to spring it on her at the airport. Please try to understand."

I sucked air into my lungs. "Okay. So where does this leave me?"

"I'll let you know what she says. If she's okay with me seeing you while she's here, fine. Otherwise, I'll make it up to you when she leaves."

My throat turned dry. This wasn't the response I'd expected. "Okay," I said hoarsely, even though it was anything but. I understood his determination to talk to his daughter before introducing her to me, but I resented the idea of an eight-year-old having the power to veto my interaction with her father for the next three weeks.

Reynolds ran his hands through my hair, distracting me from my self-pity fest. "Why don't you give Lenny a call? Or ask the excavation team if you can hitch a ride back to Shamrock Cottages?"

I swallowed past the lump in my throat. "You sure you don't want me to keep you company?"

He laughed. "In this rain? No. I'd feel happier if I knew you were at home, warm and dry."

"Okay," I said for the second time, and with an equal lack of conviction.

Reynolds bent to claim my mouth with his. Courtesy of the kiss, I forgot all about my woes and surrendered to the moment.

When he released me, I took a reluctant step back. "I'll catch up with Ellen Taylor. If she has room, I'm sure she'll let me ride with her."

His smile melted the last of my doubts, at least temporarily. "You do that. Get a good night's sleep, Maggie. I'll be in touch."

I plastered a sunny smile across my face. "Bye, Liam. Enjoy sentry duty."

Resisting the impulse to look back over my shoulder, I sprinted up the hill, leaving Reynolds behind me in the rain.

WHEN I PULLED up at the Movie Theater Café at ten to two the next afternoon, a crowd had gathered on the pavement. Everyone was staring across the road at the premises that had once housed Joan Sweetman's gallery. I followed their gaze. Two workmen were attaching a large wooden sign above the door. It was painted a garish pink with two large cupcakes framing the name.

"The Cupcake Café," I read out loud, coming to stand beside Jennifer Pearce, a lawyer with whom I'd interacted on previous investigations. Jennifer and I weren't exactly close—she was too uptight and closed to share confidences. However, we occasionally met for a coffee, and we'd developed a tentative friendship.

I liked her, in a weird kind of way, even though I wished she'd drop the ice queen act.

"Noreen won't be pleased to have a rival right across the street," murmured Jennifer.

"No, she won't."

Although business at the Movie Theater Café was brisk during the summer months, my aunt felt the pinch during the low season. A competitor, particularly one with as enticing a concept as The Cupcake Café, would be a popular addition to Smuggler's Cove's gastronomic offerings.

As though she'd read my thoughts, my aunt appeared in the doorway of her café. Her pursed lips and tight expression confirmed my suspicion that she wasn't taking the news of her new competition well.

"Hey, Noreen," I said, keeping it casual. "Quite a crowd out here."

My aunt snorted. "Dolly O'Brien is back in town. She always draws a crowd."

I raised an eyebrow. "Dolly? Philomena's sister-in-law?"

"The very one," Noreen said, folding her arms across her ample bosom. "Big boobs and big hair. She split up with that eejit of a husband of hers and decided to move back to Whisper Island." Her tone was snider than I'd ever heard her use when talking about another woman.

"Does Philomena know?" I asked, watching my aunt's expression closely.

"I don't know," Noreen said acidly. "She's coming down the street now. Let's ask her."

Julie's mother, Whisper Island's head librarian, walked briskly toward the crowd on the pavement, her arms full with a stack of books. Like mine had been, her attention was drawn to the action on the other side of the street. She blinked, as if startled, and caught sight of Noreen. The guilty expression that flitted across her face told me all I needed to know.

Jennifer cast me a wry look. "Isn't Philomena supposed to help out at the café this afternoon?"

I grimaced and nodded. "That's going to be a barrel of laughs."

In spite of their physical differences, Noreen and Philomena were close, but both had tempers when riled, and could be stubborn to a fault. Although I'd never seen them argue, I knew it would be epic when they did.

Noreen put her hands on her hips and addressed her sister. "Did you know about this?"

"Well…" Philomena darted a glance at the offending sign. "Sort of."

"What do you mean, 'sort of?' You either did, or you didn't."

Philomena looked at me for support. I held up my palms. "I'm staying out of this. You two will have to duke it out, and you might want to do it away from an avid audience."

Sure enough, the crowd had shifted its attention to the impending showdown.

"I'll text you later," Jennifer whispered. "Let's go out for a drink this week."

Inviting me to meet her for a drink as opposed to a quick coffee was a leap for Jennifer. I tried to keep my surprise under wraps and my tone casual. "Under the present circumstances, I'll need a night out."

With a parting wave to the lawyer, I ushered an indignant Noreen and a reluctant Philomena into the deserted café. Noreen stalked over to the drinks counter and poured herself a whiskey. I exchanged a look with Philomena. With the notable exception of St. Patrick's Day, I'd never seen either of my aunts consume alcohol this early in the day.

Philomena placed her books on a table and sat down. She sighed. "Okay, Dolly mentioned her café idea to me. I had no idea she was opening the place so soon."

"How long have you known about this?" Noreen demanded.

Philomena bit her lip. "Around two weeks."

"And you didn't think to give me a heads-up?"

"She asked me to keep the news under wraps until it was official." Philomena sounded defensive, and she fiddled with her rings, a sure sign that she felt uncomfortable.

Noreen jerked her thumb at The Cupcake Café's sign. "I'd say it's official now, wouldn't you?"

Her sister sighed. "I'm sorry I didn't get the chance to tell you before the sign went up, but there's nothing you could have done to stop her. Dolly has a right to set up a business in this town, and there's no law preventing that business from being another café."

"I'm your sister. You could have warned me. It would have saved me from being humiliated in front of all my customers."

Philomena blushed and her mouth hardened. "Dolly is John's sister and my sister-in-law. She told me in confidence. I don't break confidences."

"You've never even *liked* Dolly," Noreen replied with heat. "Why the sudden solicitude?"

"She's had a hard few years. She deserves a break."

Noreen rolled her eyes. "Don't we all? Sure, it's her own fault for marrying that fool in the first place. How could she not know what she was getting into?"

Curiosity overcame my resolution not to get involved in the fight. "I know you never liked Dolly's husband, but why, exactly, is he so unpopular?"

"He's had brushes with the law," Philomena said carefully.

Her sister snorted. "Seamus Murphy has a revolving door with the Irish prison system. He's been involved in all sorts of shenanigans over the years. He's currently doing a ten-year stretch, and that proved the last straw for Dolly."

"Ouch. Do they have any kids?"

"Two girls," Philomena said. "Both grown up with their own families."

"So the move here is a fresh start?"

Philomena nodded. "And I feel we should support her decision to start over."

I looked at Noreen. "Can't you give Dolly a chance? You know how hard it is to start a business."

My aunt put her hands on her hips and glared at me. "I also know how hard it is to keep one."

"Yes, but you have no idea if your core customers will be interested in cupcakes. For all you know, your regulars will be here every day."

Noreen's frown lines deepened. "What about the tourists? I need their trade to bolster my income in the lean months."

"Whisper Island is overrun with tourists." I aimed for an upbeat tone and failed. "I had to turn people away last Saturday because we were packed."

Noreen opened her mouth as if to argue the point, but closed it again. "Fine. All right. Let Dolly open ten cafés. If I have to sell the Movie Theater Café in a few months' time, I'll remind you of this conversation."

"Why do you always have to be so dramatic?" Philomena demanded. "The world doesn't revolve around you and your café."

Before Noreen could deliver another blistering response, the bell above the café door jangled, and an old lady I recognized from the knitting club stepped inside. She wore a frayed coat and a purse so old I feared it would fall apart any second. She looked around the café, her expression unsure. "I'm looking for Maggie."

I stepped forward. "Hi, Mrs. Dineen. How can I help you?"

The old woman's lips trembled. She clutched her worn purse to her skinny bosom. "I want to hire you to spy on my husband."

4

"Okay," I said slowly. "Do you want to take this upstairs? My office is private."

Mrs. Dineen slid a glance at my aunt. "Sure, there's no keeping a secret from these two."

"They're in the middle of a sisterly disagreement," I whispered. "You might feel more comfortable upstairs."

"We're considering tearing each other's hair out, actually," Noreen said, pouring herself another shot of whiskey. "You'd be doing us a favor if you stay for a cup of tea. You have no idea how much money I've invested in weaves over the past few years. I can't afford to lose any of it."

Philomena and I stared at her, slack-jawed. "You have weaves?" I squeaked.

My aunt downed her whiskey in one gulp. "So?

You don't think Philomena's platinum hair is natural, do you?"

"I was blond as a child," her sister retorted, on the defensive. "I'm only going back to my roots."

Noreen snorted. "You certainly have roots. The last time you were blond was when you were a baby."

"Well," Philomena pulled back her shoulders. "For all you know, we have Norse ancestry. Sure, aren't they looking for a Viking settlement up at that site where Maggie found another body?"

Mrs. Dineen took a step back, her eyes widening in alarm. "You found a body?"

"Well, more of a skeleton," I amended. "And it was Tommy Greer who found it."

"Oh, well he *would*," Mrs. Dineen said, recovering from the shock of my ever-increasing body count. "That child is a menace."

"I'm sorry," I said. "You've caught us all at a bad moment. Would you like a tea or coffee while we chat?"

"As long as the tea contains whatever your aunt is drinking, then yes."

Noreen switched on the kettle. "One fortified tea coming up. Go on upstairs, and I'll come up with a tray. You'll have the usual, Maggie?"

"The usual" constituted a double espresso and one of my aunt's signature berry scones. "Add a scone for Mrs. Dineen," I whispered. "I think she needs one."

I led my prospective client up to my makeshift

office in the old projection room of the movie theater. A sign on the door proclaimed we were entering the premises of Movie Reel Investigations. If Mrs. Dineen were to prove to be a paying client, she'd be the third I'd scored since I'd acquired my private investigator's license a few weeks ago.

I gestured to the comfortable leather armchair on the other side of my desk and slid onto my chair. A pen and notepad lay on the desk. I clicked the top of the pen and regarded Mrs. Dineen. "You said you want me to spy on your husband."

I let the statement hang in the air for a moment and observed her face. Her wrinkles deepened, and her thin lips pressed into an even thinner line. "Fionn, my husband, hasn't been himself lately."

In Ireland, this statement could mean any one of several possibilities, which included hitting the bottle, hitting the wife, or cheating.

"Right," I said, "would you care to elaborate?"

"He comes home smelling of perfume." Mrs. Dineen pressed her lips into a line so thin they became invisible. "I don't hold with cheap scents."

"I see. So you think your husband is unfaithful?"

"Such a crass term." She clutched her purse so tight her knuckles turned to ivory.

"If you want me to tail him, I need to know what I'm getting into."

The woman's nonexistent chin trembled. "I know he's cheating on me. We've been married for nearly fifty years. A woman can tell."

"Is this…the first time he's done this?"

"Yes. That's why I'm so sure. The late nights, the lying—"

The arrival of Noreen armed with a tray halted Mrs. Dineen's flow. The woman choked back a sob and located a tissue in her purse. My aunt deposited the tray on my desk and backed out of the room with a discretion I hadn't known she possessed.

While my prospective client dabbed at her eyes, I took my espresso and slid the tea across the desk to Mrs. Dineen. Judging by the smell, Noreen had been generous with the whiskey.

In addition to her famous berry scones, my aunt had included ramekins filled with strawberry jam and clotted cream respectively. I gestured to the basket. "Would you like a scone?"

The older woman shook her head. Her face crumpled, and her sobs resumed. I removed a box of tissues from my desk drawer and handed it to her. While she composed herself, my mouth watered at the tantalizing aroma from the basket, but I was reluctant to eat a scone if my client wasn't joining me. The last thing I wanted was for her to start giving me details while my fingers were covered in cream. In an attempt to drown my hunger pangs, I took a sip of coffee.

On the other side of my desk, Mrs. Dineen blew her nose, then reached into her battered purse. "I brought a recent photo of Fionn."

The photo she handed me showed a homely man

in his seventies, dressed in an off-white Aran sweater and neatly pressed pants of an indeterminate color.

"Do you have any idea who your husband might be seeing?" I phrased the question with care. She struck me as the sort of woman who'd like the idea of me not jumping to the conclusion that her husband was unfaithful, even if her suspicions had brought her to me in the first place.

"I do." Mrs. Dineen's nostrils flared. "That redhead from Janine's."

I slow-blinked. "The hair stylist at the salon down the street?"

"Yes." She spat the affirmation and picked up her teacup with a trembling hand.

I leaned back in my chair and stared at the photograph. I'd had my hair trimmed at Janine's a couple of times, and the only redhead I recalled was a perky twenty-one-year-old named Bethany. Unless Bethany moonlighted as a prostitute, I couldn't imagine her being involved with Fionn Dineen. However, experience had taught me to keep an open mind during an investigation. For all I knew, Bethany had a grandfather complex, and Fionn ticked all the boxes. "Why do you think your husband is meeting Bethany?"

"My neighbor saw her get into his car one night. I assume she's the reason he's taken to going out every Tuesday evening for the last six weeks." Her lips trembled. "He told me he was playing darts at Finnegan's Pub, but I checked. Darts is on Thursdays."

I scribbled this information on my notepad. "What time does he leave the house?"

"Nine o'clock sharp. And he's back at midnight on the dot." Her lips trembled. "Yesterday, he announced he was going out this Sunday evening, too. He never goes out on Sundays. I'm worried this means he's… getting serious about her."

"He might be meeting friends, Mrs. Dineen. Why don't you ask him?"

"I did, but he was cagey and refused to say where he was going or who he was going with." She blinked back tears and cleared her throat. "So will you take the job? I can pay you in advance."

"Are you sure you want to hire me? You have to be prepared to face whatever I uncover, even if it's not what you'd hoped to hear."

Mrs. Dineen straightened her spine. "Whatever's going on, I need to know. The uncertainty is driving me crazy."

"In that case, yes, I'll take the job."

Her shoulders sagged in relief. "Thank you, Maggie."

I explained my fee schedule, and we negotiated a down payment for a week's work. While Mrs. Dineen counted out the cash, I performed a rapid calculation. If I were frugal with my expenditures, I could afford to pay Lenny for a few hours to help me out. In truth, I didn't need his assistance for this particular case, but I'd promised him a few hours' work whenever I could swing it, and we both hoped I'd soon be in a position to hire him full-time.

After she'd slid the money across the desk, Mrs. Dineen stood, still clutching her purse tightly.

I leaped to my feet. "I'll show you out."

"No need." A wry smile touched her lips. "I used to work here as an usherette back in the days when this place was still a cinema. I can find my way around."

We shook hands, and my new client left. Alone in my office, I stared at the notes I'd made. There wasn't much to go on. I'd make a few subtle inquiries about Bethany and tail Fionn Dineen on his next nocturnal outing, which should occur tonight.

Speaking of which… I picked up my phone and called Lenny. He answered on the first ring. "Yo, Maggie. What's up?"

"Do you have plans for this evening?"

"Only reading the new episode of my favorite manga porn serial."

I shuddered. "Ugh. I don't even know what to do with that information." I dragged my thoughts away from animated adult comics, which I hadn't known existed until this conversation, and focused on Movie Reel Investigation's latest case. "If you can bear the thought of a night without your favorite form of adult entertainment, how would you like to tail an alleged adulterer?"

I filled him in on the basics.

"Epic," Lenny drawled when I'd concluded my

summary of the Dineen case. "I'll swing by the café when you finish work. I love stakeouts."

"This will be a *discreet* stakeout," I said, recalling Lenny's tendency to cause chaos.

"Hey," he drawled. "'Discreet' is my middle name."

I snorted with laughter. "You wouldn't know discretion if it hit you across the face. Okay, come over after you finish work, and we'll take my car."

"Awesome. I've stocked up on luminol, by the way. I thought it might come in handy."

"I'm kind of hoping we don't need to identify blood spatter on this investigation," I said dryly.

"I like to be prepared."

I smothered a laugh. "Okay, then. See you later."

After I'd disconnected, I cast another look over my notes but found my mind wandering back over the events of yesterday. Right about now, Reynolds would be arriving at Shamrock Cottages with his daughter. With Reynolds on vacation, Sergeant O'Shea would be in charge of the investigation. This thought filled me with gloom. The older police officer was lazy, incompetent, and content to cruise toward retirement by doing as little work as possible. With him at the helm, whoever the skeleton had been stood little chance of receiving justice. I wasn't prepared to sit back and do nothing. It was time to devise a game plan.

5

After my phone call with Lenny, I filled out a formal client card for Mrs. Dineen, and I made an appointment to get my hair trimmed at Janine's tomorrow morning. The girl who'd taken my call had been the stylist who'd cut my hair the last two times I'd visited the salon. She'd sounded hurt that I hadn't asked to book my appointment with her, and I felt a pang of guilt. However, getting my hair cut was the ideal opportunity for me to chat with Bethany. As a paying customer, she could hardly ignore me. And if I asked the right questions, I'd get a lot more information out of her than she'd realize.

The rest of my day was occupied by a sulking aunt (Noreen), a defensive aunt (Philomena), and a constant stream of customers who wanted to pump me for information about the skeleton. I had very little to tell them that they hadn't already heard on the Whisper Island grapevine.

I hadn't seen Reynolds since I'd hitched a ride back to Shamrock Cottages yesterday evening. I assumed he'd collected his daughter from the airport by now. Our last conversation had left me raw. My rational side accepted that it was natural for Reynolds to want to tread cautiously with Hannah, but my emotional side was bruised.

At least the prospect of tonight's stakeout infused me with enthusiasm. The instant Lenny rolled up in his garish purple VW van, I grabbed my jacket and backpack and waved goodbye to my warring aunts.

My friend rolled down his window when I knocked. "Hey, Maggie. Hop in."

"We should take my car. It's less…" I struggled for a diplomatic term, "…conspicuous."

Lenny looked appalled. "Your car is a wreck. I warned you the seats were busted when Granddad sold it to you."

"Yeah, but it's a dark wreck with no glow-in-the-dark lettering on the side. Let's face it, Lenny, your van isn't exactly subtle."

"My van rocks," he protested. "And the seats still have all their springs. Every time I travel in your car, my backside hurts. And as for the acceleration…"

I pointed to the still-bright sky. "We don't know how long our tailing mission will take. Chances are, it'll be dark before we're done. In your vehicle, we might as well put up a flashing neon sign to tell people we're on a stakeout."

"Oh, all right." Grumbling, Lenny climbed down from the driver's seat and slammed the door. He perked up at the sight of the paper bag I was carrying. "Are those Noreen's scones?"

"No. We sold out of the scones before noon. I brought some of her chocolate muffins, including the vegan ones you like."

His face lit up. "Awesome. We make a great team. Now, let's go tail an oldie who's getting it on with another woman."

"We don't know that Fionn Dineen is 'getting it on' with Bethany," I cautioned as I unlocked my car. "It's important to keep an open mind."

"I'm joking, Maggie. I can't see Bethany going near old Dineen."

This assessment tallied with my own. For Mrs. Dineen's sake, I hoped we were right.

Lenny and I got into the car, and I started the engine. Soon, we were cruising down Greer Street, the main thoroughfare in Smuggler's Cove, Whisper Island's only town.

"What can you tell me about Bethany?" I asked. "I only know her from the couple of times I went to the salon where she works."

"We're not exactly buds," Lenny said. "She went out with Mack for a while, and it didn't end well."

Mack, a fellow member of the Movie Club and Lenny's Unplugged Gamers club for board game enthusiasts, was a pharmacist whose knowledge had assisted me with previous investigations. He worked at his parents' pharmacy by day and hunted UFOs with Lenny at night. Okay, they went alien-hunting once every other week, but seriously?

I cast a curious glance in Lenny's direction before returning my attention to the road. "That's an unusual pairing. I can't see geeky Mack with perky Bethany."

My friend chuckled. "It's a more likely coupling than Bethany and Fionn Dineen."

"True. What happened to make Bethany's relationship with Mack go sour?"

"Ah, the usual. She's a fair few years younger than him. She can't be more than twenty-one or twenty-two. I guess she got bored and had a fling with a tourist. When Mack found out, he was livid and broke it off with her."

"How did Bethany react to being dumped? Or did she care?"

"Oh, she cared all right. You wouldn't know it to look at him, but Mack earns good money. Bethany liked the nice gifts and fancy restaurants. Thankfully, Mack had enough sense to see through her feeble excuses, and they haven't spoken since."

"Poor Mack. It sounds like he had a lucky escape."

"That's my take on the situation."

"If Bethany likes the good life, why has she stayed on Whisper Island?"

Lenny shrugged. "Habit, I suppose. She went to Galway to train at a salon for a while and came back to the island a couple of years ago. She's been at her aunt's salon ever since, apart from a couple of summers working abroad."

"Janine Finnegan is Bethany's aunt?"

"She's her mother's sister." Lenny leaned forward in his seat and pointed through the windshield window. "You need to take the second left. The Dineens' house is down that lane."

I flicked on my indicator and hung a left. "Where should I park?"

"Drive to the end of the lane and park behind the recycling bins. Hopefully, Dineen won't look this way when he comes out of his house. For once, I wish it didn't stay light in Ireland so late during the summer."

I obeyed Lenny's instructions and we waited in the car for five minutes until the gray-haired man I recognized from the photo Mrs. Dineen had given me walked down the path of one of the houses and got into a red sedan. He started the engine and turned left at the end of the lane.

Quick as a flash, I started the engine and followed him, keeping my pace slow until I'd turned left to follow Dineen down the main road. We drove to the crossroads next to the elementary school and followed the direction taken by the red sedan.

"Where's he going?" I asked Lenny twenty-five minutes later when we were still driving.

"My guess is Bethany's place. She lives in a house on her parents' farm."

"She has her own place on their land?" I asked in surprise. In comparison to their American equivalent, Irish farms tended to be small.

"The Conroy farm is one of the biggest on the island," Lenny said, "and Bethany's their only child. They dote on her."

"Where is their farm?"

"Not far from St. Finbar's Hill."

The mention of the place where the excavation site was located brought back the memory of the skull and the skeletal hand Alan had thrown into my lap. Despite the warm August weather, I shivered.

St. Finbar's Hill was in the extreme north of the island. By the time we saw the hill looming in front of us, sunset had been and gone, and it was already quite dark. Despite my determination not to look, my gaze was drawn to the hill and the neatly divided plots of land that constituted the excavation site. A light bobbed and weaved over the area of the dig.

My heart skipped a beat. On impulse, I slowed the car to a cruise. "Lenny, does the site still have a police guard?"

"Not as far as I know. I met the sarge and his kid this afternoon, and he said forensics finished their work yesterday. The archaeologists were back at the site a couple of hours later. Maybe they're making up for lost time."

"With the light from a lone flashlight?" I didn't buy it.

In the distance, the taillights from Fionn Dineen's car grew smaller. If I ditched him now, I'd have to wait until Sunday to tail him, and I could hardly charge Mrs. Dineen for work I hadn't done. I glanced back up the hill. The light moved from plot to plot. In an instant, I made my decision. I drove to the base of the hill and cut the engine.

"Uh, Maggie, what are you doing? Aren't we supposed to be tailing Dineen?"

"Change of plan," I said, opening my door. "I'm sorry, Lenny. I've got to see what's going on up there."

"Is this your detective's instinct talking?"

"I don't know. Female intuition, general gut instinct? Whatever it is, I feel strongly that I need to check out who's up at the dig."

He undid his seat belt. "Fair enough. I'll get out my flashlight."

"Take it with you, but don't put it on until I give you the go-ahead. We'll sneak up the hill and see who's there before we announce our presence."

"Because sneaking around on stakeouts has worked out well for us in the past," Lenny said dryly. "Remember the postman?"

This made me laugh. "On that occasion, you were drunk and loud. This time around, we're both sober."

"Righto." Lenny climbed out of the car, and I reached in the passenger side to grab the night-vision binoculars from the glove compartment.

I surveyed the terrain. "There's a nice clump of bushes we can hide behind right next to the dig."

Lenny bounced from foot to foot. "Maggie, before we—"

"Come on," I urged, already moving up the slope. My mind was fully occupied with getting up the hill without being seen. "We don't want them to disappear down the other side of the hill before we reach the site."

I'd love to say we snuck up the hill like pros, but it was more akin to a drunken scramble. My natural night vision had never been the best, and it was always worse in the dusky half darkness. By the time we reached the bushes near the excavation site, I'd acquired a scrape down my arm, and Lenny had bashed his knee on a rock.

We hunkered down near a gap in the bushes and took turns peering through the binoculars.

"Whoever's here isn't working on one of the units," I whispered. "They're looking for something."

"It's probably one of the students who left their wallet," Lenny muttered. "And we've lost our chance to tail Dineen until next week."

"I won't charge Mrs. Dineen for next week. That's only fair."

I took charge of the binoculars and zoomed in. The visitor to the excavation site was dressed in black, and their face was concealed by a dark hoodie. From this distance, it was hard to judge height accurately. I estimated the person to be at least five-foot-eight, possibly taller.

Beside me, Lenny shifted position several times.

"What's up?" I whispered. "Do you have ants in your pants?"

"No. I need to pee."

"You didn't think to say this before we climbed up the hill?"

"I tried, Maggie. You just took off."

I sighed. "Okay. Go back down and find a place to pee, preferably where the guy in the hoodie won't see you."

Lenny snuck down the hill with all the grace of a stampeding elephant. When a twig snapped, I winced. If Lenny and I were going to make our partnership official, we both needed to work on our covert surveillance skills.

I turned my attention back to the bobbing light. The person was moving toward the locked equipment shed where Professor Frobisher and Richard Carstairs had been talking on Monday. I strained my neck and zoomed in to get a closer look.

"Aaah!" An anguished roar sounded from the bottom of the hill.

I jerked around, still peering through my zoomed-in night-vision binoculars. "Oh, whoa. Just…no."

At the bottom of the hill, Lenny was performing a wild jig and clutching his man junk in his right hand.

I put my head in my hands and swallowed a groan. On the other side of the bushes, the cacophony had alerted the intruder to our presence. The bobbing light froze for a second, and then the person in the hoodie ran to the other side of the hill and disappeared from my line of vision.

Sighing, I switched on my flashlight and made my way down the hill. I'd almost reached Lenny when a deep male voice stopped me in my tracks.

"Maggie? What are you doing here?"

6

My heart leaped in my chest. I whirled around to find Reynolds staring at me, slack-jawed. "Liam?"

A little girl with a blond ponytail appeared at his side. "Dad, why is that man jumping around holding his—"

"Jeez, Lenny," I shouted. "Put it away. No one wants to see your junk."

"It hurts," he groaned. "It hurts so much."

Reynolds did a double take at the sight of my friend, who'd dropped to his knees and was rolling around in the grass, still clutching his man parts. "Please tell me he's not on something?"

"No. He's sober, I swear." At least, he was as far as I knew.

"Dare I ask what happened?" Reynolds's voice shook with laughter.

"Nettles," Lenny moaned from the grass. "I tripped while peeing and fell onto a patch of nettles."

"Ouch." Reynolds winced in sympathy. "What were you two doing out here in the first place?"

"A stakeout," Lenny gasped. "All in the line of duty."

"We were tailing a guy who might or might not be having an affair," I hedged.

Reynolds's mouth twitched. "How does this involve you hanging around the excavation site?"

"It doesn't. We were following the dude we'd been paid to track when I noticed a light up at the dig. It struck me as suspicious, so I slowed down to get a proper look."

"Why didn't you assume the excavation team was working late?"

"That occurred to me, but I dismissed the idea. The light I saw was from a single flashlight. I'm sure of that. If the excavation team wanted to put in extra hours to make up for the time lost on Monday and Tuesday, surely they'd use lighting similar to that used by forensics teams who have to work a crime scene in the dark."

Reynolds's gaze swept over the hill. "There's no light up at the site now. What happened to the person you saw?"

"He or she took off like a bat out of hell when Lenny started his caterwauling."

"I'm sorry, Maggie," my friend said. "I'm in *pain*."

"My mum puts aloe vera gel on nettle stings," the little girl interjected. "We have some in the car."

Reynolds looked blank. "We do?"

The girl nodded. "Sure. Mum put some in the first aid kit she insisted I give to you. When I handed it to you yesterday, you went, 'Uh-huh,' and shoved it in the glove compartment."

Reynolds scratched his jaw. "Oh. That sounds like something I'd do."

"Now would be a good time to make that kit reappear." Taking a deep breath to calm my nerves, I extended a hand to the girl. "I'm Maggie, by the way. I live next door to your father."

Reynolds started and turned his attention back to us. "Sorry, ladies. In my distraction over Lenny's predicament, I forgot my manners. Maggie, this is my daughter, Hannah. Hannah, this is Maggie."

Hannah's handshake was surprisingly firm for one so young. "Dad says we can go to your café one day and eat ice cream sundaes."

"It's my aunt's café, actually, but we'd love to have you stop by."

In the background, Lenny groaned. "If you can find that aloe vera gel, now would be a very good time to do so."

Reynolds opened the door of his car and reached into the glove compartment. He located the gel and tossed it to Lenny. "Use all you need," he said dryly. "No need to give it back."

"Thanks, man. I appreciate it."

We turned our backs while Lenny tended to his wounds.

"Why are you here?" I asked Reynolds. "Were you just passing?"

His smile was wry. "Not exactly. Timms called me from the station to say a passerby had reported people acting furtively on St. Finbar's Hill. In light of the recent discovery, Timms thought we should check it out. I assumed it was kids looking for more skeletons. I didn't expect to find you and Lenny sneaking around in the dark."

"Someone was up at the excavation site. I'm sure of it."

"Yeah—probably a kid who ran off when Lenny started howling."

"I guess it could have been a teenager," I said doubtfully. "If it was, why were they alone? Isn't digging for skeletons the sort of thing one does with a group of friends?"

"Having had no experience in that particular pastime, I can't say. It never occurred to me to dig up dead people in my youth."

I frowned. "Unless it was a dare, and his or her friends were waiting on the other side of the hill where I couldn't see them?"

Reynolds eyed me steadily. "You don't sound convinced."

"I'm not. I'm rolling with your theory that kids decided to dig around the excavation site in the hope of finding more bones."

He stretched his neck and sighed. "I can tell from your tone that you don't think much of my hypothesis."

"Why would teenagers be interested in the storage shed?" I demanded. "There's nothing in there to excite them."

"Maybe they wanted to break in and steal old bits of pottery," Hannah supplied. "They're bound to have cool finds in there."

"And some expensive equipment." Reynolds returned his attention to the hill. "I'll go up and take a look."

"I'll come with you."

I moved to follow him, but he held up a palm. "Would you mind staying with Hannah? If someone is sneaking around up there, I'd rather not leave her down here alone."

I raised an eyebrow. "Lenny and his aloe vera'd privates aren't considered sufficient protection?"

"Frankly, I wouldn't leave Lenny in charge of my cat, never mind my child."

"I heard that," Lenny yelled from his position behind my car. "I'll have you know I babysat my sister's baby when she visited last weekend, and everyone survived."

"Is that the same time you duct-taped a diaper on the poor kid?" I asked, struggling not to laugh at the memory of that panicked phone call.

"Hey, the sticky bits on the side didn't work," my

friend protested. "I had to take action before it fell off."

Reynolds got a flashlight and night-vision binoculars out of his glove compartment. "It's getting cold. Why don't you wait with Hannah in the car? You too, Lenny, once you've treated your wounds."

My friend staggered over to us. "Sure you don't want backup, Sarge?"

"I'm good, thanks. You just…" Reynolds waved his hands around, clearly struggling not to laugh, "… rest yourself."

My friend opened the back door of my car and collapsed face-first onto the seat. "I'm just gonna have a rest, Maggie. This getting-stung-on-the-balls business takes it out of you."

I chuckled. "I'll take your word for it, Lenny."

Through the dark, I sensed Reynolds observing me, a wry smile on his face. "I won't be long," he said. "Thanks for watching Hannah."

And then he was gone.

I looked at Hannah and forced a smile. "How do you like Whisper Island so far?"

"It's a dump." The kid folded her arms across her chest and smirked. "That wasn't the answer you were expecting, was it?"

"I—" For a moment, words failed me. I looked desperately in the direction of my car. A guttural groan from Lenny assured me he'd be no help. "Maybe you just need time to settle in."

"And maybe I just need to persuade Dad to move back to England."

Despite her rudeness, I felt bad for the kid. It couldn't be easy only seeing her father a few times a year. "I don't think that's going to happen, sweetie."

"Why?" Her lip curled. "Do you think he'll stay here for you?"

I slow-blinked, and my stomach flipped. I'd expected meeting Hannah to be awkward, but I wasn't prepared for the girl's level of animosity. "Did your dad tell you we're dating?"

"Yeah. He said it like it was some kind of treat for me to meet his girlfriend. Well, it's not. I came here to spend time with Dad, not with you."

"Hannah," I said in a gentle voice, "I'm not trying to steal your dad away from you. His relationship with me has nothing to do with how he feels about you."

She rolled her eyes. "Well, duh. I know *that*."

I sighed in exasperation. "Then what's your problem? He and your mom split up ages ago."

"Two years, four months, and one week ago exactly," Hannah shot back. "And it doesn't have to be permanent."

I squeezed my eyes shut. I sucked at dealing with kids, especially ones having an emotional moment. "They're divorced. That's as permanent as it gets."

"They can always get remarried." Although the girl's tone was defensive, a note of uncertainty had crept in.

I took a deep breath. "How do you feel about your mom dating?"

"She's my *mum*, not my mom." The kid pouted. "She's not seeing anyone at the moment."

I blinked. "I thought—"

"They broke up." Hannah's voice held a note of triumph. "Two weeks ago. Dad doesn't know yet. I want to make it a surprise."

I opened my mouth to tell her that it would make no difference, but I bit my tongue. Who was I to crush the kid's fantasy? And I'd been dating Reynolds for all of five minutes. How did I know he wouldn't leap at the chance of reconciliation with his ex?

In the chill of the settling darkness, Hannah shivered.

I opened the passenger door of Liam's car. "Why don't you wait in here? It'll be warmer."

For a moment, I thought she'd argue. Instead, she shrugged, got in, and slammed the door behind her.

Okay, then. Feeling as low as a slug, I went over to my car to check on Lenny. He was upright now, and tucking into the bag of Noreen's muffins. I slid into the back beside him. "How are you feeling?"

"A bit better," he said between mouthfuls of muffin. "How'd you get on with the mini diva?"

"Not well. She was polite when Liam was around, and then…" I rolled my eyes.

"And then she gave you some serious shade, right?"

"For a total dork, and a lousy babysitter, you can read kids well."

Lenny stuffed more muffin into his mouth. "It's a talent. So let me guess. You've been cast in the role of the evil girlfriend?"

"Apparently. This in spite of the fact that I haven't gotten past first base with her dad."

Lenny laughed. "And you accuse me of over-sharing?"

"Well, it's true. Ours is a fledgling relationship, in every sense of the word. I don't feel sure enough of Liam's feelings to know if he'd seriously consider getting back with his ex." I looked through the window. Hannah had the lights on in the car and wore earbuds. "I'd better make sure she's okay."

"She'll be fine. She's probably just sulking. You should persuade Liam to pawn her off on Julie and her summer camp kids for a day. You and Liam deserve to spend at least a day of his holidays together."

I shook my head. "That's not how it works, Lenny. Hannah's his daughter, and he hardly ever gets to see her. They deserve the time together."

"Suit yourself. Hannah might have fun with the other kids."

"Maybe she would, but she's here to be with her dad." I patted my friend on the arm. "I'll be back in a sec."

I climbed out of the car and walked toward Reynolds's BMW. He'd bought it just before Hannah's arrival, not wanting to risk her mother's wrath by transporting her around Whisper Island on his Harley. I guessed a borrowed squad car would be no less acceptable. I hadn't met his ex, but I'd formed a picture of her in my mind as Jennifer Pearce on steroids: an uptight lawyer who buried her emotions under layers of legal smarts.

The movement of a flashlight from the hillside heralded Reynolds's return. "Find anything unusual?" I asked when he reached me.

He shook his head. "Nothing and no one. The shed's locked up, nice and tight. When I shone my light through the window, everything looked neat and tidy."

"I didn't imagine the person up there."

"I didn't say you did. Just to be on the safe side, I called Professor Frobisher. He said one of the students might have forgotten something up there and gone back to retrieve it."

I shook my head. "Whoever it was, they looked at each plot and then focused on the shed."

"Why do you find that sinister, Maggie? I realize that yesterday's discovery must have freaked you. All the same, the excavation team and their shed are unlikely to have a connection to the skeleton you and Tommy found."

I pulled my jacket close. He had a point, but the nagging feeling wouldn't go away. "Do you have any idea who the dead person is?"

Reynolds shook his head. "Officially, I was off the

case as of this morning. Unofficially, I spoke to the head of the forensics team. They asked a forensic anthropologist to look at the bones recovered. She estimates that the skeleton had been in the ground for fifteen to twenty years. He was a male aged between thirty-five and forty-five, and he most likely died due to a wound inflicted by musket fire. Forensics found a musket ball in the soil near the skull, and there was no exit wound, so the most likely scenario is that the ball lodged in the victim's brain."

I shivered and wrapped my arms around me. "Are the police looking at missing persons reports?"

"Yeah. Sergeant O'Shea checked missing persons reports from the area, and requested dental records for a few potential candidates."

"Thanks for keeping me in the loop, Liam. I appreciate it. Why are you here, anyway? In the chaos of Lenny's close encounter with nettles, I forgot to ask why Timms didn't send Sergeant O'Shea."

Reynolds grimaced. "Timms tried to contact him, and he wasn't reachable."

"Dude's probably playing golf," I said with disdain.

"Probably not in the dark," he said with amusement, "but the Whisper Island Golf Club is hosting a tournament. I believe Sergeant O'Shea is competing."

I gave a disgusted snort. "So Timms called you instead, even though you're officially on vacation?"

"Yeah, but it's no biggie. Hannah and I were at a

loose end." He chuckled. "I'll be grateful when the new police officer starts next week."

"Any idea who you're getting?"

Reynolds shook his head. "I have no input on that, I'm afraid. All I know is that it's someone the district superintendent recommends."

In the car, his daughter had the lights on and appeared to be reading a comic. In reality, she snuck me a dirty look every time I glanced in her direction.

"So," I said in as casual a tone as I could muster, "how's it going with Hannah?"

Reynolds's smile spoke volumes about his love for his only child. "It's wonderful having her here. I'm enjoying showing her around Whisper Island. She loves it as much as I do."

Not according to what Hannah had told me, but I refrained from arguing the point with her besotted parent. "That's great."

"Listen, Maggie, I'm sorry for what I said yesterday. I didn't mean to hurt your feelings." He closed the space between us. "When Hannah goes back to her mother, I'll make it up to you. In the meantime, I'd like to invite you to join Hannah and me for a picnic this weekend. I've hired a yacht to go exploring, and I thought you might like to come with us for a day trip."

"Have you run this idea by Hannah yet?"

"She knows I'm planning to take her to Dolphin Island. I haven't mentioned you joining us yet. I'll talk

to her tomorrow. She took the news about our relationship pretty well."

Um…okay.

Reynolds looked over in the direction of his car.
"We'd better get going. I need to get Hannah to bed."

I stepped aside, putting space between us. "I hope
you guys have a good night."

A wicked smile sprang to his lips. He maneuvered
me out of Hannah's line of vision and brushed his
mouth against mine. "Good night, Maggie.
Sleep well."

Leaving me shivering in the darkness, and not just
from the chill night air, Reynolds got back into his car
and started the engine. As he drove away, Hannah
glanced out her window and stuck her tongue out
at me.

Oh, boy. Dealing with that little madam was going
to be tougher than I'd anticipated.

7

When I arrived at Janine's for my hair appointment, Bethany was on a smoke break. Janine led me to a chair between Jennifer Pearce and Clodagh Burke, one of the Whisper Island Historical Society volunteers who'd been at the excavation site on Monday.

Jennifer peeked out from under a pile of highlight foils. "Hi, Maggie. Sorry I haven't texted you about that drink yet. I meant to last night, but Nick surprised me with restaurant reservations."

"That's sweet. I guess he's busy this time of year."

"Tell me about it." Jennifer's laugh rang hollow. "Even the most casual member of the Yacht Club wants to go sailing in the summer, so the sailing classes are all full. And then there's his boat rental business. Nick's been working so much that we haven't had a chance to nail down the details for our wedding."

"When's that happening?" I'd known Nick and Jennifer were engaged, but this was the first time she'd mentioned the wedding.

"I'd love an autumn ceremony." She pulled a face. "Nick says it's too short notice to arrange it for this year, so maybe next spring."

The acerbic note in Jennifer's voice gave me the impression that this hadn't been the first time Nick had wriggled out of setting a date.

Clodagh glanced up from her magazine, a wistful expression on her thin face. "I married in spring. As long as you're okay with the possibility of rain, it's a lovely time of year for a wedding."

I grinned. "Isn't rain always a possibility in Ireland?"

"Very true," Jennifer said. "How's business for you, Clodagh? I see a lot of tourists going in and out of your shop."

The older woman perked up. "We're having a great summer. I could barely find time to get away to get my hair done."

Janine bustled over and gave each of us a glass of iced lemonade. "A treat on such a hot day. Bethany had to take a phone call, Maggie. She'll be with you in a moment. Sorry for the delay."

"No problem." I picked up my lemonade glass and took a sip of the delicious cool liquid. "Between your store and volunteering up at the dig, you must not have a lot of free time."

The woman's smile froze for an instant. Had I hit

a nerve? And then I remembered the skeleton. If even I'd been horrified by the discovery, it must have been traumatic for someone unused to discovering dead bodies on a regular basis.

The craft shop owner rallied quickly. "Tom hired extra help for the summer months. That's the only way I could have volunteered to work up at the dig."

"I'm sorry the experience was marred by Monday's discovery."

A muscle in Clodagh's cheek flexed. "It wasn't what I'd expected, that's for sure."

"Do the police have any idea who the skeleton is?" Jennifer asked.

"Not yet." I was reluctant to share the details I'd learned from Reynolds in case they weren't public knowledge. "As far as I know, they're still going through missing persons files and dental records to try to find a match."

Jennifer shuddered. "How awful. Hopefully, whoever it was has been buried for hundreds of years."

I exchanged a glance with Clodagh. In an unspoken agreement, we didn't disabuse Jennifer of this notion.

Our conversation about the skeleton was cut short by the appearance of Bethany. The girl was red-faced and breathless. "Sorry to keep you waiting."

"No worries. I hope everything's okay."

"Yes, it's fine. I had to run a quick errand." Bethany tugged at the hem of her ultra-short dress and smoothed her straight red hair before turning her attention to my wild mane. "Janine said you wanted a trim."

"That's right. Just the ends will do."

"Okay. I'll move you over to a sink, and we'll get started."

While Bethany massaged shampoo into my hair, I brought the conversation around to dating. She gushed about her boyfriend, a guy she'd met while working abroad last summer. "His dad has pots of money, and he helped to wrangle him a job on the island until the end of the month. Getting to see him regularly is awesome."

"What are your plans once he leaves? Will you do the long-distance thing again?"

She beamed. "No need. He's got a job lined up at the university in Galway."

"Galway isn't too far away," I said in an encouraging tone.

"Exactly. I'm starting a cosmetology course in September, and I've found a house share just outside Galway."

"Even better." I let Bethany chatter about her boyfriend and then casually mentioned a fictitious friend who was dating a much older man.

The girl screwed up her nose. "I can't imagine going out with a guy old enough to be my dad. I don't know what we'd talk about."

If Bethany rejected the idea of dating a man old enough to be her father, I was pretty sure she'd be horrified at the notion of a relationship with a guy of Fionn Dineen's age. So if she wasn't romantically involved with Dineen, why was she meeting him late at night? Although I'd learned not to leap to assumptions, my gut told me Bethany wasn't moonlighting as an escort for extra cash.

The subject of her rich and handsome beau dominated the conversation through my wash, trim, and blow-dry, making me regret I'd ever brought up the topic of dating. Boy, the girl knew how to talk.

By the time I'd paid for my cut, I was convinced of two facts. One, Bethany was as mercenary as Lenny had implied, making the strapped-for-cash Fionn Dineen an unlikely target for her affections. And two, the girl was far too superficial to want to date a man old enough to be her grandfather. Unfortunately, my conversation with Bethany hadn't revealed why Mrs. Dineen was adamant the girl had been meeting her husband on the sly.

AFTER I'D FINISHED at the salon, I walked down the main street of Smuggler's Cove. I'd told Noreen I'd help out at the café for a few hours, but one look at The Cupcake Café told me my help mightn't be necessary.

A petite blonde dressed in a formfitting summer dress stood outside The Cupcake Café, greeting passersby with a friendly smile and a tray of delectable-looking samples of her wares. Her eyes widened with recognition when she saw me. "Maggie?"

Her smile was infectious. "Hey, Dolly. It's been a while."

"Years." She looked me up and down. "The last time I saw you was at Julie's sixteenth birthday party."

"Wow. You have a good memory."

Dolly laughed. "It was easy, actually. I haven't been back to Whisper Island many times since I left."

"You're back now, I see." I gestured to the sign. "Great concept, by the way. I can't think of anywhere in Smuggler's Cove that serves designer cupcakes."

The woman beamed and enveloped me in a hug, almost upsetting her tray of samples. "Thanks, Maggie. I can't tell you how excited I am to open my own place. Would you like to try a piece of cupcake? I have samples for pistachio cream, lemon delight, strawberry crumble, and maple pecan."

I took a mini maple pecan cupcake and popped it into my mouth. "Oh, boy. This is good."

Dolly's cherry-painted lips stretched into a wide smile. "I'm delighted you liked it. Here's a coupon for a free cupcake."

I took the pink card and slipped it into my pocket. "Thanks. I'll call by soon."

After I said goodbye to Dolly, I dodged the crowd of people swarming around her free samples…and crashed straight into my childhood nemesis, Melanie

Greer. "Oh, excuse me," I said as the other woman righted her designer sunglasses.

Melanie looked slim and elegant in white chinos and a coral-colored blouse that emphasized her bronzed skin. Her dark hair was swept up in a high ponytail, and her flawless complexion was expertly made up. Although she'd given birth to four children, there didn't appear to be an ounce of saggy flesh on her perfectly toned body. As always when I encountered her, I experienced a pang of envy tinged with irritation.

Melanie gave me a quick once-over. Judging by her disdainful expression, she didn't approve of what she saw. "Hello, Maggie. I was on my way to your aunt's café."

Given how infrequently the woman had darkened the door of the Movie Theater Café since her mother's death, I raised my eyebrows. "For coffee, or…?"

"I was looking for you, actually. Tommy says you were his chaperone on Monday."

I grimaced. "If this is about the skeleton, I only took my eyes off him for a moment."

To my astonishment, Melanie laughed. "That's all it takes with that boy. He's dreadfully behaved. What he's not inclined to do is lose stuff he likes."

I blinked. "Did Tommy forget something on the bus?"

"I'm not sure *where* he left it. Tommy's digital camera is missing."

I cast my mind back to Monday afternoon. "I

confiscated it at one point, and Tommy retrieved it from my bag later. When I saw him taking photos of the skull, I told him to put it away. I don't know what happened to the camera after that."

Melanie frowned. "It's odd. He's a disaster at keeping track of the stuff he doesn't care about, but that camera is one of his prized possessions. He's devastated by its loss."

"Have you checked with the summer camp?"

"Yes. And the bus company. Neither has seen any sign of it."

"Sorry I can't help. I don't recall seeing Tommy's camera after I told him to put it away again."

Melanie sighed. "Hopefully, this will teach him a lesson about looking after his possessions."

I nodded in the direction of the Movie Theater Café. "I need to get to work."

"Yes, I suppose you do." A catlike smile curved Melanie's pink lips. "Not that Noreen will have much trade today with The Cupcake Café's grand opening." Just when I thought I'd actually had a civil exchange with Melanie, she had to go and remind me of why I'd never liked her.

"Goodbye, Melanie. I hope Tommy finds his camera." Without waiting for her response, I crossed the road and entered the Movie Theater Café.

One glance at Noreen's thunderous expression told me she'd seen me with Dolly. I sighed and slipped my purse under the counter.

"You were across the road." This statement was delivered in an accusatory tone that irked me no end.

"So? I don't know Dolly well, but she was always nice to me. Why would I shun her?"

"Don't you care that she's trying to put me out of business?"

I squeezed my eyes shut for a moment and took a deep breath. "Noreen, you'll have to snap out of it. If the customers see you with a grumpy face, they'll run over to Dolly's place, and your fears about losing business will become a self-fulfilling prophecy."

My aunt swept an arm around the empty café. "It's already happened. Everyone is across the road."

"It's The Cupcake Café's opening day. Of course people want to check out Dolly's free samples. I can't see your regular customers deserting the Movie Theater Café permanently."

Noreen's belligerence waned, replaced by a worried expression. "I'm sorry, Maggie. I know I'm not being reasonable."

"Well," I conceded, "you do have reason to worry. Dolly's wares are good, and she is opening a café directly across the street. My point is that there's nothing you can do about it, so the best course of action is to put on a brave face and come up with a business strategy to weather the inevitable customer drain. Like it or not, people will want to check out the new place. It is what it is."

"And I'm just supposed to roll over and take it?"

"No. We need to come up with a strategy to

prepare your business to survive the inevitable slump."

My aunt collapsed onto a chair. "What do you have in mind for this super business strategy you want me to conjure out of thin air?"

"I'm delighted you asked." I whipped my ever-present pen and notepad out of my purse. "You're the Movie Theater Café. Apart from the decor and the Movie Club, you don't work the theme enough."

"I do," my aunt said indignantly. "Sure, isn't the place decorated like an old movie theater?"

"Yes, but where's your movie-themed menu? Surely we can come up with a few ideas to jazz it up."

"People like my muffins and scones." My aunt sounded hurt. "No one's ever looked for fancy stuff in here."

"It doesn't need to be fancy. Come up with a muffin recipe and name it after an old movie. Make your ice cream sundaes appeal to fans of various movie franchises." My pen danced across the page, scribbling ideas faster than I could voice them. "What about hosting kids' parties? Make use of the movie theater to screen kids' favorites. Encourage the children to come in costume and offer them an appropriately themed menu."

I could see that I'd piqued her interest. "Wouldn't I have to close the café to do that? I don't like losing business."

"You could block off time on Saturday or Sunday afternoons," I said, warming to the topic. "Keep it flexible. If you have a booking, use the café to host the party. If not, keep to your regular opening times. We don't do much business late Saturday afternoon as it is. This is one way to fill that gap."

The next half hour flew by. Noreen and I hashed out ideas, eventually narrowing them down to three potential changes: a jazzed-up ice-cream menu, kids' parties, and themed movie weekends aimed at younger fans of popular movie franchises. By the time my phone buzzed with an incoming call, Noreen was in a more positive frame of mind and had a game plan.

I glanced at the display, and my heart leaped. "It's Reynolds."

Noreen patted me on the arm. "Go on. Take the call upstairs. It's not like we're overrun with customers at the moment."

"Thanks. I'll make it quick." I grabbed my phone from the counter and hit connect. "Hi, Liam," I said breathlessly as I ran up the stairs to my office.

"Hey." A pause. "I spoke with Hannah—"

I slumped into my desk chair. She'd have vetoed our weekend boat trip.

"—and she's fine with you joining us on Saturday."

I stared at the phone, a suspicion forming in my mind. What was the child up to? "Are you sure?"

He hesitated a fraction of a second too long before responding. "Oh, yeah. It'll be fine. She didn't object when I suggested you joining us."

"'Didn't object' isn't synonymous with 'embraced the idea with enthusiasm,'" I said dryly.

This made him chuckle. "The enthusiasm part was lacking. However, she didn't throw a fit. I consider that a win."

It was a baby step, but I'd take it. "What time would you like to leave on Saturday?"

"How does eight sound? Is that too early?"

"Eight sounds perfect. I'll take care of the picnic food if you stock up on beverages."

"Okay." He fell silent for a moment, and then said, "Listen, the boat trip wasn't the only reason I called you."

"Oh? Can I help you with something?" I sincerely hoped that 'something' didn't involve babysitting Hannah. I'd have to roll with the situation if it did.

"I'd like to hire Movie Reel Investigations."

I stared at the display, processing his words. "You want to hire me? What for?"

"You're going to think this sounds crazy."

"Whatever it is, it can't be any crazier than some of my previous cases," I said dryly, recalling the cold case investigation into a missing sheep. "Hit me with it."

"I want you to do some digging about that skeleton. I'm officially off the case, and I'm concerned Sergeant O'Shea will mess it up. I'll pay you privately. This won't be deducted from the station's budget, and it'll be strictly between us."

"And Lenny," I added. "He's my assistant."

"And Lenny," Reynolds conceded. "He's an eejit, but he knows how to keep his mouth shut."

I contemplated my previous run-ins with Sergeant O'Shea and shook my head. The older police officer's laziness and incompetence would be amusing if we weren't talking about a murder investigation. "Isn't the new police officer due to arrive this week?"

"O'Shea is still the senior officer at the station while I'm on my holidays. Even if he's working at a snail's pace, Sergeant O'Shea won't hand the case over to a newbie."

"I see your point," I said. "Is there no way you can intervene? Maybe contact the district superintendent?"

"Ah, Maggie, you know what police politics are like. I doubt it's any different in the U.S. Unless O'Shea does something outrageous and illegal, complaining about a fellow officer to the higher-ups is dangerous territory."

In spite of quitting his place on a prestigious London homicide team for sleepy Whisper Island, Reynolds was ambitious. He'd taken the job here for his daughter's sake, and Hannah wouldn't be a kid forever. Once she was older, Reynolds would want a more challenging position.

I switched the phone to my other ear. "It's a tough position to be in. I get that you don't want to watch O'Shea screw up, but maybe you need to let this one go. Spend time with your daughter. Enjoy your vacation."

"Maggie, I promised my ex I wouldn't work while Hannah is on Whisper Island, and I'll honor that deal. I *want* to hang out with my daughter."

"Why do I sense a 'but' coming?" I asked with a smile.

He chuckled. "*But* I'm not prepared to sit around and watch O'Shea screw up yet another investigation. He's already making mistakes."

My pulse increased in pace. "Did Reserve Garda Timms contact you?"

"Yeah." Liam sighed, and I could picture him running a hand through his close-cropped hair as he spoke. "And I called the forensic anthropologist on the down-low. There are a couple of points in this case that bother me even if they don't ruffle Sergeant O'Shea's feathers."

I reached for the notepad and pen I kept on my desk. "Care to elaborate?"

"First, all parts of the skeleton were recovered from the pit, bar one." His pause added dramatic tension to the announcement, although I knew it was unintentional. "The left femur is missing."

I frowned and cast my mind back to a long-ago anatomy class at the police academy. "That's the thighbone, right?"

"Correct. The forensics team searched the entire area, including neighboring pits. So far, no sign of the missing bone. O'Shea asked the excavation team to keep an eye out for it, but he doesn't seem too concerned."

I leaned back in my chair and fiddled with my pen. "What relevance can the thighbone have in the investigation into the person's death?"

"Maybe none. I don't know. The fact that the rest of the skeleton was found intact in the same burial location bothers me. Why was one bone missing?"

I didn't know and I wasn't sure that its absence was as relevant as Reynolds seemed to think. "What's the other point that bothers you?"

"O'Shea is working on the assumption that the current excavation and everyone involved with it has nothing to do with a body that was buried fifteen to twenty years ago. Frankly, it's the same assumption I made at first."

I leaped on this point. "What made you change your mind?"

"It turns out that another excavation took place in the same area seventeen years ago."

My mind whirred. "That's right. Ellen Taylor mentioned an excavation that focused on the old monastic settlement."

"That's the one. And here's the part that bothers me: one of the team members on the current excavation also worked on that excavation."

The scent of a trail made my blood hum. "Who?"

"The guy currently living next door to me. Richard Carstairs."

8

L enny demolished a fourth raspberry muffin. "Run this by me again. Reynolds, a police officer, wants to hire *you* to investigate the skeleton."

It was eight o'clock on Wednesday evening, and I'd called an emergency meeting in my office with my sometimes partner to discuss the new case. "Reynolds is in an awkward position," I said. "He doesn't trust Sergeant O'Shea to do a thorough job, and their boss doesn't seem to care."

"I don't get it. Why can't Reynolds give O'Shea the boot and take charge?"

"His daughter is staying with him for the next three weeks. If his ex finds out he worked on a case during Hannah's visit, she'll freak, and that could upset the already precarious custody arrangement."

Lenny raised both eyebrows. "Why would she freak? She's gotta know he's a cop."

"Yes. And Liam's workaholic tendencies were a major factor in their split."

"So by hiring you—"

"Us," I corrected. "I need your help on this case."

"By hiring *us*, Reynolds thinks he can ensure whoever was buried on St. Finbar's Hill gets justice?"

"He knows he can't guarantee justice, with or without our assistance. As Sergeant O'Shea is no closer to identifying the guy, Reynolds can at least feel like he tried to do the right thing."

Lenny cleaned his fingers with a napkin and washed down the last bite of muffin with mineral water. "Do we have a plan of action?"

I gestured to the folders on my desk. "More like a mad jumble of notes that don't connect—yet. Reynolds compiled his own unofficial case file based on what he'd gathered before his vacation began, and on info gleaned from the forensics team. He emailed it to me, and I've printed copies for both of us."

I slid a copy of Reynolds's notes across the desk to Lenny. While my friend leafed through his copy, I stood and grabbed a marker and wrote "Known Facts" on one side of my whiteboard and drew a circle around it. "Let's put my new whiteboard to good use. Here's what we know for sure. The skeleton belongs to a male aged between thirty-five and forty-five. The body was buried fifteen to twenty years ago, and the cause of death was probably a musket ball to the temple."

"'Probably?'" Lenny raised his eyebrow. "That's vague."

"It's as precise as the forensic anthropologist and pathologist were prepared to be. The skull has a hole that's consistent with an entry wound. Without the organs, it's impossible to know if other shots were fired, and none of the other bones show signs of trauma."

"Any idea what gun was used?" Lenny frowned. "If 'gun' is the correct term. Muskets were in use for centuries, right?"

"That's correct. My dad is an enthusiastic amateur historian with a particular interest in weapons. I have nowhere near his level of expertise on the subject, but I know some." I thumbed through my copy of Reynolds's file and pointed to a photograph of a musket ball. "This was recovered from the pit by forensics and is undergoing analysis in their labs. Until we know what weapon it was fired from, we're looking at a wide field of historical firearms, but judging by the size and shape of the ball, my guess is one dating from the eighteenth century."

"So we're dealing with a man who was killed within the last twenty years using a weapon that's been obsolete for over a century." Lenny stared at the whiteboard, a thoughtful expression on his thin face. "Dude, you really know how to pick the interesting cases."

"I didn't *pick* the case. I guess you could say it picked me."

Lenny flipped through his copy of Reynolds's case file. "Are there any potential missing persons from around that time?"

"According to Reynolds, O'Shea's checked the database and narrowed the candidates down to a few possibilities. He's waiting on the dental records for cross analysis."

My friend perked up. "You don't know any of their names, do you? I could do an internet search."

I shook my head. "Unfortunately, no. Reynolds doesn't know, so therefore I don't, either. He's being kept up to date by Timms, and Timms's knowledge is limited to what O'Shea chooses to share with him." Which, from what I could ascertain from Reynolds's unofficial case file, wasn't much.

Lenny turned his attention back to the white-board. "Anything else we can add to the 'Known Facts' section?"

"Yeah." I flicked to another page in Reynolds's file. "Three items, all of which fall into the factually-correct-but-probably-irrelevant category. First, the skeleton is missing the left femur, or thighbone. This doesn't appear to faze O'Shea, but Reynolds doesn't like it."

My friend consulted the folder. "It says here that the rest of the skeleton is accounted for, and the missing femur wasn't found in either of the two neigh-boring excavation site units."

"Yes. That's the part that bothers Reynolds. He's

asked the excavation team to keep an eye out for it. So far, no luck."

"What's the second item you wanted to add?" Lenny prompted.

"Seventeen years ago, a team of archaeologists excavated the medieval monastic settlement that Ellen Taylor referred to during our tour on Monday. One archaeologist was present on both that dig and the current one: Richard Carstairs."

Lenny took a sip of water. "That might mean nothing. Ireland's not a big country. There can't be that many qualified archaeologists who specialize in a particular period."

"I know. It's probably just a coincidence. Ditto the missing femur."

"What's the third probably-nothing item?"

I swirled the coffee in my cup and furrowed my brow. "This is me stretching, but I'll toss it into the ring anyway. According to Melanie Greer, Tommy's camera is missing. Remember him taking photos of the skull and me freaking out because he was breaking the excavation site's no-photos rule?"

"Vaguely. There was a lot of freaking out happening after the skull put in an appearance."

"Melanie was insistent that Tommy took good care of that camera and wouldn't just lose it."

"One of the other kids could have stolen it," Lenny said. "None of them are exactly saint material."

"Yeah, but I don't think one of them took it. After

Tommy found the skeleton, the kids were pretty shaken, and Tommy didn't ride back to town with the others on the bus. He left early with his dad."

"Why would an adult want to steal a kid's digital camera? What could be on it that the forensics team's photographer didn't catch the following morning?"

"I don't know." I massaged my temples. "I said I was stretching. However, it's yet another coincidence, and those three irregularities are all we have to go on at the moment. At the very least, we should try to find out more information about the first excavation that took place on St. Finbar's Hill."

"You live near Carstairs," Lenny said. "You could find an excuse to talk to him about the first dig."

I nodded. "I intend to. I'll also pay a visit to the library and ask Philomena if I can take a look at the archives. There's got to be information about the excavation in old newspapers. If they put on an exhibition of some kind, there might be a record of that as well. While I'm there, I'll look up info on musket rifles, as that appears to be the most likely weapon used."

"What would you like me to do?" Lenny asked.

"It's a weird request. I'd like you to research femurs."

He frowned. "Anything in particular about them?"

I shook my head. "I have no idea if an internet search will shed any light on why a femur would be missing from an otherwise complete skeleton. It's probably a total waste of time, but the absent bone is one of the few pieces of information that doesn't make sense. For that reason alone, we should pursue it."

"Fair enough. If it's okay with you, I'll ask Mack about femurs. He took plenty of anatomy classes when he was studying pharmacy."

"Okay, you talk to Mack. Be vague on why you're asking about this. Reynolds doesn't want anyone to know he's hired us to take a look at the case, and you know what the rumor mill is like on Whisper Island."

"I'll be careful what I tell him, but you don't need to worry about Mack blabbing. He's annoyingly discreet." Lenny removed a couple of scene photos that had been taken by forensics and passed on to us as part of Reynolds's unofficial case file. "The pit looks a lot different from when we saw it."

I took a look at the photograph. In contrast to the barely visible skull and the lone loose hand that had been in evidence when I'd last been in the pit, the forensics team had neatly brushed away dirt to reveal the bony outline of the skeleton. I cast my gaze over the line of the skeleton, taking in the legs. The left leg must have been buried under the dirt where I'd rolled Alan into the recovery position. *Or not...* I re-angled the photograph and let my mind recreate the scene as I'd last seen it. No, I was wrong. The left leg would have been under the pile of dirt Tommy had created during his digging spree, and that mound of dirt was right next to the place where I'd rolled Alan.

"You're thinking, Maggie," Lenny said. "I can practically see your brain at work."

"It's at work, but I don't know how to interpret the information it's processing." I shook my head. "Man, I wish I'd thought to take a photo before Reynolds showed up, and to heck with the no-photos rule."

"A lot of us were hanging around, staring at Tommy's discovery. Maybe one of the others took a photo with their phone. It's worth asking around."

"Yeah. I'll do that. Speaking of Tommy," I said slowly, "I'm going to ask him about his missing camera. Maybe we can find it if we retrace his steps. He lost it at some point between taking those photographs and going home with his dad, and that couldn't have been longer than twenty minutes total. It can't have vanished without a trace."

"Tommy's a kid," Lenny said. "Maybe he broke the camera and was too scared to fess up to his parents."

"That's a possibility," I mused. "At any rate, it's worth talking to him. I don't know how those kid digital cameras function. Is there any way the photos he took would be saved in the cloud?"

"Not the ones he'd just taken that day," Lenny replied in a definite tone. "We stock that model at my parents' electronics shop, and I sold the camera to Paul Greer a couple of months ago. It comes equipped with a limited amount of built-in memory, so Paul asked me to put in a micro SD memory card to up the capacity. To back up the info on the memory card, the camera could be hooked up to a computer via a USB cable, or the SD card could be removed and inserted directly into a computer."

"In other words, there's no way to retrieve the data from the day the skeleton was found without finding Tommy's missing camera." I stared at my notes gloomily. "I guess it was too much to hope that the solution to the mystery would fall into our laps while talking."

Lenny laughed. "Unlikely. Maybe we'll have better luck with the others who were at the site that day. Tommy wasn't the only kid with a camera, and plenty of the adults must have had phones."

"We can ask and compile a list of everyone who could have photographed the pit between Tommy finding the skull and the forensics team's arrival the following morning." I checked my notepad and scribbled an action plan. "To summarize, I'll visit the library, talk to Carstairs, and go back to the excavation site to find out if anyone took photos or saw Tommy's camera lying around. And I'll try to talk to Tommy himself."

"And I'll research femurs and talk to Mack." Lenny typed a one-fingered note to himself on his phone. "Where are we on the Dineen case?"

I pulled a face. "Nowhere until Sunday. I called Mrs. Dineen and explained that something came up yesterday and we couldn't tail her husband. That means we'll have to make following him our priority this weekend."

"Did you speak to Bethany?"

"Yeah. Unfortunately, no startling revelations came out of that conversation." I gave him a brief rundown of my visit to the hair salon.

"The boyfriend with the rich father is definitely more Bethany's type," Lenny said after I'd finished. "Whatever she's doing with Dineen, I don't think they're romantically involved."

"Neither do I, but we can't wrap up the case until we know what they're up to."

"I've made a few discreet inquiries. No one knows of any connection between Bethany and Fionn Dineen. They're not related and don't appear to share any common interests."

"It's bizarre."

Lenny grinned. "No more bizarre than skeletons with missing thighbones."

"Very true. Do you want to meet tomorrow to discuss our progress? Kelly is helping Noreen at the café, and I have time all day to work on the skeleton case."

"Sure. I'll stop by around seven and help you set up for the Unplugged Gamers. We can use the time to fill each other in on what we've found out."

"Sounds like a plan."

My friend stood and stretched his gangly frame. "I'd better make tracks. I promised Granddad I'd show him how to work his new streaming service."

"Have fun and say hi to him for me."

After Lenny had left, I reviewed my plan for tomorrow. We didn't have a lot of info to work with, and we had to hope the couple of leads we had bore fruit. I leaned back in my chair and cast my eye around my office. It wasn't much, but it was mine. Within a few weeks of receiving my private investigator's license, I had paying clients, and both of my two current cases for Movie Reel Investigations were interesting. If my lawyer's latest email were to be believed, my divorce from Joe would be official before the end of the month. In short, my life was on a positive trajectory.

The only fly in the ointment was the awkward situation with Hannah. I squared my shoulders. I'd figure out a way to win her over. I hadn't a clue how, but I'd give it my best shot.

y alarm jolted me awake at six the next morning, and I took my dog out for a pre-breakfast run. In Bran's case, it was possibly him taking me out for a run rather than the opposite way around. The Border collie-Labrador mix had begun life as Noreen's dog, and he'd moved in with me back in March, ostensibly on a temporary basis. As my stay on Whisper Island had developed permanency, so, too, had Bran's position in my life.

In addition to the dog, I had two kittens, Sukey and Felix, and an older cat I'd taken in after her owner had been murdered. In spite of Mavis treating all of us with a regal indifference, I'd grown fond of her watchful presence over the few weeks of her residency.

When Bran and I returned to Shamrock Cottages after our run, the excavation team was preparing to leave for St. Finbar's Hill. The complex I lived in consisted of eight cottages. Reynolds and I lived in numbers seven and eight respectively. Numbers one and two were currently rented out on a one- or two-week basis by families holidaying on the island. The remaining four cottages had been leased for the excavation team's leading members. I cast an eye over the people loading cars.

Susie O'Malley, the shy doctoral candidate who worked as Ellen Taylor's assistant, shared a cottage with the excavation's photographer, a red-haired woman named Ruth Dede. As the most-senior members, Ellen Taylor and Professor Frobisher each had a cottage to themselves. Finally, Richard Carstairs shared with the professor's assistant, Ben, a hipster with a sculpted beard and a man bun. Ben occasionally came into the Movie Theater Café for a takeout coffee, but I'd never served him. I'd make sure to do so the next time he came by.

I jogged over to Richard's truck where he and Ben were loading gear into the trunk.

"Morning," I said cheerfully. "How are you guys doing today?"

Ben's nod was curt and too cool for school. In contrast, Richard treated me to the full force of his charm. "Hey there, gorgeous. You're up early."

Ugh. Slime city. "The dog wanted to bring me for a run, and I let him."

The man laughed, looking more like George Clooney than ever. "He strikes me as an energetic pup."

"He sure is."

Bran sniffed Ben, showing a marked preference for the younger archaeologist and turning his back on Richard. My dog was rarely wrong about people, and he obviously shared my instinctual dislike of the older guy.

Ben leaned down and gave Bran lavish attention. "I had a Labrador when I was a kid. His name was Sooty."

"No dog now?" I asked.

"Nah. I move around too much to keep a pet."

"Where were you before this dig?" I didn't much care where Ben had been, but I needed to segue neatly into asking Richard about his previous visit to Whisper Island. The younger archaeologist's mention of travel gave me an excellent opening.

"Egypt. That's my specialty. This dig's a departure for me, but I like a challenge."

"I'd love to visit Egypt someday. It must be fun to travel for work." I flashed Richard a smile. "Do you move around much?"

He nodded. "All part of the profession. I was on a dig in Brittany before this one."

"Travel for work sounds exotic. Do you get the opportunity to see much of your surroundings?"

Ben shrugged. "It depends. I saw quite a bit of Egypt. I was out there for three years, on and off."

"What about Whisper Island? Will you have a chance to tour around the area once the dig is over?"

"I'm not sure," Ben said. "I'd like to. I have fond memories of this part of Ireland."

Richard loaded another box of what looked like rock samples into his truck. "I won't be doing any sightseeing once we're done here. I have another job lined up in Wales."

"Oh, that's a shame. Whisper Island is a lovely place." I paused for a moment. "You've been here before, right, Richard? I know it was a long time ago, so I'm sure a lot has changed."

The older guy looked startled. "How do you mean?"

I kept my smile in place and my tone casual. "The dig on St. Finbar's Hill in 2000. I heard you were part of the team."

Under his tan, Richard Carstairs paled. His grip on the box tightened. "That was a long time ago."

I'd hit a nerve. Time to keep pressing. "It must be great to revisit the site of an old dig after so many years."

The man's Adam's apple bobbed. "I'm not overly sentimental about digs. I do my job and I leave." He looked at his watch pointedly. "We'd better get going. Professor Frobisher wants us to start at seven on the dot." Without another word, he swung himself into the driver's seat and gunned the engine.

Ben appeared to be startled by his coworker's sudden urge to leave, but he rolled with it. "Bye, Maggie. I might see you tomorrow at that film club your aunt organizes. She invited me the last time I picked up a coffee."

"I'll see you then. Enjoy your day." I waved goodbye as the man leaped into the truck seconds before Richard roared off.

Although Richard's violent reaction to my mention of the previous dig intrigued me, it didn't explain how his presence at both excavations was connected to the skeleton. I was left with the looming possibility that I was wasting my time, but my instincts told me I wasn't. Even if Richard had had nothing to do with the dead man in the pit, the mention of the 2000 excavation had rattled him. I needed to find out more about that excavation: who'd been on it, what had happened, and why the mere mention of it had scared him.

AFTER A SHOWER AND BREAKFAST, I drove to Smuggler's Cove and stopped by the library. Philomena was on desk duty, although her current occupation was reading a romance novel behind the counter. She was so engrossed in her book that she didn't appear to notice that her glasses had slid halfway down her nose.

"Maggie," she exclaimed when she saw me. "This is a pleasant surprise. Are you here for work or pleasure?"

"Work." Aware of the curious glances from a

group of older ladies who'd congregated at a table in the library's main hall, I dropped my voice to a whisper. "I'm interested in any information you can give me about the excavation on St. Finbar's Hill in 2000. Photographs, documents, a list of everyone who worked on the dig. Whatever you can find, I want it."

My aunt's fingers flew over the keyboard. "I have a printed report on the excavation that was compiled for research purposes. I also have a color brochure that was part of an exhibition put on in conjunction with the Whisper Island Historical Society."

"Those are both good," I said. "I'd also like to have a look at newspapers from the time. Any reference to the excavation and its team members is of interest."

"Okay," said my aunt. "I'll find you the report and the brochure while you peruse our newspaper archives. You can find back issues of the major national papers in our digital collection. Unfortunately, the digital archive for the *Whisper Island Gazette* only goes back five years. You'll need to go down to the basement and look through the paper editions."

I raised an eyebrow. "They're not even on microfiche?"

My aunt grimaced. "I'm afraid not. Ideally, we'd like to scan all the old editions within the next two years, but it's a question of resources. Neither I nor my staff has the time to take care of the project, so it depends on whether or not we receive funding to hire someone to do the work for us." Philomena slipped out from her cubicle and led me across the main hall of the library.

"How long was the team on Whisper Island in 2000?" I asked, keeping my voice to a whisper.

"According to metadata I pulled up just now, the excavation took place between May and August of 2000. If you go back a little before that, you should find all the references made to the dig."

Thank goodness Whisper Island's only resident newspaper was published on a weekly basis and not daily. As it was, I figured I'd need to wade through twenty-five or so of the 2000 editions of the *Gazette* to make sure I didn't miss any vital information pertaining to the excavation.

Philomena escorted me downstairs to the basement. It was a dark and windowless cavern with the stale, dry air of a room that housed countless books, newspapers, and other stacks of papers. After my aunt explained how to search through the print back issues of the *Gazette* in an efficient fashion, she left me to my work.

I spent the next three hours scouring newspaper pages and making copious notes every time I discovered a reference to the excavation. The 2000 dig had been a larger-scale affair than this summer's effort. In contrast to the current team's hesitation to commit themselves to saying there had been a Viking settlement on the hill, the earlier excavation had received large donations from various academic institutions in Ireland and abroad.

The team consisted of sixty paid members, most
of whom were the premier experts in their respective
fields. In addition, twenty volunteers also helped on
the dig. Courtesy of the report that Philomena had
dug out for me, I was able to discover the names of
most of the important team members. I scanned their
listings, but made few notes until I came to Richard's
bio. A surge of excitement built as I read the two
sentences devoted to my neighbor.

*Dr. Richard Carstairs is a Cambridge-trained expert on
Early Christian Ireland with extensive excavation
experience. In addition to his academic pursuits, Dr.
Carstairs is an enthusiastic member of Fragarach, a
reenactment group specializing in bringing medieval Irish
battles to life.*

The photo that accompanied the bio showed a
clean-shaven man in his late thirties with a shock of
black hair. Had I not seen his name next to the photograph, I'd have had to look twice to recognize
Richard without his beard and messy ponytail. For the
second time, I cast my eye over the list of names, but
Richard was the only common link to the two excavations.

I pushed my chair back and sighed. What had I
expected to find? A headline about a missing person
right next to the stories about the excavation? No, that
would be too easy. Besides, the first excavation had
taken place farther up the hill. There had been no

conveniently dug-up piece of earth into which to dump a body near what was now the current excavation site.

After I finished with the newspapers, I returned them and made my way back to the main floor.

My aunt glanced up from her book. "Did you have any luck?"

"Nothing concrete," I said. "Thanks for letting me take a look. I wanted to research eighteenth-century firearms as well, but I need to get going. I'll try to come back and do that tomorrow."

Philomena put a bookmark in her romance novel, and her face grew animated. "I can do that for you."

I frowned. "Are you sure? I don't mind returning tomorrow to take care of it."

My aunt waved a hand. "Sure, what else would I be doing? It's a quiet day here. What exactly are you looking for?"

"Where on Whisper Island I'd find a weapon that fires musket balls. My guess would be an eighteenth century flintlock like a Brown Bess."

Philomena scribbled a note to herself and clicked her pen with an air of satisfaction. "You're your father's daughter all right. Dermot always loved old weapons."

"Anything I know, I learned from Dad."

My aunt gave me a sly smile. "If you're looking for info about how that skeleton died, you should email your father. He might know who had muskets on the island seventeen years ago."

"How did you hear about the musket ball?" I asked. "Someone on the excavation team?"

She nodded. "Fergal Conroy is one of the Historical Society volunteers working on the current dig. He was full of news about the musket ball when they held their monthly meeting in here yesterday evening."

While most of the special interest clubs on Whisper Island met at the Movie Theater Café, a few of the more academic ones preferred to use the library for their meetings. "Fergal Conroy," I murmured. "Is he related to Bethany?"

"He's her father," my aunt said. "A bit stuffy, but a nice fella under the starch."

I turned this new information over in my mind. If Bethany's father was a volunteer on the dig, there was a link between both cases I was working on. Yet another coincidence?

"By the way," my aunt said, cutting short my musings, "I'm still looking for that exhibition brochure. It appears to have been misplaced."

My pulse picked up the pace. "I guess that happens in libraries."

Philomena frowned, some of her previous animation dissipating. "Not here. We're a small staff, but we're diligent."

I pounced on this detail. "When was the brochure last consulted?"

"Around five years ago," my aunt replied. "A student referred to it for a school project."

"Maybe that's when it got lost."

She shook her head. "No. I was on duty that day, according to the records, and I made a note that I'd returned it to its shelf."

"If it's routine admin," I began carefully, "maybe you assumed you'd returned it to its correct location, and it actually ended up somewhere else."

"I don't do things like that, Maggie. Even when I'm tired and distracted, I don't misplace library material."

I'd irritated her, and I needed to keep her sweet. I wanted more info on that missing brochure, but now was not the moment to press my aunt. "Thanks for your help. Will I see you at the Movie Club tomorrow night?"

"I want to be there." A pained expression flitted across Philomena's face. "Dolly is threatening to come with me. I'm not sure I can face Noreen's wrath if I show up with Dolly in tow."

"She'll cope. When I spoke to Dolly yesterday, she seemed to think the move back was permanent. If that's the case, Noreen will have to get used to having her and her café around."

"I wish I shared your optimism. My sister is stubborn, and she never liked my sister-in-law, even before Dolly opened a rival café right across the street." My aunt forced a smile. "At least we have some good things happening in the family with you and Julie settling down with your men."

A pang of regret twisted my stomach. "I'm definitely not settled yet."

She waved a hand in a dismissive gesture. "Ah, sure, once your divorce comes through, it'll all be different. Here's hoping it'll be finalized before your birthday. It would be nice to have two events to celebrate."

Yeah, it would be good to shed my snake of an ex before I turned the big 3-0, but I wasn't holding my breath. "Liam's daughter is visiting him for the next few weeks."

My aunt's eyes twinkled in amusement. "How are you getting along with her?"

"I've only met Hannah once. It didn't go well."

Philomena chuckled. "She's defending her territory. That's only natural. How old is she?"

"Eight going on eighteen." I sighed. "I'm just not great with kids. I never know what to say to them. Heck, with a few notable exceptions, I didn't know what to say to kids when I was one."

"Hannah will come around to the idea of her dad seeing you. Just give her time."

"I hope so. Liam's invited me to join them on a boat trip on Saturday."

My aunt's face lit up. "That's a great idea. The weather forecast is good. I'm sure you'll all have a lovely time. Just give the girl a chance."

"I'll try. I just hope she extends me the same courtesy." I glanced at my watch. "Thanks again for your help. I need to make tracks."

"Good luck. I'll contact you when I have news about your musket."

After I left the library, I got into my car and drove out toward St. Finbar's Hill. I parked at the foot of the hill, close to the spot I'd stopped the night of the flashlight up at the dig. I walked up the hill toward the dig, taking my time and allowing my gaze to take in everything that was happening.

Professor Frobisher was hurrying toward the shed when I approached, but he stopped in his tracks when he saw me and drew his bushy eyebrows into a hairy V. "What are you doing here?"

"The silliest thing." I treated him to a beatific smile. "I think I lost a ring when I was up here on Monday. When I mentioned coming to look for it, one of the summer camp mothers asked me if I'd keep an eye out for her son's lost camera."

An irritated look passed over the professor's face. "Is that the woman whose son found the skeleton? She's been pestering everyone about that camera. Instead of indulging the boy with expensive gadgets, she should teach her kid to behave."

"He did seem very fond of his camera," I said in as casual a tone as I could muster. "As am I of my ring. I don't suppose you've seen a silver amethyst ring lying around?"

"The only jewelry I'm interested in is medieval," he snapped. "Now if you'll excuse me, I have important work to do."

Friendly dude. The professor stalked off to the shed,

clearly irritated by my pedestrian mind and preoccupation with non-academic matters.

I moved from unit to unit, asking the archaeologists if they'd seen my nonexistent ring or Tommy's missing camera. No one had. Even Ruth Dede, the excavation's official photographer, was short with me, in spite of being perfectly friendly on the occasions I'd met her at Shamrock Cottages. I got the impression that the entire team was on edge. From the filthy looks Professor Frobisher cast my way, I suspected the excavation team leader had forbidden them to talk to outsiders.

I turned to leave, and a flash of a red T-shirt caught my eye. Susie O'Malley waved in my direction. "Hello, Maggie. Have you come to find more dead bodies?"

"I hope not." I walked over to join her at her unit. She and Alan had made a lot of progress since I'd seen them at work on Monday. "Wow. That hole is getting deep."

"We found part of a brooch this morning," Susie said excitedly. "Richard says it could be a significant find."

"I hope so for your sake."

Alan rolled his eyes. "Come on, Susie. That man would say anything to get women to do what he wants."

Susie's pale face turned pink. "You're ridiculous."

"*I'm* ridiculous?" He drew himself up to his full

height and glared at her. "I'm not blind. I see the way he looks at you."

"Keep your voice down." Susie cast me an embarrassed glance. "It's just Richard's way. I don't pay any attention to him."

"What's his way?" I disliked pressing her on the issue, but I was reluctant to let this chance slip away.

Susie twisted her fingers. "He's a bit of a flirt."

"A bit of a flirt?" Alan snorted. "The man is a sleaze. I can't believe you can't see through him, Susie. I thought you were more intelligent than that."

This was the wrong thing to say to her. Susie rounded on him with a ferocious expression. "Don't you dare bring up my intelligence. It's not my fault I got an assistant's position and you didn't. You're just not good at selling yourself at interviews."

"And you think that hipster made a better impression than I did?" Alan jerked his thumb in the direction of the pit where Richard and Ben were working. "I don't know what the prof was thinking when he hired *him*. He can barely tell one end of a unit from another. He must have bought his Ph.D. because he shows no evidence of deserving one."

Susie glared at him. "That's not fair. Ben is clever and he has extensive fieldwork experience."

"But not in Ireland and not in these conditions," her coworker insisted. "Digging in the desert is completely different. Unless Frobisher was searching for a Richard-lookalike, I don't know what he was thinking."

Susie, still red in the face, turned to me. "Want to take a walk with me, Maggie?"

I slid a glance at Alan. "As long as he intends to be polite to you when you return."

The man's mouth gaped open. He snapped it shut and cast me a withering look. "I've said what I had to say. As far as I'm concerned, Susie can work another unit today, and I'll finish this one."

I stared Alan down. "I don't like bullies. And I particularly don't like men who bully women."

Susie grabbed my arm. "Leave it, Maggie. I can handle Alan."

As she hauled me away, I gave the guy the evil eye.

When we were out of earshot, Susie murmured, "I'm sorry. Alan can be temperamental at times. His father was a gifted archaeologist, and Alan can't bear the idea of not living up to his reputation. It makes him underestimate all that he's achieved so far and inclined to put others down."

"You shouldn't let him undermine you. I don't care how much you think you love him, that belittling behavior is a major red flag. Seriously, Susie. Take it from one who knows."

The girl shoved a stray strand of hair behind her ear. "You misunderstood the situation. Alan and I aren't together. Not anymore. I broke up with him a few months ago."

"It doesn't sound like he accepts that."

"No." She squeezed her eyes shut. "I shouldn't have agreed to work on this dig. I knew Alan would be here, and I figured it would be awkward. What I didn't anticipate was Professor Frobisher pairing us up for fieldwork."

"You need to talk to the professor. Get him to assign you another partner. Alan's behavior is unacceptable."

"Don't you think I've tried?" She sighed. "All the prof cares about is making this excavation a success. He has us out here every hour of daylight we can get. According to him, Alan's and my skill sets complement one another, so it makes sense for us to work together."

"Can't Ellen intervene? She doesn't strike me as the sort of woman who'd put up with a member of staff harassing her assistant."

"Under normal circumstances, I could count on her support."

"I sense a *but* coming."

"Yeah." The girl bit her lip. "Ellen's been…preoccupied lately."

"With work for the dig?"

Susie's smile was wry. "I wish. I keep having to pick up the slack for her. No, she's got some personal stuff going on, and she's constantly disappearing."

Interesting. I needed to find out more about Dr. Taylor. "It sounds like the discovery of the skeleton hasn't been the only drama on the excavation."

Susie laughed. "No. If anything, having the dig closed down for a day gave us all a break from the tension."

"Speaking of breaks, have you had much of a chance to socialize since you arrived on Whisper Island?"

"I've barely had time to sleep." She rubbed the back of her neck, and her face grew red again. "Sorry for venting."

"I witnessed Alan's behavior, and I engaged with it." I looked around at the other workers, all of whom were avoiding eye contact. "I didn't see the rest of your team running to your defense."

"It's every man and woman for him- or her self on this dig," Susie said with an edge to her voice. "For various reasons, we all need this job to go well. I want to use my contribution to score a job once I defend my dissertation. Alan wants the prof to change his mind and make him his assistant. All the others need the job in order to further their careers."

"If this excavation means so much to people, why does Ellen Taylor keep disappearing and dumping her work on you?"

Susie smirked. "Wrong question. You should've asked *who* she keeps disappearing to."

"Who—?" My question was interrupted by Professor Frobisher's strident tones.

"Susie," he yelled, red-faced and irritated. "I need you over here."

Susie grimaced. "Sorry, Maggie. Duty calls. Maybe we can chat another time."

I seized on this opening—I wanted to know more about Ellen Taylor's mysterious behavior. "If you'd like me to show you the wild nightlife of Smuggler's Cove, why don't you be my guest at tomorrow's Movie Club meeting? We're watching an old Hitchcock movie called *The 39 Steps*."

The younger woman perked up. "If I can get away early enough, I'd love to. What time does the film start?"

"We serve cocktails an hour before the movie, so if you could be at the café at some point after eight?"

Her smile was genuine. "Thanks, Maggie. I hope to see you then."

"I'm looking forward to it. Feel free to extend the invitation to your friends on the excavation team. We love having guests on movie nights." This last statement was a pure exaggeration, but having the opportunity to talk to the archaeologists in a casual atmosphere would be fantastic.

After Susie left me, I returned to my car. As I drove away from the excavation site, I ran through what I'd learned. I'd discovered nothing concrete about the skeleton, but the undercurrent of tension that existed between the various excavation team members aroused my curiosity. While I considered Alan to be a petulant bully, his remarks about Ben intrigued me. Was Alan just acting spiteful, or was there something odd about Ben's position on the team? And what had Susie meant about Ellen's disappearing acts? Who could the older archaeologist be meeting when she was supposed to be at work? Richard sprang to mind. He had a reputation as a flirt, but why would Ellen need to leave the dig to meet him?

I shook my head. I'd encountered so many oddities and coincidences on this case so far that I was over dismissing a loose thread as insignificant. I'd pump Susie about Ellen's activities, and I'd ask Lenny to work his magic to dig for dirt on Ben.

10

A fter I left St. Finbar's Hill, I spent the rest of my day dealing with domestic chaos and shooting off an email to my father regarding eighteenth-century firearms. I'd been so busy lately that I'd let certain household tasks pile up. By the time I arrived at the café to meet Lenny for the Unplugged Gamers, I'd made serious inroads into my dirty laundry, and my cottage was now a clutter-free zone.

I'd just started to sort the ingredients for the iced Irish coffees the Unplugged Gamers loved when Lenny pulled up in his van. He hopped out and burst into the café. His jaunty step and animated expression told me he'd had more luck on the research front than I'd had.

"I totally rocked my internet searches," he said, beaming. "And Mack and I brainstormed reasons to make a femur disappear. I had a theory before I went to see him, and he found it credible."

"Okay, hit me with it."

"What if the dead dude had some sort of metal plate or screws in his thigh? According to my research, orthopedic surgical devices can be used to identify bodies."

I digested this information for a moment. "The make, models, and serial numbers are traceable. Yeah, that scenario works."

Lenny's cheerful expression faltered. "Do you think the killer removed the thighbone before burying the body?"

"I can get Reynolds to check with his contact in forensics, but that scenario strikes me as unlikely. The examination of the skeleton revealed no damage to the surrounding bones. It would be difficult to cut out part of a body without leaving marks."

"So they waited until the body was likely to be a skeleton and then dug up the femur?" Lenny shook his head. "That makes even less sense."

"The only way I see your orthopedic device theory working is if the femur was stolen on the day Tommy discovered the skull."

We stood there for a tense few seconds, neither of us saying a word.

"You're implying the killer was at the excavation site," Lenny said. "That's pretty out there, Maggie."

"This entire case is pretty out there. If the killer didn't steal the femur, maybe someone who knew the name of the dead guy was at the site and took action to prevent his easy identification."

Lenny tugged on his goatee. "What are the odds that the killer, or someone who knew the murdered man, just happened to be hanging around when the skeleton was dug up?"

"Slim, but not impossible. Okay. Let's roll with your idea for a moment more." I closed my eyes and pictured the excavation site as it had been on the day of the summer camp trip. "We know that a previous excavation took place on St. Finbar's Hill within the time frame that the skeleton was put in the ground. We know that at least one team member from the 2000 excavation is also working on this dig. And last but not least, info about both excavations was shared in the *Whisper Island Gazette*. The killer could have found out that the new dig was happening in the area where they'd buried the body. Pretend you're the killer. What would you do if you discovered that the body you'd so carefully buried all those years ago was likely to be dug up?"

"I'd run."

I opened my eyes and looked right at him. "Would you really? Let's say you're the killer. You live on Whisper Island, or somewhere else in Ireland. Once you read about the planned excavation, you know it's only a matter of time before the archaeologists find the body. If you run, you'll make yourself conspicuous. If you stay, you risk the cops identifying the skeleton and linking the dead guy to you."

"So the killer got involved with the excavation," Lenny finished. "That means he or she must be part of the excavation team, or one of the volunteers from the Historical Society."

"Exactly. Assuming the killer knew about the dead man's titanium implant, or whatever might have been in there, he or she made sure to be on site if and when the skeleton was found."

"How did they grab the femur without anyone noticing? From the moment Tommy started screeching, all eyes were on that pit. Most people present never went anywhere near the skull."

"Apart from Tommy, me, Professor Frobisher, Ellen Taylor, and a doctoral student named Alan. Assuming neither Tommy nor I ran off with the femur, we have three members of the excavation team who went down into that pit, and I rolled Alan next to the area where the femur might have been. I wasn't looking at the pit the whole time, even when I was down there. For a start, I had to call Reynolds, and then give him my statement. And the sight of the skull turned my stomach. I was deliberately not looking that way."

"Did anyone have an opportunity after that?" Lenny asked.

A memory stirred at the back of my mind. "The tarpaulin. I can't believe I forgot that. Professor Frobisher asked a couple of guys to cover the pit to prevent rain from messing with the scene."

"Who was involved in putting up the tarpaulin?"

"It was the professor, Richard Carstairs, a hipster dude named Ben Dunne, and another guy," I said without hesitation. "By the way, Alan claims Ben's archaeological credentials are dubious. We need to look into him some more."

"If it's an internet search you're after, I'm your man. What do you know about Ben?"

"Not much. He specializes in Egyptian archaeology and lived there for three years. I don't know more than that."

"Leave it to me. I'll ask around and do some research." Lenny typed a note on his phone. "Do you think one of those guys could have snatched the femur?"

"I'm not sure. I guess it could be done if they knew *what* they were looking for and roughly *where* to look." I wrinkled my nose. "Surely one of us would have noticed if they'd removed an object from the pit?"

"Maybe. Maybe not." Lenny leaned forward. "What did you discover at the library?"

"Not a lot, unfortunately. The first excavation was big news in the *Whisper Island Gazette*. They even had an exhibition in the museum of some of the finds. Philomena had a brochure about the exhibition in the library catalog, but it appears to be missing."

"Ask a member of the Whisper Island Historical Society if they have a copy lying around. Or a random island oldie. A lot of them love hoarding rubbish."

"I'm not even sure that it's worth busting my behind to find. I'm hoping it mentions names of the volunteers who aren't mentioned in the official excavation reports."

"Did you have success on the photograph front?"

"No. Everyone up at the excavation site claims they had no phone and no camera, as per Professor Frobisher's rules. There's still no sign of Tommy's camera, and I didn't have time to go to the hotel in search of him. I'll put that on tomorrow's to-do list."

"I'm starting to think you're right about Tommy's missing camera being no accident," Lenny said. "If our maybe-crazy theory is true and the killer wanted to make sure no one connected them with the dead man, perhaps Tommy took photos of the pit before the killer had a chance to steal the femur."

"Exactly." I wrinkled my nose. "The excavation stinks. Maybe it's not the excavation itself, but a person connected to it. Either way, something's not right, and I can guarantee you that Sergeant O'Shea will never solve a case this complex."

"When are you due to talk to Reynolds about what we've discovered?" Lenny asked.

"We haven't set a time. He was taking Hannah to the beach today, and I said I'd email him with a summary of the day's discoveries. As you can imagine, he doesn't want to discuss the case in front of his daughter."

Lenny grinned. "Have you seen her since the night on the hill? That kid has spunk."

"Reynolds invited me to join them on a day trip on Saturday. I'll use the opportunity to try to win her around."

My friend roared with laughter. "Good luck with that."

"She's only a kid. It's got to be tough seeing her dad just a few times a year."

"There are days I'd happily reduce contact with my dad." Lenny pulled a face. "He's driving me around the bend lately with all his wild ideas for the shop. It's as if he's lost a sense for the electronics people want to buy versus the gadgets he's interested in. Don't get me wrong. I love gadgets. They just don't appeal to our customers."

The bell above the café door jangled, and Julie, Günter, and Mack swept in. My cousin smiled up at her new boyfriend with a besotted expression. An unfamiliar pang of envy settled in my stomach. I wanted that carefree happiness for Reynolds and me —assuming he cared about me as much as I cared about him.

Mack, our pharmacist friend, sat beside me. "Hey, Maggie. Lenny tells me you two are busy with cases. I'm glad your P.I. business is taking off."

Lenny slid a tray of iced Irish coffees across the table, and we each took one. "The more customers Maggie gets, the more likely it is she'll be able to hire me full-time."

"It's still early days," I said with caution, "but that's the goal."

"We met Reynolds and his daughter down by the harbor," Julie said. "She's a sweet little thing."

Lenny snorted with laughter. "Your name's not Maggie."

Julie cast me a look of sympathy. "I'm sorry. It must be tough dealing with a resentful kid."

"It'll be fine." At least, I hoped it would. "We've only met once so far, and Hannah used the opportunity to throw some attitude my way."

"Poor kid. She'll be feeling territorial, especially if you're the first of her father's girlfriends she's met."

"She made certain to inform me that her mother is newly single," I said dryly. "A fact she's looking forward to sharing with her father."

Julie's brow creased. "And she thinks this means her parents will reconcile?"

"She hopes so at any rate."

"Kids can be difficult," my cousin said. "Hannah probably just needs time to adjust to the idea of her father moving on."

"The logical side of me knows this, just as it understands why Liam was reluctant to tell her about us. Unfortunately, my emotional side forgets I'm an adult in this situation, and I need to respect that she's a kid."

Lenny and Mack set up *Elysium*, the game we'd chosen to play that evening. For the next half hour, I used the game to distract myself from all thoughts of Reynolds and his daughter. My experimental iced Irish coffees went down well, and I volunteered to make a second batch once we'd downed the first ones.

Mack helped me to carry the iced coffees over to our table. "I heard the district superintendent is arriving tomorrow with the new police officer."

"Yeah. I hope he or she is more competent than Sergeant O'Shea."

Lenny and Julie dissolved into laughter.

"They can't be much worse," Günter said with a grin. "O'Shea's busy with the golfing tournament. I doubt he's paying much attention to the skeleton."

"Speaking of the skeleton, did you or Julie see anyone taking photographs after Tommy found the skull?"

Günter raised an eyebrow in amusement. "Apart from Tommy himself?"

"Yes. I was just wondering if anybody else had broken the rules," I hedged. "Because if so, they'd need to give their photographs to the police."

This was baloney, and Günter's bemused expression told me he didn't buy my story for one second. "With the exception of Tommy and the excavation team's photographer, I didn't see anyone with a camera or a phone."

"Same here," Julie said. "I didn't see anyone snapping photos. Why do you ask?"

"Because Maggie is on the case," Günter said smoothly. "In every sense of the phrase."

My cousin's eyes widened. "Did someone hire you to investigate?"

"I can't answer that question," I hedged. "Suffice it to say, I'm very interested in any information you might have concerning that skeleton. Can you remember any missing persons cases around here in the last fifteen to twenty years?"

Julie frowned and considered the question. "Not on Whisper Island. I recall reading reports about missing people on the mainland. None of the stories stand out, though."

"So no islander reported a friend or family member who'd disappeared?"

"I can't think of anyone." She turned to our pharmacist friend. "Can you, Mack?"

The guy shook his head. "Like Julie said, there was the odd article in the national newspapers about people gone missing, but no one with a connection around here."

"Thing is," Lenny said, "people leave Whisper Island all the time for work. Whole families have left since I was a kid."

"And tourists come and go," Günter added. "If you were going to kill someone, what better place to do it than somewhere no one would think to look?"

"True. Unfortunately, it doesn't bring us any closer to identifying the skeleton." I sighed. "I'm going to talk to Tommy Greer tomorrow and ask him exactly where he last saw his camera. It's a long shot, but worth trying."

"Ask Caoimhe, too," Lenny said. "She has an identical camera to Tommy's, only in pink."

I regarded my friend with wonder. "Do you remember everything your customers buy?"

"That purchase stood out because Paul bought both cameras at the same time."

I screwed up my forehead. "Why would Paul Greer buy Caoimhe a camera?"

Lenny blinked. "Because she's his kid. Tommy and Caoimhe are twins."

My jaw descended. I recalled the chubby, sarcastic little girl from Monday's trip, and compared her to handsome Paul and beautiful Melanie. "Whoa. Tommy's a miniature version of his father. I'd never have guessed Caoimhe was part of their family."

Noreen had mentioned that two of the Greers' four children were twins, but I tended to tune out any mention of my ex and his wife. Even during my time working at the hotel earlier in the year, I'd only caught a glimpse of their youngest kid. Paul and Melanie lived in a house on the hotel grounds and appeared to keep their kids away from the family business.

A wave of sympathy for Caoimhe washed over me. It must be tough to be the homely kid in a good-looking family. No wonder she had a chip on her shoulder. I'd make an effort to be nice if I saw her tomorrow.

"If you want a chance to have a chat with the twins," Julie said, "tomorrow is the last day of summer camp, and we're hosting a party for the parents. Seeing as you were a chaperone on Monday, it wouldn't raise any eyebrows if you were there."

"Okay, but I don't feel comfortable questioning the twins without their parents' permission." I pulled a face. "Seeing how well I get along with Melanie, I'm not sure she'd let me."

"It's all in the phrasing," my cousin said. "Ask Melanie if Tommy found his camera, and let it roll from there. Caoimhe's nosy and a tattletale. She'll stick close in case she misses something."

"Thanks, Julie. I'll take you up on that suggestion."

After the Unplugged Gamers meeting dispersed, Lenny volunteered to help me tidy up. "If you tackle the twins, I'll try to track down that missing brochure. One of the island's old fogies is bound to have a copy in their attic."

"Thanks, Lenny. Want to hold a meeting before the Movie Club tomorrow?"

My friend nodded. "Sure thing. I'll get here by seven. That'll give us plenty of time to swap notes and come up with our next move."

I admired his confidence. I truly did. Meanwhile, I was fast getting the impression that our case was developing more tentacles than a cephalopod.

11

A fter my morning shift at the Movie Theater Café the following day, I inhaled a sandwich and drove to the elementary school, where I arrived just in time for the summer camp's party.

When I pulled into the school parking lot, it was packed. I scored the last place in the teacher's section and crossed my fingers that my status as a one-time summer camp chaperone permitted me to park there.

Inside the auditorium, the kids had erected food and beverage stands for their parents. The accordion doors had been pulled open so that the party spilled onto the lawn beyond. In one corner of the garden, Günter, Oisin, and a few guys manned the barbecues, while Julie and the other camp instructors helped the kids serve their parents drinks, cakes, and snacks.

I scanned the crowd and spotted the Greer family at a table in the garden. The oldest of their four kids must be around ten, but I didn't see him at the table. Tommy and Caoimhe were eight, and the kid on Melanie's lap was the little boy I'd seen with her a few months ago during my stint working undercover at the hotel.

Dodging running kids and loitering parents, I weaved my way through the crowd and stopped by the Greers' table.

Caoimhe was the first to spot me. Her pudgy face adopted a disdainful expression, putting a dent in my determination to be nice to her. "Am I supposed to call you Ms. Doyle or Maggie when you're not our official chaperone?"

"Maggie's fine." I regarded the rest of her family. "Hi, there. Mind if I join you for a sec?"

Paul and Melanie stared at me as if I'd sprouted horns. Although I'd reached an uneasy truce with them after I'd unmasked Melanie's mother's killer earlier this year, we'd never be friends. There was too much proverbial water under the bridge between Paul and me, courtesy of him breaking my teenage heart, and Melanie wasn't the sort of woman who played nicely with other females.

To my surprise, Caoimhe moved up the bench before her parents could respond. "You can sit next to me."

"Thanks." I sat, wishing I'd thought to grab a glass of water before I'd joined them.

"What can we do for you, Maggie?" Melanie

asked, finally finding her voice. "Is this about the skeleton?"

My reputation as a dead-body magnet preceded me. "Actually, yes. I was wondering if Tommy found his camera."

Paul shot his son a look of annoyance. "No, and it's not looking like he will."

Tommy turned bright red. "Sorry, Dad. I swear I put it in my bag."

"Did you leave your backpack lying around anywhere?" I asked.

Tommy screwed up his face for a moment and then shook his head. "Not after you told me off for taking pictures. I put the camera in my rucksack and I wore it the whole time between then and Dad arriving to take me home."

I turned to Caoimhe. "Did you see anyone take the camera out of Tommy's backpack?"

The girl blinked behind her thick lenses. "No,"

"Did you bring your camera along on Monday's trip?"

"Yeah." She jutted her chin. "I didn't take it out while we were at the excavation site. Ms. O'Brien said we weren't allowed to take photos. Tommy broke the rules."

"So neither of you has any idea what happened to Tommy's camera?"

The twins shook their heads.

"Why are you interested in Tommy's camera?" Paul asked.

"The photographs he took," his wife said sagely before focusing on me. "What could possibly be on Tommy's photos that wouldn't be on those taken by forensics?"

Not for the first time, I was reminded that Melanie was smarter than I liked to give her credit for. My betrayed teenage self had preferred to slot her into the role of beautiful but stupid. I guess clinging to my intellectual superiority had made licking my wounds less painful. "Tommy's photos probably don't reveal anything of importance," I said. "It just struck me as curious that his camera went missing right after he'd photographed the skull."

Melanie shivered and drew her cardigan around her shoulders. "A coincidence, I'm sure. Boys can be careless."

"I wasn't careless." Tommy stuck out his lower lip in a gesture more typical of a younger child. "I really like that camera. I was upset when Ms. Doyle confiscated it. I wouldn't go and lose it after I'd finally gotten it back."

After he'd swiped it from my bag... I didn't give voice to this thought. "If you didn't lose the camera, what do you think happened to it?"

He regarded me with disdain. "Someone stole it, of course."

"Tommy, really," said his mother. "Why would your fellow summer campers want to steal your camera? Many of them have cameras of their own, or phones with built-in cameras."

The boy shrugged. "I didn't lose it, and it couldn't have fallen out of my bag. I made sure to zip it properly."

His twin rolled her eyes. "Knowing you, the bag was wide open and an invitation for anyone to take your stuff."

"I closed it, I swear." Tommy glared at his sister. "It wouldn't surprise me if *you'd* taken it, just to get me into trouble. It'd be just the sort of thing you'd do."

Caoimhe pouted. "Mum, tell Tommy to be nice to me. He shouldn't accuse me of things I didn't do."

Melanie sighed. "Did you take the camera, Caoimhe? Please be honest."

The girl frowned at her brother. "I didn't take your stupid camera." The words were delivered in a manner that told me there was more to this story than Caoimhe would admit, but I wasn't getting any information out of the kid in front of her family.

When Tommy started to argue, his father cut his protestations short. "For one afternoon, I want you two not to fight. Why don't you go and play with your friends?"

Tommy sneered. "That's no problem for me, but Caoimhe doesn't have friends."

His sister turned red in the face. Behind the thick lenses of her glasses, she blinked back tears.

"Come on, Caoimhe," Paul said in a gentler voice. "Will you help me get food from the barbecue?"

Her lips trembled. Without looking at any of us,

she got to her feet and trooped after her father. Tommy, not willing to miss a moment to torment his sister, ran after them and tugged Caoimhe's braid.

Melanie pursed her lips and bounced the toddler on her knee. "The twins can be a handful. Caoimhe in particular."

"It's not easy when you don't have a particular friend. I was never a kid with lots of friends, but I had a best friend from kindergarten." An idea struck me. "How does Caoimhe feel about boat trips?"

Melanie stared at me in bewilderment. "I have no idea. She's never objected to going out on her grandparents' yacht."

"Sergeant Reynolds invited me to join him and his daughter on a boat trip tomorrow. He wants to take Hannah out to Dolphin Island to visit the bird sanctuary. Caoimhe is the same age as Hannah, and it would be nice for Hannah to have a companion her own age. I know it's short notice, but would Caoimhe like to join us?"

"I'll ask her, but not now. She's been known to say no to activities she enjoys if approached in the wrong mood." Melanie's smile was wry. "If she's prickly now, I dread to think what she'll be like when puberty hits."

Seeing Melanie interact with her children made me reassess my feelings toward the woman yet again. I'd never like her, but she clearly loved her kids, and she was perceptive enough to realize that Caoimhe required extra TLC.

I got to my feet. "Thanks for letting me ask the twins about the camera."

"Is your number the same as the one you used when you worked at the hotel?" Melanie asked.

I nodded. "Once you've spoken to Caoimhe, let me know if she's coming or not, and if so, we can discuss a time for me to collect her."

Melanie's youngest kid hit his head on the edge of the table and began to wail. She scooped him up and kissed the sore spot. "Okay. I'll send you a text. If I wait until we're on our own, she might agree."

After I'd left Melanie's table, I found Julie and said goodbye to her and Günter. I needed to run to the grocery store and then get home to take Bran out for a run before I had to prepare the Movie Theater Café for tonight's Movie Club meeting. As I drove to the store, I replayed the conversation with the Greers in my mind. Caoimhe had been adamant that she hadn't taken Tommy's camera, and I believed her. However, something in the way she'd said it had made me suspicious. Even if she wasn't responsible for its disappearance, had she seen who'd taken the camera? And if so, was she in danger?

A shiver snaked down my spine. I was being absurd. I needed to pull myself together. My curiosity about the photos on Tommy's camera was pure speculation. I had no concrete reason to suppose they showed anything different from what the forensics team's camera had snapped the following morning. And until and unless I established a definite link between the skeleton and the excavation team, I was shooting in the dark with my theory that the dead man was connected to one of them. In spite of my cold dose of logic, I couldn't shake the sense of unease.

12

After I'd shopped, I took my dog for a fast run interspersed with sprints. In spite of pushing myself to the brink, the workout failed to distract me from thoughts of suspects and skeletons. When Bran and I jogged up the drive after our run, Reynolds and Richard Carstairs were sitting on the bench outside Reynolds's cottage. While the guys drank beer, Hannah was showing off her hula-hoop skills on the lawn.

Bran, sensing a potential new friend, tugged his leash out of my hand and sped over to Hannah. The girl was startled by the dog's sudden and enthusiastic appearance, but Bran's excited whine earned him a pet. A few generous licks later, he'd dissolved the last of her reserve.

Jeez. How come my dog knew how to get on the kid's good side, but I didn't? I took a step forward.

"Calm down, Bran. There's no need to lick her to death."

Hannah jerked at the sound of my voice. She looked from me to the dog and back again. "I didn't know he was yours."

"I'm not sure he is, actually. I get the impression that he thinks I belong to him. Ditto the cats."

A flicker of interest danced across Hannah's face. "You have cats? Dad has a kitten. Her name is Rosie."

I seized this opening gambit. "Two of Rosie's siblings live with me. You can come over and meet them whenever you like. They enjoy hanging with their sister."

"Dad rescued Rosie from a drainpipe," the girl said with more than a hint of pride.

I was about to tell her I'd already known that because I'd been present at Operation Kitten Rescue. I swallowed the words. I needed to tread carefully. Bombarding the child with time I'd spent with her father when she hadn't been around wasn't the way to win her affection. "Your dad's a good guy. Whisper Island is lucky to have him in charge of the police station."

This brought a reluctant smile to her pretty face. Despite never having seen a photograph of Reynolds's ex, I assumed Hannah took after her mother. The girl's fair hair and tanned skin were similar to her father's, but her heart-shaped face bore little resemblance to his square jaw and high cheekbones.

"Hey, Maggie," Reynolds called. "Do you want to join Richard and me for a beer?"

I glanced at my watch. I had to get back to Smuggler's Cove in just over an hour to set up for the Movie Club meeting. "If you have a non-alcoholic beer in your fridge, sure. I'll just jump under the shower first." I looked at Hannah. "Is it okay if I leave Bran with you?"

As if sensing the girl's hesitation, the dog rubbed against her legs and gave her hand a generous lick. "Okay," she said. "I guess I can play fetch with him."

At the sound of the word "fetch," Bran tore across the lawn to the front of my cottage. I grinned at Hannah. "This is my cue to get his box of toys from the hallway." I ran after him and opened the door to our home. Bran ran straight to his box, making big puppy eyes at me until I picked up the box and placed it outside. "You'll find his ball, toy bone, and an assortment of other stuff in here. Thanks, Hannah."

The girl stared down at her scuffed shoes. "I like animals."

In other words, she liked my dog, but that was all she was prepared to commit to at the moment. As my Irish aunts would say, fair enough.

I washed and dressed quickly, leaving my curly hair to dry naturally. I'd regret this decision later when it turned into a frizzy mane. For now I didn't want to waste the opportunity for a casual chat with Richard Carstairs. Since I'd questioned him yesterday about his previous visit to Whisper Island, he'd been avoiding me.

When I joined them in front of Reynolds's house, Bran hurtled across the lawn to catch the ball Hannah had thrown to him. Her father had brought out his fold-up garden table and laid it with a lemonade glass for Hannah, and two alcohol-free pale ales for us. Carstairs stuck to his bench and his German brand of bitter.

I raised my bottle to the two men. "*Sláinte*."

Carstairs eyed me warily. "Ellen says you're a private detective."

"Yeah," I said vaguely. "I get a case here and there. Mostly missing items and suspected adultery."

The archaeologist didn't look convinced. I was pretty sure he suspected my questions about the previous excavation were borne of a deeper interest than idle curiosity. "Are you working on anything interesting at the moment?" His attempt to keep his tone casual failed.

"I can't give specifics due to confidentiality agreements. The majority of the work I do is far from the exciting scenarios we see on TV shows." I deliberately didn't meet Reynolds's eyes in case he mentioned my propensity to fall over dead bodies. "How's your work progressing on the dig?"

Carstairs took a swig from his beer bottle before answering. "We're getting there. Slowly. The commotion on Monday set us back by more than a day. The police dug up two units in addition to the one where the skeleton was found. I've had to sift through the mess in an attempt to salvage whatever was there."

I winced. "I'm sorry. That must be an archaeologist's worst nightmare."

"Not quite." His lips twisted into an ironic smile. "My worst nightmare is knowing material of archaeological significance is under a site that's being bulldozed to make way for yet another unnecessary office block."

I pulled a face. "I see your point."

"Whisper Island isn't likely to erect office blocks on every corner," Reynolds said. "Holiday homes, maybe."

The archaeologist laughed. "The island's popular with tourists."

"At this time of year, yes. It was pretty dead when I first arrived. Right, Maggie?"

"Yeah. The winter months are bleak."

Richard took another pull on his beer bottle. "I only work on British Isles digs during the summer months. During the winter, I head south."

"Aren't you a professor at Cambridge?" I recalled a Cambridge connection from the man's résumé.

Again, a flicker of wariness darted across Richard Carstairs's face. "That was a long time ago. I concentrate on fieldwork now."

Bran's ball flew in our direction, and Reynolds caught it in the palm of one hand.

Hannah bit her lip. "Sorry, Dad. I almost hit the window."

Her father squeezed the ball and tossed it to the panting dog. "No harm done."

Richard drained his beer bottle and got to his feet. "I need to type up notes from today's finds."

"Maybe we'll see you at the Movie Club later," I said, keeping my tone nonchalant. "Susie and a few of the others said they'd stop by after work."

Carstairs scratched his beard. "I heard something about a Hitchcock film."

"We're watching *The 39 Steps*," Reynolds said, running with the bait I'd thrown him. "We drink cocktails and watch old films. I'm taking Hannah."

"I'll see if I have time. You two have a good night."

After Carstairs had gone into his cottage, I pounced on Reynolds. "How did you persuade Noreen to bend her no-one-under-eighteen rule?"

His eyebrows shot up. "I didn't know that was a rule. I asked her if Hannah could tag along, and she agreed."

Crafty Noreen. She was determined to throw Hannah and me together at every opportunity in the hope the girl would grow to like me.

"How's the case coming along?" Reynolds had dropped his voice to a low whisper.

"Slowly." I glanced at Richard's cottage, wary of being overheard. "I'll email you later with the details, or fill you in tomorrow."

He nodded to my bottle. "I'm going to get a glass of water. Do you want another drink?"

"I'm good, thanks."

At that moment, my phone buzzed with an incoming message. I picked it up and glanced at the display.

Maggie, Caoimhe says she'll join you on your boat trip tomorrow. Please let me know what time you're collecting her. Thanks. Melanie

I glanced at Reynolds. "I need to tell you something really quick before you grab your drink. I kind of invited an extra guest on the trip to Dolphin Island."

Reynolds groaned. "Please don't tell me you've asked Lenny. With his track record, the boat will sink before we leave the harbor."

This made me laugh. "No, it's not Lenny. I asked Caoimhe Greer, Paul and Melanie's daughter."

He stared at me as if dumbstruck. "You can't stand Paul and Melanie."

"True. I'm not sure I can stand Caoimhe, either, to be perfectly honest."

His eyebrows shot up. "Then why did you invite her?"

"I suspect she knows more about Tommy's missing camera than she's admitted. Plus," I added straight-faced, "she's the same age as Hannah and has no friends. I'm not sure how your daughter deals with socially inept kids."

Reynolds chuckled. "You know how to sell a person, Maggie. Let's ask Hannah what she thinks."

"Ask me what I think about what?" Hannah flopped onto a chair and reached for her lemonade glass, while Bran lay at her feet and gazed adoringly at her. That dog was a flirt. He was also smart enough to recognize a sucker who'd be willing to play fetch with him for hours on end.

"I've asked a girl to join us on our boat trip," I said. "I hope that's okay with you. She's eight, and her name is Caoimhe."

Hannah glared at me over the rim of her glass. "Are you hoping to distract me so you can kiss Dad?"

"Maggie means a lot to me," Reynolds said with quiet firmness. "I expect you to be polite to her."

My chest swelled with pleasure at his words. I turned back to Hannah. "I like kissing your dad, but that wasn't my motive for inviting Caoimhe. She's the kind of girl who doesn't make friends easily."

"You're landing me with a freak?" Her voice dripped with disdain.

"Hannah," her father said sternly, "be nice."

"Caoimhe's not a freak. She's just awkward. Haven't you ever found it tough to make friends?"

Hannah shrugged. "I guess."

"So it's okay with you if Caoimhe tags along?" Reynolds asked. "If she comes, I don't want you to be mean to her."

From his tone of voice, I inferred there had been issues in the past with Hannah not being nice to people. I wasn't surprised and I had to admit I was relieved that Reynolds wasn't quite the blindly besotted father I'd judged him to be on the night I'd first met his daughter.

"I'll be nice to her, I swear. Seriously, Dad, that whole punching business was so last year."

"Last school year," Liam said softly, "meaning three months ago."

I winced and experienced a pang of guilt for dragging Caoimhe on a day trip with a girl who apparently punched her peers.

"It was self-defense."

"The girl called you names. You gave her a black eye."

Hannah scuffed the toe of her shoe against the ground. "I said I was sorry."

Her father sighed. "I know you did, and I believe you're contrite. I just don't like to hear you making disparaging remarks about people, especially kids you haven't met."

Hannah threw her arms up in the air. "I'll be nice as pie to Caoimhe, okay?"

I placed my beer bottle on the table and stood. With a show of reluctance, Bran shuffled to his feet and joined me. "I'd better get ready to go. It's my turn to prepare the café for the Movie Club meeting."

"See you later, Maggie," Reynolds said.

Prompted by a warning look from her father, Hannah muttered a reluctant goodbye.

I gathered up Bran's toys and ushered him into

the cottage. As I got dressed for the Movie Club, I questioned my decision to throw Hannah and Caoimhe together. In spite of what I'd told Hannah, I'd invited Caoimhe along to have a chance to pump her for info about her brother's missing camera. It was now clear to me that I couldn't do that—not morally at any rate.

Caoimhe was a kid with social issues, and Hannah didn't appear to be much better at peer interaction. As much as I yearned to coax Caoimhe into telling me what she knew, I couldn't use a vulnerable girl for my own ends. No, the day trip would be exactly as I'd described to Hannah: a chance for two girls of the same age to get to know one another. The mystery of Tommy's missing camera would have to wait for another day.

13

O f all the Movie Club meetings I'd attended since moving to Whisper Island, tonight's was the busiest.

"Where did all these people come from?" I whispered to Lenny while we shook cocktails and mixed drinks for the club members.

"You gave an open invitation to the excavation team, remember? Apparently, Paul Greer did the same with his golf tournament pals."

"There has to be sixty people present. Will there be enough room for everyone to sit in the movie theater?"

"Yes. It seats fifty, and Noreen asked Mack and Günter to carry in some of the chairs from the café when the people start filing in for the film screening."

Among the guests was Dolly O'Brien. She'd swept in an hour ago, dressed to the nines, and had greeted Noreen with gushing enthusiasm. My aunt's initial reaction to her rival's hearty greeting had been frosty. Before long, her innate good manners had won out and she'd given Dolly a grudging tour of the café.

"Noreen's face is too expressive for anyone not to notice she's seething," Lenny said. "She needs to cut that out, or everyone will go to Dolly's place."

"That's what I told her, but Noreen's stubborn, and she's scared. Not a good combo. I'm hoping she'll put into practice some of the suggestions I made for jazzing up the Movie Theater Café's offerings."

Before I could elaborate on those plans, Jennifer Pearce approached the counter, accompanied by her fiancé, Nick Sweetman. Exquisitely groomed and tailored, Nick and Jennifer could have stepped out of the pages of a glossy magazine.

The lawyer smiled when our eyes met. "Hello, Maggie. Once again, I must apologize for not contacting you. Work has been insane this week."

To my embarrassment, I'd forgotten all about Jennifer's suggestion of a drink. "No problem. I've been pretty busy, too."

The lawyer pulled out her smartphone and checked her calendar. "How about Monday evening? Nick has to work late, and I'll be home alone."

"Monday sounds good. I'll check my planner to be sure." I gestured to the cocktail shaker. "What can I get you to drink? A sidecar?"

The lawyer laughed. "Yes, please. You have an excellent memory for people's favorite drinks."

"It's easy with the regulars." I turned to her fiancé. "What would you like, Nick?"

He perused the cocktail menu. While she was a regular attendee, Nick only occasionally showed up to the Movie Club. Now that it occurred to me, I hadn't seen him for months. After a thorough scrutiny of our offerings, Nick replaced the menu on the counter. "I'll have a whiskey sour."

"Coming right up."

The bell above the door jangled, and a fresh swarm of excavation team members flowed in. Susie looked very friendly with Ben, who was in full flirt mode. Alan brought up the rear, staring moodily at Susie and Ben.

Ellen Taylor and Richard Carstairs entered the café directly after Alan and made a beeline for the counter. They were laughing at something that must have been said before they'd entered the café. Was Richard the person Ellen was sneaking off to meet? If I had an opportunity later, I'd ask Susie to elaborate on the remark she'd made about Ellen's disappearances.

"Hi, there," I said when their laughter had subsided. "Can I offer you something to drink?"

Ellen linked arms with Richard, and her gaze swept over the crowd waiting for their cocktails. "I'll have a dry martini, Maggie."

"Same for me," Richard said.

While Nick fiddled with his phone, Jennifer

regarded the newcomers with open curiosity. "Aren't you attached to the dig on St. Finbar's Hill?"

"That's right." Richard turned the full force of his charm on her. "Are you planning to come up and visit us?"

"May I?" Jennifer's face lit up. "I thought tours were by special arrangement only."

"We'll make a special arrangement. My esteemed colleague here can fix it with our boss."

"Hmm?" Ellen's vague response rang false. "The prof's not happy we're so far behind schedule. I'm not sure he wants more visitors."

I blinked. Ellen wasn't an effusive woman, but she was hugely enthusiastic about her work. She'd been thrilled at my request to show the summer camp kids the site. Had Professor Frobisher forbidden her to invite visitors to the site? Or was there another reason for her reluctance to give Jennifer a tour?

The lawyer's face clouded with disappointment. "Oh, no worries. I quite understand. I'd imagine you lost time when the site was closed earlier in the week."

Richard had been staring at Ellen in bewilderment. He turned his attention back to Jennifer. "I'd be happy to show you the work I'm doing at the site. Stop by whenever you're in the area."

Her face lit up. "That would be wonderful. Thank you so much. Nick and I are huge fans of historical and archaeological research, especially local. We're looking forward to your exhibition at the end of the dig. Aren't we, Nick?"

"Yeah, I guess." Nick sounded anything but a guy who was looking forward to an exhibition of archaeological finds. He finally put his phone back in his pocket and glanced impatiently at his watch. The gesture struck me as odd, given that he'd been staring at his phone display seconds before, and that surely had the time. "We should go into the theater before all the good seats are taken."

Surprise flooded Jennifer's face. "It's a little early. We just got our drinks."

"The last time I came, I got a lousy seat." Nick looped his arm through his fiancée's. "See you all later."

Without looking at the archaeologists, Nick hauled Jennifer through the crowd.

"What was that all about?" I whispered to Lenny. "Nick was pretty rude."

"Beats me," Lenny murmured under his breath. "It's been so long since he came to the Movie Club I'm surprised he remembers where he sat during his last visit."

After Nick and Jennifer left, Lenny and I finished serving drinks to the archaeologists. Just as I was about to corner Susie, Noreen announced a last call for drinks before the movie, and a swarm of people descended on the bar. In the middle of my cocktail-shaking frenzy, I spotted Reynolds and Hannah arriving, accompanied by a silver-haired man with a pencil moustache, and a teenage girl of around sixteen. The girl's jet-black hair was divided into numerous snake-like braids, and her heavy makeup matched the Goth vibe of her clothes.

The newcomers joined the throng at the bar. When Reynolds reached the top of the line, he winked at me. "Hey, Maggie. You're looking good tonight."

I'd made an extra special effort with my appearance, knowing he'd be there. I smoothed down the skirt of my royal blue A-line dress. "Thanks."

Reynolds gestured to the silver-haired man. "This is Superintendent Conlan. Superintendent, this is Maggie Doyle and Lenny Logan."

The older police officer shook hands with us. "Sergeant Reynolds has been kind enough to give me and my daughter the grand tour of the island."

"That doesn't take long." I said with a laugh. "What would you all like to drink?"

"I'll have a virgin mojito, and Hannah'd like a lemonade." Reynolds turned to his guests. "What'll you have? My treat."

The older police officer examined the menu. "Just a whiskey for me. No ice."

"Same," the girl said in a deep, throaty voice that added to her whole Gothic vibe, "and make mine a double."

I glanced from her to Reynolds and back again. "Given that neither Sergeant Reynolds nor your father have objected, I'm guessing you are over eighteen, right?"

An icy silence descended. The girl's steely gaze bored into me. "I'm happy to provide you with ID."

She whipped a wallet out of the folds of her flowing skirt and shoved it across the counter. I opened it…and found myself staring at an official An Garda Síochána ID card for Garda Sile Conlan.

"Ouch," murmured Lenny. "That's awkward."

I took a deep breath, plastered a smile on my face, and slid the ID back to its owner. "Welcome to Whisper Island, Garda Conlan."

"Thanks," she replied in a dry drawl and looked around the café. Her expression was inscrutable, and I couldn't tell if she liked what she saw or regarded it with disdain. "You work here full-time?"

"No. I'm a private investigator." I didn't know why I felt the need to get specific, except maybe to have the satisfaction of surprising her.

She merely raised an eyebrow and shifted her gaze to Lenny.

"Lenny Logan, Maggie's sidekick."

Garda Conlan's lips twitched. "Is that so? You got a license to be her sidekick?"

"Once he moves to full-time work for me, he'll take the private investigator's course," I said quickly, not wanting Lenny to reveal just how many hours he'd been working for me recently.

"Excellent. It's good to remain on the right side of the law." She slid a pointed look at my friend. "Wouldn't you agree?"

Lenny regarded her straight-faced. "Absolutely."

After Reynolds and his guests had been served, Lenny and I took the final orders before heading for the movie theater. We lingered outside the theater doors, letting others go before us.

"That Goth chick looked familiar," Lenny whispered. "What's her name again?"

"Garda Síle Conlan."

"Silly?" Lenny raised an eyebrow. "Are you sure about that?"

"Well, maybe it's pronounced Shilly. Isn't 'S' more of a 'S-H' sound in Gaelic?"

"How is her name spelled?"

"S-I-L-E."

Lenny busted out laughing. "It's pronounced *Sheila*, Maggie."

"Why on earth isn't it spelled like Sheila?"

He looked smug. "Because S-H-E-L-I-A is the Anglicized version of S-I-L-E."

I held up a finger. "Don't say it. I need to sign up for Julie's class. I'll get on it next week."

My friend scrunched up his forehead. "I swear I've seen that girl before, but I can't remember where."

"I haven't seen her around the island."

"Well, no. Irish police aren't supposed to work in an area where they have family and fr—" Lenny froze mid-sentence and his face turned into a mask of horror. "Whoa. I know where I've seen her."

"Where?" I prompted, curious to know more

about the prickly new police officer who dressed like a rebellious teen.

Lenny's eyes met mine. "Juvie community service."

It was my turn to gape. "Seriously? The new police officer is a former juvenile delinquent?"

"I note your lack of surprise that *I* ended up in trouble with the law," Lenny said dryly.

"Oh, well," I said, waving a hand in a dismissive gesture. "You got it out of your system young." I paused, and then added, "Mostly."

"I had no idea Sile's father was a Guard," Lenny said. "He must have been tickled pink when she got nabbed for stealing cars. She was in rehab too, if I recall correctly."

"Fabulous," I said, deadpan. "Whisper Island has a former juvenile delinquent and a lazy old man in charge of maintaining law and order for the next three weeks. This makes me all the more determined to help Reynolds crack the skeleton case."

Lenny grinned. "Plus we've got Sunday night's stakeout to look forward to. The next few days are going to be wicked."

"Wicked or not, I hope we manage to wrap up at least one of our cases. I can't charge Mrs. Dineen more money with no results."

"Want to bet that Old Man Dineen is just heading out for a break from his wife?"

I frowned. "Mrs. Dineen doesn't strike me as a

nag. No, something's up with her husband, and it's up to us to find out what."

"Didn't you say you'd emailed your dad about the musket ball?" my friend asked. "Have you heard back from him yet?"

"Yeah. I sent him the details and a copy of the forensics photo of the musket ball from Reynolds's file. Long story short, Dad agrees with my theory that the musket ball was probably fired from a late eighteenth century flintlock musket. The problem will be finding who had access to such a weapon on Whisper Island. I've asked Philomena to help me out with that."

Lenny bounced from foot to foot. "I love being a P.I. Between murder, mayhem, and muskets, life on Whisper Island is way more exciting than it used to be. Sunday's stakeout can't come fast enough."

"I have to survive tomorrow's boat trip first." I linked arms with my friend. "Come on. It's time to forget about work. Let's go watch *The 39 Steps*."

14

On the morning of the boat trip, I stopped by the Movie Theater Café, where Noreen helped me to pack a scrumptious picnic. It included elaborate sandwiches, scones, muffins, and sticky caramel slices. I added a large thermos flask of coffee for Reynolds and me, and iced tea for the girls. Armed with the enormous basket, I trudged out to my car.

Across the road, Dolly O'Brien had just opened The Cupcake Café. She waved across to me. "Lovely day for a picnic."

"It is," I yelled, "especially one on a yacht."

I slid behind the wheel just as a group from the excavation team entered The Cupcake Café. I glanced through the front windows of my aunt's café, noting the empty tables and the worry lines on her forehead. A pang of regret hit me. Much as I wanted to, I could do nothing to help alleviate Noreen's worries.

My next job was to collect Caoimhe Greer. Her grandparents owned the Whisper Island Hotel, and her parents managed the business. In addition to working at the hotel, they lived in a property on the grounds.

As I turned into the drive that led to the hotel, I caught a glimpse of a guy jogging through the gardens. He looked familiar enough to make me look at him twice. I frowned. If it weren't for the guy's clean-shaven jaw, I'd have sworn it was Richard Carstairs. I checked the jogger for evidence of Richard's trademark gray ponytail, but the bandana around his head made it impossible to tell. I shook my head. My obsession with the skeleton case was making me see things that weren't there.

I hung a left and drove through the gates to an elegant house that was separated from the hotel grounds by a ring of trees. It was my first visit to the house Paul and Melanie had built for their young family. Although I hated to admit it, the house was far from the ostentatious mansion I'd envisioned. Instead, it was a tasteful villa with floor-to-ceiling windows and a generous private garden.

Caoimhe, dressed in bright pink, was waiting for me on the doorstep. Melanie hovered behind her daughter, fussing over the contents of the girl's back-pack. "Are you sure you haven't forgotten anything?

Should we double-check to see that you packed your inhaler?"

"*You* packed my inhaler, Mum, and you've checked the bag three times already."

"Morning," I said brightly and strolled over to join them.

"Hello, Maggie." Melanie's smile was tight. For once, I knew it wasn't because of me. "I have a portable booster seat that should work in your car." She eyed my rusty vehicle with visible apprehension. "The backseats have seat belts, right?"

I suppressed a smile. "They do."

"Paul?" Melanie called over her shoulder. "Can you come out here and put Caoimhe's booster in Maggie's car?"

My former boyfriend appeared at her shoulder, unshaven and more casually dressed than I was used to seeing him. "No problem. I'll show Caoimhe how to fasten the belt around it."

Melanie's hands fluttered. "She should have everything she needs. If there's any problem, give me a call. I'll have my phone on me all day."

Her daughter rolled her eyes. "Seriously. I'm eight. I'll be fine."

Her mother hovered like a worried hen, finally hugging her daughter tight. "Have fun, darling. And don't forget to apply extra sun cream after lunch."

Caoimhe hoisted her backpack over one shoulder and followed her father over to my car.

"I promise I'll take good care of her," I said to the girl's mother.

She gave a stiff nod. "Caoimhe can be difficult. She doesn't find it easy to socialize."

"I got that impression on Monday's trip."

Melanie sighed. "I hope it'll improve as she grows older. I hate seeing her ostracized at school, but we can't force the other kids to play with her. At least the bullying has improved since your cousin became her teacher."

From my own experience during childhood summers on Whisper Island and from Julie's stories, I knew Melanie had been a notorious bully in school. The fact that she now found herself the mother of a bullying victim was pretty ironic.

I took a step away from the door. "I'd better get going. I'm not sure what time we'll get back. It shouldn't be later than eight. I'll leave my car at the harbor, so I'll drive Caoimhe home."

"Thanks, Maggie."

Paul had finished putting the booster seat into my car.

I slid behind the wheel and started the engine. We waved to Caoimhe's parents on our way down the drive, and then I hung a left and took the coast road to the harbor. My guest was silent for most of the drive, but she perked up when we reached Carraig Harbour. We climbed out of the car, and I retrieved the picnic basket and my backpack from the trunk.

Reynolds and Hannah were waiting for us by the entrance to the elevator.

Oh, boy. Could I overcome my anxiety about elevators, or would I delay us all by taking the rickety iron staircase down to the pier? I took a deep breath and wiped my clammy palms on my shorts. "Hey," I said brightly. "Are you all set to have fun today?"

Hannah looked at Caoimhe with interest. The other girl hung back and took a step closer to me.

I put a hand on her back and urged her forward. "Hannah, this is Caoimhe. Caoimhe, Hannah."

The girls sized one another up. I shared a concerned look with Reynolds. I recalled my time as a little girl all too vividly. Girls could be complicated.

Hannah took a step toward Caoimhe. "I like your T-shirt. Where did you find Star Wars gear in pink?"

Caoimhe blushed. "My dad got it custom-made."

The girls stepped into the elevator.

Reynolds took my hand. "Would you prefer to take the stairs?" he asked in a low voice. "We don't mind waiting for you."

I swallowed past the lump in my throat. "I can handle it," I said with a bravado that didn't match my feelings.

Reynolds grinned. "You're terrified. Come on, admit it."

"That's about the size of it."

He tugged me into the elevator. "Close your eyes and imagine you're already on the boat."

"Given my past experience of being sick on boats, that's not an enticing prospect."

"If you get seasick," Hannah said, "why did you agree to come out on the yacht today?"

"I thought it would be a nice chance to get to know you." I patted the pockets of my shorts. "I brought seasickness pills."

Pity I hadn't brought anti-anxiety medication.

The elevator doors closed, and we began our descent. I kept my eyes tightly closed the whole time. A rivulet of sweat snaked down my back, and my palms felt clammy. I concentrated on Reynolds's hand around mine and counted my breaths. The descent seemed to take forever, and when the door slid open and salty sea air gushed in, I sagged in relief.

"See?" Reynolds's voice rumbled in my ear. "That wasn't so bad."

"You didn't spend the last five minutes fending off a panic attack."

He laughed. "The lift took twenty seconds at most."

"Well, it was a *long* twenty seconds."

"Here we are." Reynolds pointed at a small yacht at the end of the pier. "I hired it from Nick Sweetman."

"It's cute," I said.

Caoimhe screwed up her nose. "It's much smaller than Granddad's yacht. But then, he's rich and could afford to buy his own."

"When would my dad find the time to sail a yacht

regularly?" Hannah demanded. "He's busy keeping Whisper Island safe."

"Okay, girls," I said, keen to ward off the impending fight. "Time to go aboard. Who wants to help me explore?"

Although the tour of the boat didn't take long, it proved a distraction and gave the girls the opportunity to tease each other over the bright orange life vests I insisted they wear, and to discover two board games in an unlocked closet. They settled on *Monopoly* and were soon playing happily. In spite of her prickly attitude with me, Hannah proved to be skilled at diffusing Caoimhe's defensive remarks. By the time we were halfway between Whisper Island and Dolphin Island, Hannah had coaxed Caoimhe out of her defensive shell.

I left the girls to their game and joined Reynolds at the wheel—or whatever the steering area of a boat was called.

He grinned when he saw me. "No catfights?"

"Not so far. Hannah's actually pretty good with Caoimhe."

Reynolds slipped his arm around my waist and pulled me close. "I've missed you," he murmured. "It's nice to have a chance to spend time with you again."

"Even if we have two mini chaperones to preserve my modesty?"

He laughed. "Even then."

For the first stretch of our voyage, we made the

most of our time alone, keeping the conversation light and avoiding any mention of work. The view through the window was spectacular. The blue sky was speckled white, and the water stretched before us like a shimmering green-blue carpet. An array of boats dotted the sea, and they diminished in number the farther we traveled from Whisper Island.

"If you want a better view, use these." Reynolds picked up a pair of binoculars and handed them to me.

I held them to my eyes and peered through the lenses, adjusting the zoom when I spotted an object I wanted a closer look at. A large yacht bobbed in the distance. A lone sunbather lay on the deck, enjoying the warmth of the sun. As we drew closer, I noticed the yacht wasn't moving.

"I hope that person's slathered in sun cream," I said to Reynolds. "If I tried sunbathing in sun this direct, I'd fry."

He angled the boat slightly to the left. "We'll arrive at Dolphin Island in around fifteen minutes."

"Should I tell the girls to pack up the game?"

"They can leave it out if they want to finish it on the trip back."

I looked through the binoculars again and zoomed in on the looming cliffs of Dolphin Island. I hadn't been there since I'd moved to Whisper Island in January, but I recalled visiting the smaller island one summer when I was a child. In addition to the dolphins that were frequently spotted in the vicinity of the island, Dolphin Island was home to one of the largest bird sanctuaries in Ireland, as well as a nature reserve containing endangered flowers and plants. With the exception of the people who worked there, no one lived on Dolphin Island, and there were no hotels or guesthouses. It was a day-trip destination only.

I swung the binoculars to my left, and the large yacht with the sunbather came back into my range of vision. This close to the yacht and at this zoom level, I could pick out the details of the deck. The gleaming wood shone under the sunlight. Two deck chairs were visible, and the sunbather wasn't lying on either of them. I shifted to the right. And drew in a breath.

"Liam, someone is lying facedown on the deck of that yacht. It's the person I mentioned earlier. Farther away, I assumed they were sunbathing. This close, I can see they're not on a deck chair. And I think there's something sticking out of them."

"Are you sure?" He took the binoculars from me and held them to his eyes, adjusting the zoom. He swore under his breath. "Take another look, Maggie. Does that gray ponytail look familiar?"

Our eyes met.

I grabbed the binoculars and peered through them. "From this distance, it's hard to tell for sure, but he reminds me of Richard Carstairs. Whoever he is, he's not sunbathing. We've got to check it out."

"I'm on it." Reynolds swung the boat around and powered toward the larger yacht. The minutes ticked by at a snail's pace before we pulled up next to the other vessel. He killed the engine. "I'm going to board the other yacht. Stay here with the girls."

In spite of my urge to join him, common sense prevailed. We couldn't leave two eight-year-old girls alone on a boat they couldn't sail. I didn't know my way around boats, but at least I knew how to work the radio and call for help if necessary.

The instant he clambered from our boat and up the ladder that led to the deck of the larger yacht, the girls appeared from below deck.

"Where's Dad?" Hannah demanded.

Caoimhe peered out the window. "Why have we stopped?"

"Liam's checking on the man on the boat next to ours. We think he might be sick."

Caoimhe's eyes grew wide. "Do you think he's had a heart attack? Do you have a defibrillator on board?"

"I don't know. We can check the first aid equipment."

"We have a defibrillator at the hotel," Caoimhe said sagely. "Mum insisted we get one after a man had a heart attack in the hotel gym."

Hannah shuddered. "Did he die?"

The other girl shook her head. "He had bypass surgery and survived."

Suddenly, Liam shouted from the other boat. From his tone, we could all tell something wasn't right. I bolted out onto the deck and ran to the railing.

I shielded my eyes from the sun and craned my neck. "What's wrong?"

Liam appeared above me, leaning against the rail of the bigger boat. His pallor and grave expression told me we had a problem. "Can you come up here for a sec, Maggie?"

I glanced at the girls, both of whom were craning their necks to get a glimpse of the action on the other boat.

Reynolds ran a hand through his close-cropped blond hair. "Hannah and Caoimhe, go downstairs and stay put. Maggie and I will be back in a minute."

With what I hoped was a reassuring smile for the girls, I scrambled up the ladder and onto the deck of the luxury yacht. I froze the instant I took in the scene, my breath coming in short and sharp bursts. As I'd seen through the binoculars, the man lay on the yacht's deck, facedown and unmoving. One glance at the knife in his neck told me the dude was dead.

15

Reynolds turned to me, his face pale under his summer tan. "I went through the motions and checked for a pulse, but there's no chance."

"Not with a neck wound of that nature." And not with the amount of blood seeping from beneath the body. In spite of the warm sun, I shivered. "May I check him out?"

"Be my guest…but wear gloves."

I gave him the side-eye. "Where am I going to get disposable rubber gloves on a yacht in the middle of the Atlantic?"

A smile tugged at the corners of his mouth. "Catch." And he tossed me a package containing one pair of disposable gloves.

I stared at the package and shook my head. "Seriously? You carry these around even when you're on vacation?"

"Hey, I'm on a day trip with Maggie the Dead-Body Magnet. I came prepared."

I put my hands on my hips. "So not funny."

He grinned. "It's force of habit. I always have a Swiss Army knife, disposable gloves, and a pocket flashlight. I feel naked without them."

As I traveled with a similar ensemble, I made a mental note to add disposable gloves to my collection. Heck, I'd throw in foot covers and a plastic cap just to get one up on Reynolds.

After I'd gloved up, I went over to the body and hunkered down, careful to avoid the blood. I touched the dead man's skin. Even through the rubber of my gloves, the skin felt cooler than it should under the direct sun. He'd been dead a while. "The beard, the build, the ponytail. I don't need to see an ID to know this is Richard Carstairs."

Reynolds nodded grimly. "Yeah. It's him, all right."

I shook my head. "It's so weird. I saw a guy who looked so like him jogging through the hotel grounds less than an hour ago. Now that I know Richard was probably dead by then, it's eerie."

He regarded me sharply. "How alike were they?"

I scrunched up my forehead and cast my mind back to my drive to Caoimhe's house. "I only saw him from a distance, but I was immediately struck by the likeness."

"We'll check if Richard had family on the island. A brother or cousin would explain the lookalike you saw." Reynolds regarded the corpse with a frown. "I'm no doctor, but I've encountered enough corpses to know Richard's been dead for more than an hour."

"I agree with your estimate." I stood and surveyed the deck. "I can't see how he got a knife in his neck by accident. If he had a wound through the stomach, I'd be prepared to consider the possibility that he tripped and fell, but this? No way."

"Yeah," Reynolds muttered. "I guess this throws a new light on the skeleton investigation. Carstairs was the only link between the two excavations."

"The only link that we know of," I corrected. "I'm not done digging for info. Have you checked his pockets yet? Maybe there's some clue as to why he's on this big yacht alone." I paused. "He was alone, right?"

Reynolds nodded. "My first act was to check the boat for more bodies—dead or alive—and my second was to call the police station and ask for backup." He squeezed his eyes shut and groaned. "Robyn will have a fit."

"Who's Robyn?"

He opened his eyes, and the sadness within had me longing to reach out and kiss him. "Robyn is my ex—Hannah's mother. She's already tried to micro-manage this visit from afar. When she discovers Hannah was with me when I found a corpse, she'll go ballistic."

"Hannah's safely on the other boat. It's not like she's seen the—"

"Oh. My. Goodness," a girl's voice said from behind me. "Is that guy *dead?*"

We whirled around. Hannah and Caoimhe stood on the deck, staring in horror at the prone figure.

"Wow. This is so cool. Wait until I tell Tommy." Caoimhe turned to Hannah. "My brother dug up a skeleton on Monday. Now I'll get to say I found a dead body."

"Sergeant Reynolds found the corpse," I said sternly, "and we told you two to stay put."

Caoimhe rolled her eyes. "We're not deaf. We could hear you two talking up here. Not every word, but enough to get the gist."

Hannah stared at me warily. "Caoimhe said you find dead people a lot."

I sighed. "It's happened a few times."

The girl gave me a look of grudging approval. "That's kind of cool in a weird sort of way."

"That's what I said when Tommy found the skeleton," the other girl added. "Mum and Dad were horrified. They didn't think it was cool at all."

"Oh, my mum will go mad when she finds out. Which she doesn't have to." Hannah raised her voice for this last sentence. "Right, Dad?"

Reynolds rubbed the back of his head, and the worry lines etched on his forehead deepened. "I can't not tell her, love. Even if I wanted to hide the discovery from her, it'll be all over the news."

His daughter pouted. "That sucks. She'll be on the first plane back to Ireland, assuming she ever left."

"What do you mean?" I asked. "Did your mother come with you on the plane?"

The girl regarded me with disdain. "Well, duh. I'm eight. The airline won't let me fly without a chaperone."

Reynolds picked up the thread. "Robyn escorted Hannah to Shannon Airport on Tuesday morning and caught the next flight back to London after I'd collected her."

No wonder he hadn't wanted me to drive him to the airport. The picture I'd formed in my mind of his ex was of a domineering woman who tried to control everyone around her. This was probably unfair, but he'd used the word "micromanage" to describe how Robyn tried to control Hannah's visit. For all I knew, she might simply be very organized, and her attempts to organize him had irritated Reynolds.

An awkward silence hung in the air since the mention of Hannah's mother. A change of subject was the smartest move at this juncture, and I went for the most obvious one. "You mentioned you'd searched the boat. Apart from the body, is there anything suspicious on board?"

"Not that I could tell from my cursory search," Reynolds replied, "but I wasn't looking for clues. I wanted to make sure no one else was hurt, and that the k—" his gaze darted to the girls, "—wasn't still on board."

"Killer." Hannah rolled her eyes. "You can say the word, Dad. Caoimhe and I aren't stupid. Even if

Maggie hadn't already said it didn't look like an accident, the knife in his neck would have clued us in."

Reynolds winced. "I wish you'd stayed put like I told you to. I was going to cover him with a blanket before I came to get you."

His daughter laughed. "The first thing we'd have done is come up with a plan to sneak a peek. Right, Caoimhe?"

The other girl bobbed her head. "Definitely. No way would we want to miss out on the fun."

"There are many adjectives I could use to describe this situation," Reynolds said in a dry tone, "and 'fun' isn't one of them."

"Would you mind if I took a look below deck?" I held up my gloved hands. "I won't touch anything unless necessary."

"Can we come with you?" Caoimhe bounced from foot to foot in excitement. "Me and Hannah can act as your forensics team."

I suppressed a smile. "The real deal will be swarming all over the yacht before long. I don't think they'd be happy if so many of us had searched the boat."

Not to mention the fact that I didn't trust the girls not to touch stuff or go through drawers and closets.

Reynolds shot me a grateful smile. "You two can stay with me. Seeing as you're here and it's going to take a while before backup arrives, you can watch me look for the dead man's ID. Just keep your distance, okay?"

Caoimhe turned to Hannah. "Your dad is awesome. Mine would never let me check out a corpse."

"This is the first time he's let me," Hannah confided. "Although I did take a peek at some crime scene photos he had in his briefcase. Those were seriously gross."

Reynolds sighed and looked at me. "I'm pretty sure this isn't my finest parenting moment. I don't feel comfortable leaving them out of sight on another boat for too long. And I know there's no way I'll persuade you to stay there with them."

"Nope. I'm not letting an opportunity to check out the scene of the crime pass me by." I gave him a cheeky wave. "I won't be long."

I climbed down the short staircase to the area below deck. I was sure it had a formal name, but I wasn't familiar with sailing terminology. I looked in each room. The sleeping areas had a musty scent and didn't look like they'd been occupied in a while. The galley—the one boat term I did know—was small and well equipped with modern cooking appliances. Everything was neat and in its place. The only sign that someone had been in here recently was a large pink box with the words "The Cupcake Café" emblazoned across it in chocolate brown letters.

I took a step closer to the box. The sticker that had served as its seal was still intact. I debated my next action for all of half a second. Reynolds would be annoyed, but I couldn't see how peeling off the sticker would do any harm. After I'd done so, I lifted the lid with care and peeked inside the box.

Rows of delicious-looking cupcakes had been neatly arranged according to flavor. I counted the cupcakes. There were thirty-nine in the box. Why thirty-nine and not forty? Forty would have fit perfectly in a box of this size and tied in with the distribution of eight cupcakes per flavor. Instead, there were only seven of the maple pecan variety I'd sampled on The Cupcake Café's opening day. Had the customer ordered thirty-nine cupcakes, or had Dolly simply forgotten to put one in? Frowning, I closed the box and replaced the sticker. It was a minor point, but it bothered me.

I spent the next few minutes looking around the bottom level of the boat. Nothing of significance leaped out at me. When I rejoined the others on the deck, Reynolds held a wallet in his hand, and his expression could have given the Grim Reaper a run for his money.

"Did you find an ID card?"

His eyes met mine, and he handed me a driver's license. "Whoa." My gaze darted to the body, then back to Reynolds. "Richard Carstairs's real name was Ryan Murphy?"

"I don't know. He has another driver's license made out to David Wallace."

"Wow." Hannah took a step closer to the body. "Richard Carstairs is the guy who lives next door to you, Dad. The one you had a beer with the other day."

"Yeah. He is—or was—part of a team of archaeologists who are excavating a site on Whisper Island. A few of them have rented cottages in our complex until the end of August."

"Do you think he killed the skeleton?" Caoimhe demanded, her voice rising with excitement. "Maybe someone bumped him off in revenge."

Reynolds and I exchanged glances.

"Aw, screw it. There's no point in lying to them." I turned to the girls. "We don't know for sure there's a connection, but it's one heck of a coincidence if there's no link."

Reynolds was more cautious. "Until the body is examined by a doctor, we can't say for sure his death was unnatural."

"Oh, come on, Dad. His head's hanging off. Caoimhe and I aren't stupid. It's totally obvious that foul play is at work." Hannah looked at Caoimhe. "I got that phrase from an old episode of *Murder, She Wrote*. Mum doesn't usually let me watch crime series on TV. For some reason, she doesn't think Jessica Fletcher counts."

"You're lucky," Caoimhe confided. "My mum doesn't approve of kids watching TV. I have to rely on YouTube."

I laughed at this image. Melanie didn't strike me as the most tech-savvy individual. She probably had no idea what her kids could find on the internet apps she and Paul allowed them access to.

Reynolds examined the wallet again. "Did you notice anything odd downstairs, Maggie? Any of Richard's stuff?"

I paused for a moment before answering. "There was a cake box in the kitchen."

"Yeah. I saw that. From that new place across from your aunt's café."

"The Cupcake Café." I paused. "It contains thirty-nine cupcakes."

"Oh, no," he groaned. "Please tell me you didn't break the seal?"

"Of course not," I said indignantly. "I took great care to peel back the sticker and replace it after I'd looked inside."

The girls found this revelation hilarious.

Reynolds shook his head. "You're incorrigible."

"Don't you think thirty-nine is an odd number?" I demanded.

"Thirty-nine *is* an odd number," Caoimhe pointed out. "Mathematically speaking."

"Why would someone order thirty-nine cupcakes?" I demanded. "Why not forty? Was it for a birthday?"

Reynolds sighed in exasperation. "So Dolly forgot to put in a cupcake. What's the big deal?"

"I don't know that there's *any* deal, big or small. I merely find it strange. And that bothers me. Ever since Tommy found that skeleton on Monday, I keep finding things that don't add up, or are just plain weird. That sets off alarm bells."

Caoimhe blinked, owl-like. "Tommy's missing camera."

I nodded. "Yeah. That's on my list of oddities."

Reynolds scratched his neck. "To get back to the cupcakes, the box and Richard's body are the only signs that anyone has been on this boat recently."

"Right," I agreed. "The cupcakes look fresh, and Dolly's place only opened three days ago."

Hannah turned green. "All this talk of cupcakes is making me sick. What about you, Caoimhe?"

Her friend pulled a face. "I don't think I ever want to see a cupcake again. They'll always make me think of dead bodies."

Reynolds and I exchanged amused glances. "I'll take the girls back to the other boat," I said. "I'm sure they'll find another board game to play to distract them from the body."

"Are you going to dust the cupcake box for finger-prints?" Caoimhe asked. "Can we watch?"

Reynolds shook his head. "That's a job for the forensics team. They'll dust for fingerprints and take photos of everything to get a clear picture of what everything on the boat looked like at the time of the m—death."

"Murder." Hannah blew out her cheeks. "You guys are ridiculous. It's not like we don't know the dude was bumped off."

With those sage words, Hannah and Caoimhe

clambered over the side of the yacht and climbed down the ladder to the boat below. I darted over to Reynolds, stood on my tippy-toes, and brushed his lips with mine. "Do you want me to bring you up a sandwich?"

He shook his head. "No thanks. My appetite is gone." He paused. "Is the coffee in the thermos from the Movie Theater Café?"

"It is. And yes, I'll bring you a cup."

He laughed and caught me up in his arms. We stared into each other's eyes for a couple of tense seconds before Reynolds claimed my mouth with his. For a glorious moment, all thoughts of dead bodies and odd-numbered cupcakes melted from my mind. By the time he released me, we were both breathless and grinning like teenagers.

"Thanks for supervising the kids, Maggie."

His breath tickled my neck. I forced myself to take a step back and put some distance between us. "No problem." I gave him a mock salute. "Happy corpse duty."

16

It took four hours before Reynolds could hand off the case to Sergeant O'Shea. The older police officer had been in the middle of a game for the golf tournament and was livid to be called into action, especially as Reynolds was on the scene. It took some not-so-gentle persuasion to convince him that Reynolds was on vacation and therefore not obligated to deal with the investigation.

Once we'd left the irritated sergeant in the company of the forensics team, Reynolds sailed our boat to Dolphin Island, where we spent the rest of the day exploring the bird sanctuary. We arrived back at Carraig Harbour just before eight that evening.

"Our carefree day trip didn't go quite as planned." Reynolds slid me a look and chuckled. "I should have known we'd have an adventure with you along."

"It was the best day ever," Caoimhe said. "I had so much fun."

Hannah nodded, wide-eyed. "Me, too. Can we do it again before I go home?"

"Go out on a boat, or find a dead body?" her father asked, deadpan. "Because I'm hoping you don't mean the latter."

"The whole experience was fantastic," Hannah gushed, "and Caoimhe totally got into the swing of helping me try to solve the crime."

Reynolds and I exchanged an amused glance.

"Would you like me to talk to Caoimhe's mother to see if you two can meet again while you're on Whisper Island?" I asked.

"Yes," both girls said in unison.

"Maybe Hannah can come and swim in our pool," Caoimhe said, suddenly shy. "Swimming's the one sport I like, even if I'm not all that good at it."

"You have a pool?" Hannah sounded impressed.

"Well, it's the hotel's pool," Caoimhe amended. "We're allowed to swim there sometimes. My grand-parents own the hotel, and Mum and Dad work there."

"Cool," Hannah said. "I'd love to."

"I'll speak to Melanie and see what we can arrange." This statement was delivered with more confidence than I felt. I dreaded telling Melanie that her daughter had seen a dead body in my company, especially after Tommy's discovery on Monday.

"Thanks, Maggie," Reynolds said. "And thanks for

joining us today, Caoimhe. I was glad Hannah had some company, especially with all the drama."

Caoimhe smiled shyly. "Thank you for inviting me."

We said goodbye to Reynolds and Hannah, and I drove Caoimhe home.

An anxious Melanie hovered on the doorstep of the Greer residence, giving me the impression she'd been worrying about her daughter all day. *Ugh.* I hoped the news of the dead guy hadn't reached her. Maybe I should have called her about it earlier, but Caoimhe was safe and I'd thought the news would be better delivered in person.

The girl's hand lingered on the passenger door handle. "She's going to bust a gut."

"I know." I grimaced. "I'll talk to her. Come on. Let's get it over with."

I got Caoimhe's booster seat from the back, and we trudged up the pebbled drive like the condemned on their way to their executions.

Melanie's gaze darted anxiously from me to her daughter. "Hi, Caoimhe. How was your day?"

The girl's face grew animated, making her look almost pretty. "Totally wicked. I had the best time."

Her mother slow-blinked. "Then why the long faces when you two got out of the car?"

"You're going to be so mad. I swear it wasn't Maggie's fault. She's been awesome, and the whole thing was a ton of fun."

Melanie fixed me with a hard gaze. "Oh, no. Please don't tell me you found another body?"

"Technically, Reynolds found it," I said hastily, "and Caoimhe was never in any danger. In fact, she handled herself like a pro. You have a very level-headed daughter."

Melanie's lips pressed into a thin line. "Say goodbye to Maggie and go inside."

After a moment's hesitation, Caoimhe ran over to me and gave me a hug. "Thanks so much for inviting me today. I'd love to meet up with Hannah again if you can persuade Mum."

I laughed. "I'll do my best. Get a good night's sleep."

When her daughter had disappeared into the house, Melanie rounded on me. "What happened?"

I gave her a brief rundown of the day's events, careful to emphasize how well Hannah and Caoimhe had gotten along. "Despite the drama—or maybe even because of it—the girls had a great time."

Melanie shook her head, a bemused expression on her face. "This is the first time Caoimhe has been invited out with another kid where she's come home with a smile on her face. I don't get it."

"Kids are ghoulish, Melanie," I said with a laugh. "And neither girl was ever in any danger. By the time we finally reached Dolphin Island, they'd both decided they wanted to be crime scene investigators when they grow up."

This made Melanie laugh, a rare sound from her

lips. "Okay, you win. Hannah is welcome to visit us. I think I have Sergeant Reynolds's number somewhere. I'll send him a text to arrange a date."

"Hannah will be delighted." I took a step back. "I'd better get going."

"Bye, Maggie. And thank you."

I trudged back to my car, deep in thought. Realizing that Melanie had a good side sucked. And what sucked even more was recognizing I resented the fact that she wasn't all bad. I'd preferred shoving her into a box labeled with a capital 'B' and feeling morally superior.

When I arrived back at Shamrock Cottages, Lenny lounged on the bench in front of my cottage, reading a comic. He leaped to his feet when I got out of the car. "Hey, Maggie. I was hoping you'd get back soon. Reynolds said you wouldn't be long."

"I had to drop Caoimhe Greer home." I slid my key into the lock. "I can tell you have news. Want to join me on my deck for a cocktail? I could use one after the day I've had."

Once we were settled on the deck with a jug of Gin Basil Smash, Lenny looked around. "Where's Bran? He's usually up in my crotch within five seconds of my entering the premises."

I laughed. "He's staying with Noreen for the night. With all the commotion earlier, I wasn't sure when we'd get back, so I asked her to feed the cats and take Bran overnight. He can go for a walk with her and her new dog. Now, come on. Tell me your news."

Lenny beamed and leaned forward. "Two things, actually. First, I have a lead on the exhibition brochure. The Spinsters told me they have a bunch of junk in their attic and we're welcome to go through it. They're positive they went to that exhibition and would have picked up a brochure."

The Spinsters—Miss Flynn and Miss Murphy— were regular patrons of the Movie Theater Café. They were retired schoolteachers who shared a house in Smuggler's Cove. From my first days working at the café, I'd liked them, and I was particularly grateful to Miss Murphy for a 101 in Tea Preparation.

I took a sip from my Gin Basil Smash. "What's the second thing you discovered?"

"The 2000 excavation and volunteers from both the Historical Society and the Folklore and Heritage Society. Do you remember Sheila Dunphy?"

"The president of the Whisper Island Folklore and Heritage Society? Yeah. Didn't she try to block the excavation like she did back in the Sixties?" I'd met Sheila during a previous investigation. She was a passionate defender of a fairy tree located on the hotel grounds and had frequently protested against excavation and building plans that would remove it.

"She didn't try to block that excavation," Lenny said. "Far from it. She's interested in the island's history. She's president of the Folklore and Heritage Society, and she's an active member of the Historical

Society. The only reason she protested against the excavation plans in the Sixties was because they involved cutting down the fairy tree."

"So what's her connection to the 2000 excavation?" The penny dropped, and I whistled. "Wait a sec…was she a volunteer on the dig?"

"Bingo." Lenny looked pleased with himself. "She's promised to tell me all about it over lunch on Monday and show me a scrapbook she made at the time."

"That's fantastic. Well done, Lenny. If you talk to Sheila, I'll ask the Spinsters if I can root around in their attic tomorrow. Did you have any luck finding info on the young archaeologist, Ben?"

"Nothing nefarious so far. His credentials check out. I'm going to keep digging." He took a sip of his drink. "So how was your day?" Lenny asked. "Did Hannah throw more attitude your way?"

"The answers to those questions are 'dramatic' and 'no.'" I filled Lenny in on the events of the day, including the news about the murder and Carstairs's various identities.

Unsurprisingly, Lenny was thrilled. "Whoa. So Richard Carstairs, the only dude on both excavations, got whacked?"

"Yep. And there have been way too many coincidences for me to dismiss this as yet another. There's got to be a link." The mention of links jogged a memory. "Speaking of coincidences, I saw a guy jogging through the hotel grounds this morning who looked so like Richard."

"Could it have been him?" Lenny asked.

I shook my head. "The timing's all wrong. I collected Caoimhe just before eight this morning. While Reynolds and I were giving our statements to Sergeant O'Shea and Timms, I overheard the pathologist estimate Richard's time of death at between seven and eight. There's no way he could get from the Whisper Island Hotel to the area we found the yacht in a few minutes."

Lenny considered this information for a moment. "Could he have been killed on the hotel grounds and then transported to the yacht?"

"No. Even if time wasn't a factor, the cake knife he was killed with was still in his body when we found him."

"Cake knife? Are you sure?"

I nodded. "I paid close attention to what the forensics team said to each other, and it looked like a cake knife to me."

"What about Dolly's cupcakes?" He frowned and shook his head. "Are they connected to the knife? I'm trying to find the significance between the cupcakes and Richard's death, but I can't. I mean, half of Whisper Island has picked up a box of her produce since Wednesday. We don't get many new businesses in town, and hers is a novel concept."

"I have no idea," I said. "The most likely explanation is that Dolly—or whoever packed that box—

forgot the fortieth cupcake. I'm going to call by her café tomorrow to ask. Even if she's been inundated with orders, we might get lucky and she'll remember who picked up the box."

Lenny scrunched up his forehead. "Who'd want Carstairs dead? The person responsible for killing the skeleton?"

I cradled my cocktail glass between my palms and sighed. "I don't know. Maybe. Richard had a reputation for being a ladies' man, and he had multiple identities. That gives us a number of reasons for someone wanting him dead."

"Was he romancing anyone involved in the excavation?"

I shrugged. "He was friendly with Ellen Taylor, but I'm not sure it went farther than talk. Susie said Ellen keeps slipping away from the excavation to meet someone, and I got the impression that person was a man."

"And you think Richard was the guy she was meeting?"

"Actually, no. Susie didn't say anything about Richard running off. I need to ask her to elaborate."

"Who else on the excavation had a motive to kill Richard?" Lenny asked.

"Alan Doherty implied Richard was flirting with Susie, but it's hard to say if that statement was motivated by paranoid jealousy."

Lenny tapped the arm of his chair in an absent rhythm. "Do you know where Carstairs got the yacht?

From your description, it sounds kind of fancy for a guy on a field archaeologist's salary."

"The forensics team found papers identifying it as being part of Nick Sweetman's fleet. He must own a number of boats."

"Ten, and only two are the size you're describing." At my incredulous expression, he added, "I used to be a member of the Yacht Club."

"You?" I shook my head. "You're so not a yacht club kind of person."

"I'm not," he agreed, "but before Noreen offered her café to island interest clubs, there weren't many options. I founded the Unplugged Gamers with Mack and Paul, and Noreen started the Movie Club. Once I had stuff to do that was more interesting, I quit the Yacht Club and the Golf Club."

"Back up a sec. *Paul Greer* was a founding member of the Unplugged Gamers?"

"Well, yeah. I told you he was a member when you joined. He stopped coming after you became a regular."

I was momentarily bereft of speech. "I had no idea."

"I mentioned it the very first time you came to one of our meetings. You were looking into his mother-in-law's death at the time, and I figured he stayed away because of that."

Now that he mentioned it, I had a vague recollection of Lenny telling me about Paul being an Unplugged Gamer. When Paul had never shown up to a meeting, I'd forgotten. "I feel bad if he stayed away because of me."

"Don't. It's his choice. If he lets himself be browbeaten by Melanie, that's his problem."

"Do you think she told him to stay away from the club?"

"Oh, yeah. She's jealous of you. She wouldn't want him anywhere near you, especially if she's not present."

I blinked. "I didn't pick up on that vibe at all."

Lenny raised his Gin Basil Smash. "That's because you're you, Maggie, and we love you for it."

I didn't quite get what he meant, but it was time to steer the conversation back to safer territory. "Before we get to your news, tell me about Nick's boats. I'm assuming a person renting one has to give some form of ID and prove they can operate the vessel."

My friend nodded. "Especially a yacht of the size Richard Carstairs was on."

"Could one person sail a yacht?"

"For a short trip? Yeah, no problem. The question I'd have is why Richard Carstairs would hire a boat that large if he intended to make a solo trip."

"Unless it was the only one Nick had left? I'd imagine tourists snap up those boat reservations."

"Maybe." Lenny didn't look convinced. "It just strikes me as strange. We need to find out if Carstairs had arranged to meet someone today."

"We?" I teased. "We're only supposed to be investigating the skeleton."

Lenny laughed. "We'll find a solid link between the two. Might as well get a head start."

"We need to know where Carstairs was going," I mused. "The boat was pointed in the direction of Dolphin Island, but he might have been on his way somewhere else."

"Want to make a list of tasks and divide them up? I know how much you love your lists."

I laughed and grabbed my notepad and pen from the table. "Oh yes, I do. Let's go back to the items we listed as 'Known Facts' on the whiteboard in my office. One: the skeleton belongs to a male aged between thirty-five and forty-five. Two: the body was buried fifteen to twenty years ago. Three: the cause of death could have been a fatal musket shot to the skull. This could place the murder at the time of the earlier excavation, and the age of the victim could make him a contemporary of Richard Carstairs."

Lenny frowned. "Meaning they might have known each other?"

"Correct. A fourth known fact: the skeleton is missing the left femur. We've already discussed the possibility that this was stolen from the burial site soon after Tommy discovered the skull, possibly to avoid identification if the femur contained an identifiable orthopedic device."

"Where do we go from here?" Lenny asked. "Want me to keep looking for that brochure?"

"Yes, please. And use your amazing internet research skills to dig up dirt on Richard Carstairs.

While you're busy with that, I'll follow up on the cupcakes and visit the Spinsters. If they have the brochure, I'll let you know.

"Sounds good. Where are we on the Dineen case?"

I grimaced. "Nowhere. I've continued to ask questions, but no one knows anything about what Fionn's doing on his nocturnal excursions. Mrs. Dineen told me he's due to go out at around nine on Sunday night. This time, I'll tail him to the bitter end. Do you want to join me?"

His face lit up. "Sure. I have to catch up on computer repairs tomorrow, but I'm free in the evening. I'm working the morning shift at my parents' shop on Monday, but I'll concentrate on digging for info on Richard Carstairs in the afternoon, after my lunch with Sheila."

"I'm keeping my fingers crossed that there's a logical explanation for Fionn Dineen spending time with Bethany that doesn't involve them having an affair. Mrs. Dineen is a lovely woman. I'd hate to see her hurt."

"Agreed." My friend drained his glass and glanced at his watch. "I'd better get going. I asked Granddad to collect me from the entrance to Shamrock Cottages at nine-thirty. I promised him I'd fix his sink."

"Poor you," I said. "You're always fixing stuff for people, including me."

He grinned. "Ah, but at least you pay me."

"Yes, but not nearly enough. As soon as I get more cases, we can look at increasing your wages."

My friend's smile widened. "Forget about the wage increase. If you can swing it to send me on a P.I. course, that would be awesome."

"I'll do my best." If Lenny were licensed, we could actively pursue contracts with companies looking for discreet and thorough internet investigations.

I walked my friend down to the gates. "The scene on the yacht was like something out of a book or a TV mystery show," I said. "I can't put my finger on why."

"How do you mean?"

"It seemed, well, staged? Like the killer was trying to send a message, but we're too clueless to decipher the code?" I shivered. "Maybe I'm reading too much into it. The whole situation was surreal."

"Will Reynolds get updates from O'Shea?"

I laughed. "I doubt it. O'Shea is unhappy his beloved golf tournament has once again been interrupted, and this time, it's for a case he can't ignore."

"Does Reynolds have any idea if O'Shea's made progress on identifying the skeleton?" Lenny asked. "If we had an idea who he was, it'd be easier to check for a link between him and Richard Carstairs—or whatever he was really called."

"Judging by the conversation I overheard between Reynolds and O'Shea on the yacht today, O'Shea's drawn a blank finding a missing persons file that matches the skeleton. He mentioned putting the new police officer to work on those files on Monday."

"Síle? Good luck with that. She doesn't strike me as the type to care much about putting in actual work."

I stared at my friend in surprise. "You're not usually judgmental."

He shrugged. "Maybe she's changed since I knew her. I doubt it, though. Plus she took pleasure in showing you her Garda ID and watching you squirm. You were only doing your job."

I escorted Lenny to the door of the cottage. "Want to arrange a time to update Reynolds on what we discover over the next couple of days? Maybe on Monday evening?"

"Sure." Lenny inclined his head in the direction of Sergeant Reynolds's cottage. "Want to include the kid?"

"She comes with the territory. We'll find something for her to do while we talk. Why don't you guys all come for dinner?"

My friend grinned. "And eat your cooking?"

"I'm improving, I swear. Besides," I said haughtily, "even I can't screw up a barbecue."

17

Famous *last words.* I set the fire extinguisher beside the mini barbecue and regarded the smoking remains of my bacon and sausages with a growling stomach. Bran sniffed the air and lay at my feet, emitting a high-pitched whine. "Guess I can't tempt you to eat this mess, huh?"

The dog's answer to this question was to bury his nose in his paws.

I sighed. So much for wowing Hannah with a delicious barbecue.

Liam Reynolds peered over the tall fence that divided our yards and flashed me a bone-melting grin. "Was that supposed to be breakfast?"

"Yeah," I said gloomily. "Funny enough, I couldn't persuade Noreen to stay and sample my cooking when she brought Bran home. I wanted to do a trial run with the grill before I invited you and Hannah over for dinner tomorrow. Lenny and I planned to use the opportunity to update you on our progress."

His eyes twinkled with amusement. "Have you ever used a barbecue before?"

I shook my head. "My dad and brothers insisted on manning the grill when I was growing up, and Joe did the same when we got married."

While grilling slabs of meat represented the sum total of Joe's culinary abilities, I had to admit—albeit grudgingly—that he'd done it well.

"Gross, Dad. What's that horrible smell?"

The tall fence blocked Hannah from view, but her father hoisted her up to take a look at the smoking mess I'd created.

I waved away the noxious fumes. "Go on. Voice your disparagement for my culinary efforts."

The girl surveyed the scene with an air of disdain and wrinkled her nose. "You're nothing like Mum. She's an excellent cook."

Of course she is. I sent silent stun rays in the unknown Robyn's direction, and immediately felt bad for being jealous. It wasn't her fault I'd never met a meal I couldn't burn.

"Why don't you and Lenny come over to our place for dinner tomorrow? Bring a salad or dessert, and I'll supply the meat," Reynolds suggested. "Would that be okay with you, Hannah?"

The girl's horrified expression told me it was anything but okay. "Is Lenny that weirdo with the purple van?"

It was on the tip of my tongue to argue the "weirdo" description. Reynolds beat me to it. "If you mean 'weirdo' in a negative context, cut that out right now. Lenny is…" he struggled for the right word, "… an original."

"He's also a good friend of mine and my partner in crime detection," I said. "Plus he bakes awesome brownies."

He truly did, but I'd have to tell him to make the kid-and-cop-friendly variety for tomorrow.

"What time works for you to stop by?" Reynolds asked. "How does six sound?"

"Six is perfect for me. I'll check with Lenny and get back to you."

"Don't I get a say in this?" Hannah demanded.

"You do," her father replied with an air of strained patience. "However, unless your objections are sound, the invitation stands."

"I don't want to cause a hassle," I said quickly. "I can always email you with our discoveries."

The girl's eyes widened. "You mean detective work? Is this about the dead guy we found?"

"Sort of," I hedged. "More to do with the skeleton at the excavation site."

"Cool." She looked at her father. "Okay, they can come. As long as you don't make me go to my room when the conversation gets interesting."

A look of pained resignation settled on Reynolds's face. "Robyn is already threatening to take Hannah back to London. I guess I can't screw up any worse than I already have if I let her listen in."

"Especially as it's not officially your investigation," Hannah added sagely. "Right, Maggie?"

With considerable effort, I resisted the urge to laugh. "I'm staying out of this one."

"Okay, we'd better get going if we want to visit the caves this morning." Reynolds hoisted Hannah back to the ground and out of sight. "See you tomorrow, Maggie."

After Reynolds and his daughter had gone back inside their cottage, I dealt with the charred mess. In my defense, the stuff on the grill had looked pretty awesome before it had gone up in flames. One shower and two bowls of cereal later, I was ready to start my day.

My first stop was Smuggler's Cove and The Cupcake Café. I parked down the street, out of sight of the Movie Theater Café. If Noreen saw me enter her rival's premises, so be it, but I didn't want to wave the fact in her face.

When I entered the café, Dolly was behind the counter, chatting effusively to a customer. I waited in line until she was finished.

"Hello, Maggie. Lovely to see you." Dolly beamed at me beneath her mass of teased blond hair. Today, she was wearing a tight rainbow-colored dress that left little to the imagination. Most women couldn't pull off that look. On Dolly, it worked.

I glanced around the busy café where two waitstaff served tables. "Do you have a moment to talk? I want to ask you a few questions about the murder yesterday."

Dolly's smile faded. "Yes, of course. We can talk in the kitchen. She signaled to one of her employees. "Lorraine, I'll be in the back if you need me."

I followed Dolly into a pristine kitchen fitted with modern chrome appliances. She gestured to a table. "Take a seat. Would you like a coffee?"

"I'm good, thanks." I got straight to the point. "Have the police spoken to you yet?"

Dolly tried to frown. Or at least, I think she did—her stiff forehead made me suspect she'd had treatment. "Not yet. I suppose it's inevitable that they'll want my statement."

I nodded. "It's routine. After all, your cupcakes were among the only items discovered on board the yacht."

Dolly stared at me for a long moment, a bewildered expression on her heavily made-up face. "Cupcakes? Whatever are you talking about?"

It was my turn to frown. "The box with thirty-nine cupcakes that I found in the yacht's galley? The box and label said they were from The Cupcake Café, and I recognized the flavors from your menu."

Her mouth gaped, revealing perfect white teeth. "I had no idea."

"What did you think I was referring to when I said the police were going to want to talk to you?"

A flush stained her tanned cheeks. "About me and Richard, of course."

"You and Richard?" My pulse picked up in pace. "You guys were an item?"

"Not really. If we had been, his death would have devastated me. Not that I'm not upset," she added hastily, "but we barely knew one another."

"I'm afraid I'm not following you, Dolly. Were you dating Richard, or weren't you?"

Her face grew redder. "Can I ask you to keep this a secret? I don't want people on the island finding out."

"Of course. Before you continue, I need to be open with you. My questions aren't random curiosity. I'm investigating the skeleton on the excavation site, and I suspect Richard Carstairs's death a few days later is connected. Whatever you tell me will be shared with my partner, Lenny, and the police if necessary. Otherwise, I won't share any information."

"I appreciate your transparency, Maggie." She took a deep breath. "Okay, here's my story. After I broke up with my husband, I started online dating. I wasn't looking for a relationship. I guess I just needed to know I was still attractive, even at fifty-plus."

"And you met Richard?" I prompted gently.

She nodded. "We got together three or four times in the spring. Always at hotels, and we used fake names. At first, it felt risqué and exciting, but the feeling wore off. I'd been with my husband since I was twenty-one. He was my first…" She trailed off, embarrassed. "Well, you know what I mean. I guess I wanted to prove to myself that I was still desirable, but I've had to accept that I'm a traditionalist at heart. The next time I date, I want to be romanced and take things slow."

"Seeing Richard on Whisper Island must have come as a shock."

Her laugh rang hollow. "Tell me about it. He waltzed into the café on opening day and ordered half a dozen cupcakes. He couldn't place me at first, although I knew him the instant he walked through the door." Dolly couldn't quite keep her bitterness at not being recognized out of her voice.

"What did he say once he realized who you were?"

"Not much. He kept it casual, like we were old acquaintances." She paused. "Which I guess we were."

"Was that the only time Richard came into your café?"

Dolly nodded. "Yes. I mean, he might have come in while I was in the kitchen and been served by one of the other girls, but I didn't see him again."

"Can you recall an order for thirty-nine cupcakes?" I prompted. "It's a strange number to order unless it was for a birthday."

Dolly thought for a moment. "Now that you mention it, I might recall that particular order. Let me check my computer."

"I hoped the number might jog your memory."

Dolly took a pair of spectacles from a shelf and opened the laptop computer that was on the kitchen counter. "It is a strange number, but we've been rushed off our feet since we opened on Wednesday. I've had orders come in over the telephone, via our website, and in person. Regardless of how the order was made, it should be in here."

I went to stand by Dolly's side, careful not to crowd her but super curious to know what info her order list would reveal.

Dolly's pink manicured nails clicked over the keyboard. "Here we are. An online order for thirty-nine cupcakes came in on Thursday afternoon. Eight each of pistachio cream, lemon delight, strawberry crumble, and raspberry ripple, and seven maple pecan."

"That's it," I said, my voice rising in excitement. "That's the box I found on the yacht. Who placed the order?"

"Someone called Mark Garry." Dolly frowned. "Does the name ring a bell to you?"

"No." Given Richard's penchant for using aliases, it might have been him. "Did you see the box being collected?"

Dolly clicked another key on her laptop. "It says that it was collected on Friday afternoon and the customer paid in cash, but the person who rang up the sale isn't working today. I could call her, though."

"Would you mind? It's very important that I find out who bought those cupcakes."

"Sure. I'll call Denise now." Dolly took her phone off the shelf and tapped a few keys. "Hi, Denise. Dolly here. Listen, can I ask you a question about an order you filled on Friday? No, there's no problem. I just want to check a detail for my records. It was an order for thirty-nine cupcakes and it was collected at just after two o'clock on Friday afternoon. Can you remember what the person collecting it looked like?" There was a pause. "Oh? Okay. Thanks, Denise. You've been a great help. See you tomorrow, dear."

I could barely contain my excitement. "And? Did she remember the guy?"

Dolly nodded. "A man in his fifties. Good-looking with a baseball cap, a beard, and a gray ponytail. She remembered him because he flirted with her, and she noticed he walked with a slight limp."

"Up to the mention of the limp, her description sounds like Richard. Maybe he hurt his leg. I'll have to ask the excavation team." Although a man with a newly injured leg would hardly go jogging the next morning, would he? Maybe I had been mistaken about the guy I'd seen on the hotel grounds.

"I'm glad I could help you, Maggie." Dolly wore a worried expression on her pretty face. "I do hope the cupcakes had nothing to do with his death. Maybe he had an allergy to one of the ingredients."

"Oh, no. No one ate the cupcakes. All thirty-nine were in the box when I saw them."

Dolly's shoulders sagged in relief. "Of course. How silly of me. You wouldn't have been so sure of the number ordered if some of the cupcakes had been missing. How did he die? All I've heard so far is that he's dead and the police are treating his death as a murder inquiry."

"I'm not sure if the police have released the info about the murder method yet," I said. "Trust me when I say it had nothing to do with your cupcakes. I came to talk to you today because I was curious to know who'd placed and collected the order. Someone must have been on the boat with Richard."

Dolly shuddered. "And you thought the killer might have bought my cupcakes?"

"It's a possibility. But from Denise's description, it sounds like Richard picked up the box himself. Thanks again for your help. I'll see myself out."

When I left Dolly's café, I took my time walking back to my car, brooding over what I'd learned. Even if Richard ordered those cupcakes, the number must have been significant. He was unlikely to gorge himself on thirty-nine cupcakes, surely? So who had he arranged to meet on Saturday? Could that person be his killer?

18

After I left the café, I drove home and took Bran out for a run. I had time to kill before I visited the Spinsters at three o'clock. They'd invited me for afternoon tea, followed by the opportunity to look through their attic. I couldn't say the prospect of wading through dusty junk inspired me, but I wanted to get my hands on that exhibition brochure.

When I'd returned to my cottage and showered, I grabbed my trusty pen and notebook and reached for the handle to my back door. My hesitation bothered Bran. He rubbed himself against my legs and whined, eager to get outside again.

"Let's go out front this time," I said, urging him toward the front door of the cottage. "I can make lists and spy on my neighbors."

The particular neighbors I wanted to spy on were the four cottages occupied by members of the excavation team. I was hoping a casual greeting might lead to a less casual chat.

Sure enough, fifteen minutes after Bran and I had adopted faux casual poses on the bench in front of our house, Alan Doherty cycled up the driveway and stopped in front of Susie O'Malley's cottage. He rapped on the door a couple of times before peering through the window. A morose expression on his face, he returned to his bike and wheeled it over the gravel courtyard.

As he passed me, I called out to him. "Hi, Alan. How are you doing?"

The young man looked startled, and it took him a moment to place me. When he did, he scowled at me, clearly recalling our last encounter. "Maggie," he muttered.

"Why don't you sit a while?" I patted the bench beside me. "I have some fresh lemonade in the fridge. Or beer if you'd prefer."

Hesitation flickered across his face, followed by curiosity. For a few seconds, the warring emotions duked it out. Eventually, curiosity won. "Sure. Lemonade sounds good."

He parked his bike and came over to sit with me. Bran immediately engaged in the obligatory crotch sniffing he subjected everyone to—unless he disliked them, which hardly ever happened.

I fetched two glasses of cool lemonade and joined Alan on the bench. "Your dig is turning out to be quite an adventure."

The young man's shoulders slumped. "Tell me about it. I feel like the entire excavation was cursed before we ever arrived on Whisper Island."

"Oh?" I kept my voice casual and took a sip of lemonade to allow him time to gather his thoughts.

"Yeah." He shoved his large work-worn hands in his pockets. "We had funding problems, you know? And a couple of last-minute changes in staff. It was a relief to finally get started on the dig, and now…this." His gaze wandered in the direction of the cottage that Richard Carstairs had shared with Ben.

"Learning of Richard's murder so soon after the discovery of the skeleton must have been a terrible shock."

Alan didn't say anything for a long while. Finally, he nodded. "I didn't like the guy. You heard what I said about him."

"But you didn't wish him dead?" I prompted gently.

"No." The tone was vehement. "That old police officer—what's his name?"

"Sergeant O'Shea," I said in a dry tone. "He and I aren't friends."

This made Alan laugh, but his anxious expression was soon back in place. "He kept asking me questions like he thought I'd killed Richard. I didn't like the guy. Everyone knew that, but I'm no murderer."

"Why didn't you like Richard? He seemed pretty popular."

Alan cast me a sardonic look. "Yeah—with the ladies. None of the men could stand him."

"That surprises me. I saw him talking with Professor Frobisher several times."

"On work matters. They didn't socialize. Not," he amended, "that the prof fraternizes with the staff. He prefers to keep his distance."

"Wouldn't Richard have been more his peer than a member of staff, though?"

Alan laughed. "Not according to the prof. The only person he occasionally deigns to talk to in a social context is Dr. Taylor."

Alan's assessment of the professor as a snob and Richard as a ladies' man tallied with my impressions of both men. Time to move into more controversial territory, preferably without prompting Alan to lose his short temper. "I don't understand why Sergeant O'Shea would focus on you. Did you tell him where you were on Friday night and Saturday morning? Surely he can rule you out."

Alan was mid-sip and choked on his lemonade. "Sorry," he spluttered. "Wrong pipe."

When he'd recovered, I tried a different tack. "I'd imagine the police are asking everyone for alibis for the time of the murder."

"I guess so. After your old-movie thing, a few of us went to a pub. We stayed there until closing time, and then walked back to our bed and breakfast."

"And on Saturday?" I prompted. "I saw a bunch

of your coworkers heading into The Cupcake Café in Smuggler's Cove. Were you with them?"

He shook his head and dug his free hand deeper into his pocket. "I went sailing, but I swear I didn't see Richard."

"I went sailing, too," I said as though this made us compadres. "There were lots of boats out in the bay. Can't your companions back up your story?"

He flushed. "That's the problem. I went on my own. I needed time to think." He made a vague gesture in the air. I got the message.

"Susie?"

"Yeah." He looked miserable. "I was hoping this dig would bring us closer together. She broke up with me a few months ago. I was so sure all she needed was a bit of space and then everything would be back to normal."

"Your behavior to her the other day is more likely to get you a restraining order than a second chance," I said. "If you'd spoken that way to me, you'd be singing soprano."

He winced. "I apologized to her after you left. I don't know what came over me. I guess it all got to be too much. First, the prof picking that eejit Ben over me, and then Susie flirting with that swine, Carstairs."

The anger in the young man's voice didn't match the worry lines etched on his forehead.

"Did you see Richard's boat out in the bay on Saturday?" I asked. "It was a sizeable yacht called *Poseidon*."

Alan's Adam apple bobbed. "With a red stripe?"

"That's right."

"Then yeah, I saw it." His gaze fell to the glass he was holding. "I didn't know Richard had hired it."

"Did you see anyone on board when you passed the yacht? Richard was alone when we found him, but his killer must have been on the boat shortly before."

Alan shook his head. "To tell you the truth, I went sailing to clear my head. I wasn't paying attention to other boats except to not crash into them."

It was a flimsy alibi, but I needed to keep him sweet. "Do you mind telling me what you meant about Ben not being qualified? I found your statement intriguing. I can't imagine someone as fastidious as Professor Frobisher would hire a fraud."

Alan's jaw tightened. "I didn't say Ben was a fraud. He's a qualified archaeologist with a great degree from the University of Liverpool."

"So what's the problem? Apart from him getting a job you wanted, that is."

The guy's nostrils flared, displaying genuine annoyance this time. "He asks stupid questions. Maybe because his area is Egyptian archaeology. If he doesn't know the basics about excavating in mud and rain, he has no business being on a dig in the west of Ireland. I have no idea why the prof picked him, except, perhaps, he was dazzled by Ben's credentials."

"Credentials that aren't much use on a dig on Whisper Island?"

"Apparently not. He's clearly read up on the

Viking Age in Ireland, but you can tell it's not his area of expertise. Excavating in the desert is not the same as excavating in mud."

I filed this info away for later. If Lenny didn't turn up any dirt on Ben Dunne, I'd tackle Professor Frobisher. He must have had his reasons for hiring the guy.

Alan drained his glass and started to get up.

"Before you go, I have one more question." I smiled sweetly at the young man, and then went for the jugular. "Do you know who killed Richard?"

Alan's face underwent a smorgasbord of emotions, the most notable of which was panic. He swallowed audibly. "No. I mean, he wasn't popular with the men, and I'm sure he broke a few female hearts. I still can't imagine anyone wanting to kill him."

I raised an eyebrow. "Can't you hazard a guess? Who do you suspect?"

His mouth opened and closed before setting in a hard line. "Why are you so interested in the murder? Is it because you found the body?"

"Partly. I also live next to several of your team members. As you can imagine, I'm wondering if I have a killer lurking nearby." I adopted my best damsel-in-distress face.

"I doubt if any of this lot have the gumption to kill a man," he muttered. "Thanks for the drink, but I've got to go."

He leaped up and jumped on his bike. I waved

nonchalantly and stayed on the bench while he peddled down the drive and disappeared from sight. I believed *almost* everything he'd told me. Although my gut instinct said that Alan Doherty wasn't the killer, it also told me he knew more than he was willing to say. Whatever it was, I needed to persuade him to confide in me.

I KNOCKED on the door of Primrose Cottage on the stroke of three, using the heavy brass handle. Miss Flynn, the thinner of the Spinsters, opened the door. Her gray hair had been pulled back in a severe bun, and she wore her summer version of her winter tweeds: plaid skirt and a blouse with a round collar. As always, her precious loop of pearls was around her neck.

She smiled warmly when she saw me, emphasizing her laughter lines. "Maggie, my dear. Please come in."

"Hi, Miss Flynn," I said as I stepped into their ornament-filled hallway. "I'm grateful to you and Miss Murphy for letting me poke around in your attic."

"We're delighted to help." Miss Flynn gestured for me to follow her through the house and into the back garden.

The lush green lawn was lined by neat flower beds. An array of brightly colored blooms stretched around the perimeter, wafting a subtle floral scent.

Bent over one such flower bed was the second resident of Primrose Cottage. Miss Murphy glanced over her shoulder at our approach and beamed at me. "Lovely to see you, Maggie." She got to her feet slowly, and winced when she put her not inconsiderable weight on her left leg. "Arthritis," she explained. "It makes tending the flowers difficult, but I refuse to be beaten." She gestured to the garden table on which a glass of water and a newspaper lay. "Would you like to have tea now, or after you've finished in the attic?"

"After, if that's okay."

Miss Murphy nodded. "Miss Flynn will take you up and show you around. I find the ladder hard on my knees."

"See you later. Enjoy your gardening."

Miss Flynn led me back into the house and up the stairs. With the use of a hook, she pulled on a trap door, and a wooden ladder unfolded. I let her go first in case she fell, and I scrambled up after her.

"I'm afraid it's a bit of a shambles up here," she said in an apologetic tone. "We desperately need to do a proper clear-out."

"Don't worry about it. And if you want help clearing this place out at some point, just let me know."

Miss Flynn patted my arm. "Thank you, dear. I might very well take you up on that offer." She led me over to two bookcases next to several large cardboard boxes. "This is where we threw a lot of our old brochures. Plays, exhibitions, and that sort of thing. I know we attended that exhibition in 2000, and I feel sure we'd have picked up a brochure when we were there. Unfortunately, that's all I can remember about it. I can't remember the precise circumstances. If I recall correctly, Milly and I didn't stay at the exhibition for very long."

"Thanks, Miss Flynn. I'll be sure to put everything back neatly."

The elderly woman laughed. "Don't worry about that. Most of this stuff is destined for paper recycling once we get around to sorting it out."

"I'll make a date with you to do that."

"You're a good girl, Maggie. Good luck with your search. I hope you find that brochure."

After Miss Flynn had retraced her steps down the ladder, I surveyed the area of the attic she considered most likely to contain my quarry. I started work on the bookshelves, seeing as they were more accessible than the content in the boxes. Pausing for the occasional sneeze from the dust, I sorted through stacks of old magazines, information leaflets, and newspapers. I set aside a complete collection of a vintage British magazine. If the Spinsters were willing to part with it, they could sell the collection online and make a bit of cash.

The minutes ticked by in a cloud of dust and the smell of aged paper. I worked my way through the bookshelves and the boxes, but no luck. After I'd replaced the contents of the final box, I stood and stretched. What now? I'd exhausted the possibilities in the corner of the attic that Miss Flynn had deemed most likely to contain the brochure. The rest of the room was covered in stacks of boxes, old furniture, and—bizarrely—a baby grand piano.

I strummed the keys of the out-of-tune baby grand, and contemplated my next move. Where would I find a lone brochure in the middle of this mess? My gaze swept the room again, looking closely at each area before moving on to the next. Out of one box protruded the spine of an *Encyclopaedia Britannica*. I'd start there.

I had no luck in the box containing a complete set of vintage encyclopedias—yet another find worth listing online. The two boxes on either side of it were equally hopeless. Maybe it was time to call it quits. I was parched from the dust, and I'd never get through all this junk in one afternoon. Although I wasn't particularly fond of tea, a hot drink was just what I needed for my dry throat. I put back the contents of the last box. This had proven to be a treasure trove of museum brochures from the Spinsters' tour of Italy and Greece in the Seventies. Right subject matter for my brochure, but wrong era.

As I repacked the box, I noticed an accordion file organizer wedged between the box I'd just examined and its neighbor. Curious, I tugged the organizer free and looked inside. My heart sank. Yet another stage production brochure for a Brian Friel play that had been performed at a theater in Galway. I flicked it open, and my gaze fell upon the date: the twenty-fourth of May, 2000. Right around the time the first excavation was taking place. A quiver of excitement zipped through my stomach. Careful to keep the contents in order, I sorted through each of the pockets of the accordion folder. More theater productions. An exhibit of rare books at Whisper Island's library. And there it was, nestled between a leaflet about a school production of *Calamity Jane* and yet another theater brochure.

With shaking hands, I extracted the exhibition brochure. For the next fifteen minutes, I read each page with care, noting the names mentioned and examining the accompanying photographs. Most of the pictures were of the objects discovered in the course of the excavation. Others were of the various people associated with the dig. I recognized my aunt Philomena, as well as Sheila Dunphy, the woman Lenny had arranged to meet this afternoon.

On the second to last page, I struck gold. A group photograph of the entire excavation team was too grainy to make out specifics, but the names underneath caught my attention. Although R. Carstairs was among them, his wasn't the name that leaped out at me. Next to Richard, a C. Carstairs was listed. My fingers tingled with excitement. I'd heard no mention of Richard Carstairs having a wife, so this C. must be his sister or his ex. All the grainy group photograph told me was that she was blond and petite.

I examined the other photos on that page. And let out a squeal. Right at the bottom of the page was a clear picture of four people, one of whom was listed as C. Carstairs.

And I recognized her. It was Clodagh Burke, the craft store owner and one of the Whisper Island Historical Society volunteers at the dig.

19

The Spinsters allowed me to keep the brochure. After I'd finished having tea with them, I returned to Shamrock Cottages with a sliver of time to spare before I was due to meet Lenny for our stakeout. On fast forward, I showered, fed Bran and the cats, and climbed back into my car.

At five minutes to nine, I pulled up at the corner of the Dineens' street. Lenny loitered by a tree, dressed all in black but destroying the inconspicuous look with the addition of a fluorescent green bandana.

"Nice outfit," I drawled when I opened the passenger door for him. "You might want to lose the bandana before nightfall."

"But it glows in the dark," my friend protested. "I thought I could use it instead of a flashlight."

I sighed. "We need to give you a lesson about

tailing people. The goal is to blend into the background, not stand out like a flaming beacon."

Lenny grinned and settled into the passenger seat of my clapped-out Yaris. "It'll be fine, Maggie. Old Man Dineen's got a squint. I doubt he can see all that well."

"He's also in possession of a driver's license. That doesn't inspire confidence."

"There he is now." My friend pointed down the lane to where Fionn Dineen was climbing into his car. "Let's see where he goes on his nocturnal outings."

I glanced through the windshield. "It's still very bright. We'll have to be careful to keep our distance."

"If he heads for the Conroy farm, it'll start getting dark before we reach it."

"True."

I lingered for a few seconds after Dineen had pulled onto the main street, and then hit the gas pedal. Our quarry drove in the same direction as he had on Tuesday night.

"Looks like he's heading for Bethany's place again," I said. "While I'm driving, take a look at this, particularly the page I've bookmarked." I shoved the exhibition brochure across the dashboard.

Lenny grabbed it and flicked to the relevant page. "Whoa. Clodagh Burke was *married* to Richard?"

"That's my guess. They look way too cozy in that photo to be brother and sister."

"Dude, that's major." My friend bounced with excitement. "This means she was linked to Richard

Carstairs and involved in both excavations. We'll have to tell Reynolds."

"We can tell him at tomorrow night's barbecue. He's hosting it, by the way." I screwed up my nose. "My trial run went up in flames—literally."

He snorted with laughter. "Am I allowed to say I'm not surprised?"

I slid him a look. "As long as it isn't 'I told you so'".

"Hey, before I forget—" Lenny rummaged through his backpack and drew out an envelope, "—I met Philomena when I was walking to meet you. She asked me to give you her research results. She said you'd know what they were."

I snuck a glance at the envelope before turning onto the road that Dineen had taken. "It's probably about that musket ball. Sergeant O'Shea must have gotten the test results back on the one found up at the site, but if he has, he hasn't passed the info on to Reynolds. Until we know otherwise, I'm sticking to mine and dad's amateur guess that the musket ball was fired using an eighteenth to early nineteenth century flintlock musket."

Lenny drummed the envelope. "I wonder what Philomena turned up."

I rolled my eyes. "Go ahead and open it. You know you want to."

"Are you sure?" His voice sounded hopeful. "It's addressed to you."

"I can't read while I'm driving, and you're my assistant on the case."

My friend required no further encouragement. He ripped open the envelope and drew out my aunt's neatly typed notes. With building impatience, I waited until he'd scanned the pages. "Well?" I asked finally, no longer able to contain my curiosity. "What does she say?"

"Philomena mentions two potential sources of a Brown Bess flintlock musket on Whisper Island. Have you been out to George Fort?"

George Fort was a star fort located on the southwest of Whisper Island. It had been built by the British as a military presence and outlook post in the seventeenth century. "I visited it as a kid," I said, "but I haven't been back in years."

"They have a small military museum there. I should have thought of it when you mentioned old weapons, but I'm not all that interested in history." Lenny tapped the sheets of neatly typed paper. "According to Philomena, the museum's focus is the various Irish rebellions in the seventeenth and eighteenth centuries and the fort's role in maintaining British supremacy. The collection of old weapons includes a Long Land Pattern Brown Bess flintlock musket dating from the Irish Rebellion of 1798, as well as several other variations."

A tickle of excitement built in my stomach. Finally, we were getting somewhere. "We need to visit the fort and see who had access to that weapon fifteen to twenty years ago."

My friend raised an eyebrow. "How will they remember those details?"

"They'll have a record of who worked there. And they'll recall if a similar weapon was stolen from their collection at some point."

"I guess it's worth a shot." Lenny grinned. "No pun intended."

"You said Philomena mentioned finding two potential sources of the Brown Bess used to shoot the skeleton. What's the second?"

My friend scanned my aunt's notes. "The Historical Society. They don't own historical weapons per se, but some of their members put on reenactments and they'd need the real deal or replicas for those."

A memory stirred in the back of my mind. "According to his bio, Richard Carstairs was involved with historical reenactments. Ask Sheila if either he or Clodagh were in any arranged by the Whisper Island Historical Society."

"Will do. What about Clodagh? Do you want to talk to her, or should I?"

"I'll go to her store on Monday," I said. "She strikes me as the sort of woman who'd be more inclined to open up to another female."

"Will her shop be open on Monday?"

I frowned. "Why wouldn't it be?"

"The first Monday in August is a bank holiday in Ireland. Most bigger shops, cafés, and restaurants stay open, but some smaller shops are closed, or have reduced opening hours."

I digested this info. "Okay. Maybe I'll wait until Tuesday to confront Clodagh. And I guess I should tell Reynolds before I talk to her in any case. He might want to come with me."

We drove in silence for the next while. I kept a discreet distance between us and Fionn Dineen's car and I chewed over the case. From my friend's uncharacteristically serious expression, he was doing the same.

When we reached a crossroads at the far end of the island, I slowed the Yaris. "I don't see Dineen's car. Which direction is the Conroy farm?"

"Turn left, and then take the first right. The road's little more than a dirt track, but it'll bring us up behind the farm and right near Bethany's house."

I followed his instructions, feeling every bump in the road courtesy of the vehicle's lousy suspension. "That's Dineen's car."

"Pull in behind him and we'll sneak up to Bethany's house."

"Do the Conroys have any attack dogs or other feral beasts we should be aware of?"

"I'm sure they have dogs hanging around the place," Lenny said, unperturbed by the prospect of being savaged. "Most farms do."

"You really know how to reassure a person," I said dryly. "Okay, let's do this thing." I slipped my flashlight and portable detection kit out of the glove compartment and climbed out of the car.

Outside, the light was fading fast, basking the landscape in a purple-orange glow. I peered around but there was no sign of Fionn Dineen.

"Is that Bethany's house?" I pointed to a neat bungalow perched on the edge of the Conroys' land, surrounded by an elaborately decorated wooden fence.

"That's the place," Lenny whispered. "I visited a couple of times while she was seeing Mack. It's a floral nightmare, inside and out. "

I swallowed a laugh. "Sounds awful. Okay, let's see if we can find a way onto the farm."

As we crept along the perimeter, the sound of mooing cows and squealing pigs floated through the air. With supreme nonchalance, Lenny ambled up to the gate and punched in a code.

I stared at him, slack-jawed. "How on earth do you know the code to the Conroys' gate?"

"Strictly speaking, this is the gate that leads to Bethany's part of the property. I haven't a clue what code her parents use for the gate on their side."

"You're dodging my question. How do *you* know the code?"

My friend shrugged. "Bethany asked me to fix her computer once or twice. She gave me the code, and I figured she wasn't the type to change it."

"How can you remember someone else's code?"

"It's easy when it's their year and month of birth."

He shook his head. "People are ridiculously naive about passwords. If Bethany catches us, we'll tell her the buzzer on her gate didn't work."

We stepped through the open gate moments before it swung shut. "What's our excuse for showing up at her place this late?"

"We'll say you're having car trouble. With the wreck you drive, no one will doubt the story."

"Gee, thanks," I said in a sardonic tone. "I don't disparage your van."

"My van is reliable."

"Your van is purple," I pointed out. "With glow-in-the-dark paint and pictures of dubious plants on the side."

"Hey, it's easy to find at night."

This was true, and the reason I never wanted to use Lenny's van on a stakeout.

We reached Bethany's gate and surveyed the house.

"What's the plan?" Lenny asked. "Do we walk up and ring the doorbell?"

"Yeah. If you consider my car a wreck, let's roll with the breakdown story. We'll lure Bethany to the door and see if she has company."

"And hope that company is Fionn Dineen," Lenny added.

"Exactly."

I opened the floral-patterned gate and strode up the short path to Bethany's front door. I pressed the bell. And waited. And waited some more. I shifted my weight from one foot to the other.

"Want to try again?" Lenny whispered. "Maybe she didn't hear the first time."

"She'd have to be deaf not to hear a bell that loud." But I stepped forward and pressed it for a second time.

As the seconds ticked by, I had to reach the reluctant conclusion that the door would remain closed. I exchanged a glance with Lenny. "Do you think they're hiding out?"

"I'm not sure." He jerked a thumb in the direction of a wooden barn around fifty feet away from the house. "Did you notice there's a light on over in that barn?"

I had noticed, and it was next on my list of places to look. "Want to check it out?"

He grinned. "Heck, yeah."

"We've got to hope the barn isn't equipped with a sensor light," I said.

"It wasn't the last time I was out here."

"All the same, let's try to make this quick."

Although the light was fading fast, visibility was still good enough to make our flashlights unnecessary. Keeping an eye out for guard dogs and other predators, we snuck across the yard. No lights were activated as we drew closer to the building, and the faint sound of music wafted through the walls.

Lenny chuckled. "What are they doing in there? Having a disco?"

"Hoist me up on your shoulders, and we'll find out." I pointed to the window six or seven feet above the ground.

My friend's mouth gaped. "No way. You'll kill me."

"Hey, I'm not that fat," I protested. "You'll live."

"You're not fat at all, Maggie, but I'm not exactly built like Reynolds. I'll crumble under your weight."

"Oh, for heaven's sake," I said with barely concealed impatience. "*I'll* try to hoist *you* up. How does that sound?"

My friend's mouth stretched into a grin. "Like I need to start bodybuilding?"

I laughed. "Come on. I won't be able to hold you for long. Just get a look in that window and tell me what you see."

On the third attempt, I managed to push Lenny far enough up the wall for him to see through the window. Under his weight, I struggled to breathe. My arm muscles ached, but I gritted my teeth and held tight.

"Wow, dude," Lenny drawled. "You should see this."

"What are they doing?" My arms turned to jelly but I kept my friend aloft.

"Dan—" Lenny cut the sentence short. "Aw, no. They've seen me. They're looking straight up at the window."

I wobbled under his weight, but straightened at

the last second. "Don't panic. We'll stick to the break-down story. We'll—"

And then disaster struck.

From out of nowhere, a Rottweiler leaped at me. I sucked in a breath, took a step back, and lost my balance. I staggered into a fall, and my friend's weight pressed down on me. The ground rushed to meet me before I had a chance to let go of Lenny and break the fall with my hands. I landed hard, and my friend crashed on top of me. We rolled in an undignified heap across the yard, each struggling to get free of the other and only succeeding in making our situation worse. Our rolling jumble of limbs came to an abrupt halt when two large paws pressed against my back, pinning us in place.

The dog got up in my face and growled menac-ingly. My pulse raced, and the rancid smell of his breath made me gag.

"What's going on, Snuggles?" The voice was Bethany's.

"Snuggles seems to have identified us as his next meal," I said in a calmer tone than I'd thought myself capable of with a Rottweiler snarling in my face. "Any chance you could dissuade him of this notion?"

Bethany took a step closer and peered down. "Maggie? And *Lenny*? What are you two doing here?"

Before I could spin her my breakdown tale of woe, her dog growled again, and pressed his nose against mine.

"Go home, Snuggles," Bethany commanded. "Naughty doggie."

The dog drew back a few inches. He looked from me to his owner, and then back again. With a show of great reluctance, he bared his teeth at us one last time and backed off.

Lenny and I got to our feet, careful to maintain our distance from the dog.

I brushed dirt from the front of my jeans and regarded our unwitting hostess. "Snuggles is a bit of a misnomer, don't you think?"

Bethany screwed up her perfect nose and stared at me with a blank expression. "A mis-what?"

"Snuggles's name doesn't match his personality."

Bethany regarded me placidly. "He's a trained guard dog, but perfectly harmless—as long as he's with family or friends."

The implication was clear: I was neither.

Footsteps sounded behind Bethany and Fionn Dineen came into view. "What's all the racket?"

"We have visitors." Bethany flicked a section of red hair over her shoulder. "Or trespassers, depending on why they're on my family's property."

"Hey, Mr. Dineen." Lenny's voice sounded as though he'd been sucking on helium. I knew how he felt. If we wanted Movie Reel Investigations to thrive, we seriously needed to work on our stakeout technique.

Dineen drew his bushy white eyebrows together and scrutinized us. His gaze settled on Lenny. "You're

Gerry Logan's grandson. The one with the mad purple van."

"That's me," my friend squeaked. "I didn't expect to see you hanging out with Bethany."

Fionn Dineen blushed, but Bethany gave a tinkly laugh. "You'll have to promise you didn't see us."

"Sure," I said, quick to seize the opportunity, "as long as you forgive us for trespassing on your land. I had car trouble."

Bethany raised a perfectly plucked eyebrow. "Is that why Lenny was spying on us? We saw him through the barn window."

"About that—"

"You won't tell the missus will you?" Fionn Dineen's pale eyes grew panicked. "I don't want to spoil the surprise for her."

"'Surprise' isn't the word I'd choose," I said deadpan. "How about 'shock'"?

The old man wheezed a laugh. "I hope not. After what happened at our wedding, I owe Bridget a proper waltz, even if it's taken me fifty years to give her one."

I slow-blinked. "Waltz?"

"That's what I was trying to tell you, Maggie," Lenny said. "They were cavorting around the barn like tango dancers."

"The waltz looks nothing like the tango," Bethany said, amused. "Do you remember me winning all those ballroom trophies when I was a kid, Lenny?"

My friend nodded a moment too late. "Uh, sure. You were some kind of champion."

"I'm teaching Mr. Dineen to waltz before his golden wedding anniversary party." Bethany squeezed her student's hand. "He's getting good."

"It's supposed to be a surprise for Bridget," Mr. Dineen said. "Both the party and the waltz. You see, she had her heart set on waltzing at our wedding, and I messed the whole thing up. Got the steps wrong and trod on her train. She was a sweetheart about it, even when she discovered a tear in the fabric."

"And you've decided to finally get it right in time for your golden wedding anniversary?" I asked gently.

The old man nodded. "I've rented the ballroom at the Whisper Island Hotel and all. We'll have top-notch catering. The works. Everyone I've invited has been asked to keep quiet."

"We won't tell anyone about your dancing or the party," I assured him. "It'll be a lovely surprise for your wife."

His shy smile broadened into a grin. "I hope so. She's as dear to me today as the day we married."

The man's affection for his wife was heartwarming. Our stakeout hadn't gone according to plan, but at least the Dineen case would have a happy ending. I glanced at Lenny. "We'd better make tracks."

"What about your car?" Bethany demanded. "Didn't you say it had broken down?"

"Do you have any car oil?" Lenny asked, quick as a flash. "That should do the trick."

"I do," Mr. Dineen said before Bethany could answer. "I bought a container of the stuff just the other day. Come on and I'll get it out of my car for you."

Twenty painful minutes later, Lenny and I were back in my car, motoring away from the Conroy farm.

"Well, that was embarrassing," I said, turning out of the Conroys' lane and onto the coast road. "The one positive is that we'll be able to reassure Mrs. Dineen that her husband isn't being unfaithful."

"What will you tell her?" Lenny asked. "Like, how can you reassure her without blowing the surprise?"

"I'll figure something out." We continued down the coast road, passing the few settlements that were on this part of the island. It was almost pitch dark and the road was deserted. I flicked on my high beams. Almost as soon as I did so, I eased my foot down on the brakes. "Hey, isn't that Ellen Taylor? I recognize her jacket."

I pointed through the car window to a cliffside cottage. A light above the door cast a pale glow, but it was sufficient to illuminate the woman standing in front of the open door. It was definitely Ellen.

Lenny sat up in his seat and stared out. "What's she doing at Nick's place?"

I pulled over to the side of the road and killed the engine. "Nick?" I demanded. "As in Nick Sweetman, Jennifer's fiancé?"

"Yeah. He owns that cottage. He lived there

before he moved in with Jennifer, but I heard he kept it to rent out during the summer months."

My breathing slowed. "Maybe that's it. Maybe she's having a fling with a tourist. That would explain all her disappearances from the excavation site."

At that moment, a dark-haired man appeared in the doorframe. He leaned down to give Ellen a passionate kiss, obscuring his face from my line of vision. Lenny clicked open my glove compartment and took out my night-vision binoculars.

"Well?" I demanded the instant he looked through them. "Can you see the guy?"

Lenny's hesitation in answering and the sinking sensation in my stomach combined to confirm my worst fears.

My friend lowered the binoculars, his expression grim. "That's Ellen Taylor all right. And the dude slobbering all over her is Nick Sweetman."

20

Discovering Nick was being unfaithful to Jennifer put a dampener on my mood that carried over into the following day. Not even the happy circumstance of informing a relieved Mrs. Dineen that she had every reason to trust her husband managed to lift my spirits. What would I say to Jennifer? That I'd tell what we'd seen was clear. When my ex had cheated on me, I'd been the last one to find out. No way would I put another woman through that, even if I ran the risk of her not believing me.

After I'd finished work at the Movie Theater Café, I walked back to my car with feet that felt like lead. Before I started the engine, I dug my phone out of my purse and dialed Jennifer's number.

"Hey, Maggie," she said when she answered. "Are you enjoying the bank holiday?"

"I had to work at the café today, but it was pretty quiet."

"Oh, of course. Noreen's place was open today. I forgot."

"What did you get up to?"

"Nick took me sailing." Her voice oozed with happiness. "I think I've gotten him to the point of committing to a wedding date."

I winced and felt a gnawing sensation in the pit of my stomach. "That's…great."

"When did you want to meet tomorrow? I've taken the day free from work to make it an extra long weekend, so my day is wide open."

I ran through my options. Telling Jennifer her fiancé was a liar and a cheat was not a conversation I wanted to have in a pub or a restaurant. "Do you want to come over to my place? I want to go out to George Fort in the afternoon, but I'm free after that."

"George Fort?" Jennifer's voice rose in excitement. "Can I come with you? It's been ages since I was out there. I hear they've improved the exhibit and now have an audio-visual tour."

I hesitated before responding. Was a museum the place for our conversation about Nick? The place probably had a café where we could talk, but I'd planned on tackling the topic in privacy.

"If you don't want me tagging along on a work trip, that's fine," Jennifer said in an upbeat tone that made me feel awful. "I totally understand."

"Oh, no, it's not that," I replied hastily. "I'm

happy for you to come with me. When we're done, we can go back to my place and I'll make you one of my killer cocktails."

She laughed. "Sounds like a plan."

I considered our respective locations. "Want to meet in the parking lot at the fort? Maybe around ten o'clock?"

"Perfect. I'll see you then. Have a great day, Maggie."

"You, too. Bye, Jennifer."

With a heavy heart, I disconnected. In spite of her natural reserve and introverted personality, Jennifer was making an effort to socialize with me. From what I'd observed, she didn't have many friends. Overtures from her meant a lot. And I was going to break her heart.

I arrived back at Shamrock Cottages with just enough time to feed Bran and the cats and grab the pasta salad I'd prepared earlier out of the fridge. In spite of—or perhaps because of—his eccentric persona, Lenny didn't share the native Irish tendency to be fashionably late. He pulled up in his purple van just as I was leaving my cottage to go next door for the barbecue.

"Yo, Maggie," he hailed with a cheerful wave. "I made brownies. They're the cop-and-kid-friendly variety, as requested."

"Thanks," I said, deadpan. "I don't think Reynolds wants to arrest someone on his vacation and in his own home."

"Just avoid the ones in the sandwich bag. I made those for Mack."

I eyed the plastic container filled with brownies. On the top layer, I spied a sandwich bag filled with what I presumed were the illegal variety. "For heaven's sake, Lenny. Leave those in your car."

"They'll go gross in the heat," he protested.

I sighed. "Fine. Leave them at my place, but they're going nowhere near Reynolds."

After we'd left the brownie bag in one of my kitchen cabinets, we went next door. Balancing the pasta salad I'd prepared earlier, I pressed the doorbell. To my amazement, the door was opened by Caoimhe Greer. "Hey, Caoimhe. How are you doing?"

The girl's wary expression gave way to a shy smile. "Well, thanks. Hannah invited me for a sleepover."

"Oh, fun. I loved those when I was your age."

Hannah appeared behind Caoimhe. Her greeting was less enthusiastic than her friend's. "Hi, Maggie. Dad's in the garden, fighting with the grill."

I laughed. "He can't do a worse job than me. You remember Lenny, don't you?"

Hannah smiled at the sight of my friend. "Vividly. Did the aloe vera gel help?"

"Yes," Lenny replied earnestly, "although I was sore for a couple of days."

At Caoimhe's look of confusion, Hannah supplied, "Lenny fell into a patch of nettles while peeing outdoors."

Caoimhe took a moment to fully comprehend the

implications of this statement. "Oh, ouch. I wish that would happen to Tommy."

Hannah led us through the cottage to the back-yard, where her father was cursing at the barbecue in at least two languages. "The charcoal's not cooperat-ing," he said by way of explanation. "I can't get it to do more than belch a few wisps of smoke."

Lenny deposited his tray of brownies on the table and rolled up his sleeves. "Want a hand?"

I looked at the girls. "Will we leave them to it?"

Hannah's stare could have frozen fire. "Actually, we were going to go to the games room and play snooker. Right, Caoimhe?"

Her friend blinked owlishly behind her thick glasses. "I guess."

I opted to ignore the rebuff. Every time I thought I was making progress with Hannah, I got a sharp reality check. "Okay, then. Have fun."

The girls hightailed it in the direction of the complex's communal games room, leaving me and the guys to operate the barbecue.

"What's the neighbor situation?" Lenny asked Reynolds. "Will we be overheard if we talk shop? Or were you and Maggie planning to get all lovey-dovey first?"

I laughed and planted a kiss on Reynolds's cheek, inhaling the scent of his aftershave mingled with char-coal. "That's about as far as I go with public displays of affection."

Reynolds laughed and gave me a swift kiss on

the lips. "As for the neighbor situation, the cottage next door is currently vacant. Ben Dunne didn't want to stay there after Richard got murdered, so he's moved to Mamie Byrne's B&B with the rest of the excavation crew. I saw Susie O'Malley earlier, but her cottage is too far away for her to overhear anything."

"So who wants to go first?" I asked. "I have something to share, and from Lenny's goofy expression, he does, too."

"Heck, even *I* have something to share," Reynolds said, "and I feel totally out of the loop, seeing as I'm not supposed to be actively investigating. Let me get you guys a drink and we'll get started."

Once my friend had been supplied with an alcohol-free beer and I with an alcohol-laden glass of white wine, Lenny grinned at me. "Ladies first. Maggie found a gem in the Spinster's attic of doom. Is the mess up there as bad as they described?"

"Probably not, but my standards are low." I went over to the chair where I'd slung my purse when we'd arrived and retrieved my big find. "In among the chaos, I did manage to find this."

At the sight of the exhibition brochure, Reynolds whistled. "Well done. Does it contain anything useful?"

"Oh, yes." I flipped to the last page and showed him the photo of a young Richard Carstairs standing next to C. Carstairs, a.k.a. Clodagh Burke.

"Wow." He looked impressed. "So not only was

Clodagh involved in both digs, but she was married to Richard?"

"That's what I'm assuming. We can't rule out that she was his sister or otherwise related to him, but they look nothing alike, so I'm rolling with wife."

Reynolds squinted at the photograph. "If his name wasn't written under the photo, I wouldn't know this guy was Richard Carstairs. The jaw's different. Even discounting the beard our Richard sported, they're not all that alike."

I held his gaze. "Are you thinking what I'm thinking?"

"Huh? I don't get it." Lenny frowned, and then comprehension dawned. "Wait a sec. Didn't you two find a bunch of IDs on Richard?"

"Yes, we did. So the Richard Carstairs we knew could have been anyone."

"And the dead guy in the pit might well be the real Richard Carstairs," Reynolds finished. "It's not much of a stretch under the circumstances."

"The trouble will be convincing Sergeant O'Shea to consider the possibility and take the necessary steps to prove or disprove the theory." I stared glumly at my wine glass. "I know you're not supposed to work on vacation, but I wish you could pull rank on this."

"I have no rank to pull. O'Shea and I are both sergeants, and he has more years under his belt than I do. My position as head of the station is unofficial and merely represents the spoken wish of the district superintendent."

I wrinkled my nose. "That sucks."

"Yes, but now we come to the piece of news I have to share." Reynolds's wide grin told me it'd be good. "My esteemed colleague is busy all weekend with the golf tournament. According to Timms, he's left Garda Conlan in charge of the station. In spite of the clothes and the attitude, Sile Conlan has a reputation for doing the right thing. In fact, that's what got her kicked off the Galway homicide squad and sent here."

"So the whole intro by Daddy was just a cover?" Lenny demanded.

"Kind of. He is the district superintendent, and I'm sure he pulled strings to make sure she wasn't relegated to an admin position." Reynolds grinned. "From what I've heard, paperwork and people skills aren't among Sile's strengths."

"You mentioned she has a rep for doing the right thing," I pressed. "Do you think you can persuade her to set the wheels in motion to confirm if the skeleton is the real Richard Carstairs? Maybe mention the missing femur, for example?" I frowned as I mentioned the femur, my mind racing back to the conversation I'd had with Dolly. The guy her employee had sold the cupcakes to had had a limp. Could that be connected to the skeleton's missing femur? If so, how?

"I can see the wheels turning in your mind, Maggie," Reynolds said dryly, making me laugh.

"Always."

He glanced at his back door. "I don't want to be seen at the station while I'm on holidays, so I invited Sile to join us after her shift ends."

"Smart," I said, impressed. "Maybe the three of us can persuade her it's a lead worth pursuing."

He raised his beer to his lips and looked at Lenny before taking a swig. "So what did you discover from Sheila Dunphy?"

Lenny beamed and pulled a folder out of his backpack. "Sheila backed up Maggie's theory that Clodagh was Richard's wife, and she let me copy photos she'd taken of the 2000 excavation team. She mentioned that Clodagh Burke had been involved in the earlier dig with her first husband, and she said they'd both been involved with a reenactment of a battle that took place on the island in 1796."

"The year ties in with the weapon I think killed the skeleton," I said. "My guess is a Brown Bess flint-lock musket."

"Your guess is correct." Reynolds grinned. "I persuaded Sile Conlan to take a look at the forensics report. The historical weapons expert they consulted gave a list of potential firearms that the musket ball could have been fired from, and the Brown Bess was his first guess."

"I'm trying to find out who could have had access to a Brown Bess on Whisper Island seventeen years ago," I said. "I'm taking a trip out to George Fort tomorrow for some research."

Reynolds nodded in approval. "Smart."

I looked at the photographs Lenny had copied from Sheila Dunphy. They included one of Clodagh and Richard Carstairs where the side of Richard's head was visible. "Do you have those crime scene photos, Liam? I want to check Dead Richard's profile and see if it matches this guy's."

Reynolds fetched his case dossier from his home office and spread the photographs he'd persuaded forensics to share with him on his yard table. "You're right. The shape of the earlobe is different. I don't think we're dealing with the same man."

"Why would Clodagh Burke not point out that the Richard Carstairs on the current dig was an impostor?" Lenny demanded.

I exchanged a loaded look with Reynolds. "If Clodagh knew the original Richard was buried on the site, it would give her a compelling reason not to reveal that the Richard we knew wasn't the real deal. Also, we don't know what the fake Richard knew about the guy whose identity he'd stolen. Can we dial back to the research you did on Richard? Did it mention a wife anywhere?"

Lenny shook his head. "I checked the records in Ireland and the UK. I found Richard's birth certificate, but no mention of a marriage, and no mention of a divorce. However, if he'd married in another country, that wouldn't show up. If Sile Conlan is willing to help, she can get access to foreign registries faster than I can. We can even split the workload. The places I'd start looking are the countries where

Richard worked over the course of his career up until the 2000 dig."

"The fake-identity aspect has me convinced that missing femur is relevant," I said. "We need Sile to look up Richard Carstairs's medical records and see if there's any mention of an orthopedic implant."

Reynolds and Lenny had succeeded in coaxing the charcoal to cooperate, and Reynolds placed the first pieces of meat on the grill.

"What should we do next?" I asked, my mouth already watering at the tantalizing cooking smells. "I wish we had access to Tommy's missing camera. I feel sure there's something important in those pictures that someone didn't want seen."

"The missing camera could be a classic red herring, Maggie," Reynolds said. "For all we know, Tommy simply lost it, and there's nothing sinister about its disappearance."

"I'd like to be sure."

"Um, Maggie?" A small voice wrenched my attention away from the men. I pivoted on my heel. Caoimhe hovered at the back door, Hannah at her side. Both girls wore guilty expressions, although Caoimhe's was guilt on steroids.

Reynolds groaned. "Were you two eavesdropping? I thought you said you were going to the games room."

"We did say that," Hannah conceded, "but we weren't serious. We knew you'd start talking about the murders, and we didn't want to miss out on the fun."

"We hid in the hallway," Caoimhe elaborated. "Only we couldn't hear anything, so we snuck into the kitchen."

"Promise me you won't tell anyone what you overheard." Reynolds's tone was severe. "This isn't a game, girls. Two men are dead."

"We know." Caoimhe stared at her sneakers. "That's why I have something to tell you."

"Tommy's camera," I whispered. "Did you take it?"

The girl shook her head. "I didn't lie about that part. I didn't take his camera." She slipped her hand into the pocket of her shorts and withdrew an SD card. "But I did take this and swap it with a blank one."

21

I sucked in a breath and experienced the buzz an investigator got when they knew they'd stumbled on a major clue. "This is the SD card that was in Tommy's camera when he took pictures of the pit? Are you sure?"

Caoimhe exchanged a glance with Hannah, and then nodded. "Yeah, I'm sure. After you told him off for taking photos, he put the camera back in his bag like he said he did. When he wasn't looking, I opened his bag and exchanged this SD card for a blank one. Tommy takes pride in his photographs, and I knew he'd freak when he discovered the SD card was empty. He'd think his precious camera was broken and have a fit."

"Why didn't you tell us this earlier?" Reynolds asked. "You must have known it was important."

"I didn't want to get into trouble." The girl bit her lip. "See, I don't think someone stole the camera. It probably fell out, and that makes it my fault that it's lost. Tommy had the backpack zipped tight, like he said. I had to shove the camera back in quickly because he moved and he'd have noticed me standing behind him. I didn't have time to zip the bag shut properly."

"Can we have a look at the photos on the SD card?" I reached out a hand, and Caoimhe dropped the card onto my palm.

Lenny gestured to the grill. "Will you take over here for me, Maggie? I have a program on my laptop that can zoom in on photos. For the fancy stuff, we'll need help."

"Sure." I took the tongs, barely registering the meat on the grill.

Lenny pulled his laptop out of his backpack and fired it up.

Before we could get started on the content of the SD card, the doorbell rang. Reynolds moved toward the back door. "That'll be Sile. I'll fill her in on the basics, and then we can all look at that card together."

I examined the meat. "I think the steak's nearly done." My words were more confident than I felt. Assessing cooking meat wasn't one of my strong points.

The girls came to my side. "It looks charred," Hannah said, but her tone wasn't as critical as I'd expected. "Maybe put on a few sausages next."

I put the steaks on warm foil and placed several

sausages over the heat. "Want a cold drink after all that excitement?" I asked the girls.

"Yeah. I can grab colas from the fridge."

Hannah disappeared into the kitchen to get the drinks, and Caoimhe turned baleful eyes on me and Lenny. "I'm really sorry for not mentioning the card earlier. Will you have to tell Mum and Dad what I did?"

"The SD card is Tommy's property, so yeah." At the sight of her forlorn face, I added, "I'm happy to come with you when you tell them, and I'll stress how brave you were to confess, especially when you knew you were doing the right thing even if it meant you'd get into trouble."

Her shoulders drooped. "Okay. My parents will be mad, but they're not total ogres. I'll probably be grounded though, and that means I won't be able to see Hannah again while she's on Whisper Island."

"Let me talk to your parents, Caoimhe. Maybe we can come up with a solution." Given Melanie's obvious relief at her daughter finally making a friend, I didn't think she'd be heartless enough to ban the girl from seeing Hannah, but I could imagine Caoimhe getting extra chores and maybe no pocket money for a while.

Reynolds reappeared at the back door, trailed by Garda Sile Conlan. She'd changed out of her police uniform and wore a similar outfit to the one she'd had on at the Movie Club night: flowing black skirt, Doc Martens boots, and leather bustier top. Her dark hair was no longer in multiple braids and was instead loose and straightened. Her petite build made her look younger than her years, but she looked older than the sixteen I'd mistaken her for now that I saw her in natural light. If she'd been in juvie community service with Lenny, she had to be close to our age.

After Reynolds had introduced her to the girls, Sile focused on Lenny and me. She looked from my friend to me and back again. "I know you from somewhere, right?"

Lenny grinned. "Juvie community service. Remember the summer we spent in Cork painting an old folks' home?"

"Vividly." Her eyebrows went skyward. "Kenny, wasn't it?"

"Close. The name's Lenny."

She clicked her fingers. "That's right. Lenny Logan. I remember the alliteration. I also remember you were a total geek."

Lenny's grin froze. "And proud of it. Nothing wrong with being a geek."

Reynolds raised his eyebrows at me. I took the unspoken hint. Time to intervene before Sile antagonized Lenny further. He was a mild-mannered guy but he could be stubborn when he didn't like someone. If we wanted to crack this case before Sergeant O'Shea hit his last tee, we all had to cooperate.

"Has Liam brought you up to speed with the case?" I asked, hoping to distract Sile from baiting Lenny.

The woman fixed me with a hard stare. "Yes, but I'd like to see those photos for myself."

"The food's ready." I gestured to the grill. "Want to eat and browse at the same time?"

"Sounds good to me," Reynolds said.

Once we'd all been supplied with a plate of salad and meat—or salad and tofu in Lenny's case—we gathered around the laptop. We clicked through photos that Lenny had copied from Sheila Dunphy, plus the exhibition brochure I'd scored from the Spinsters. "We were just about to look at the SD card from Tommy Greer's camera when you arrived," I said. "Lenny, can you do your stuff?"

My friend inserted the SD card into his laptop and opened it. We found twenty-four photos that Tommy had taken on the day trip. We clicked through the cave pictures, a butt photo I'd missed when I'd deleted a few and, finally, the photos of the pit. We all crowded around the laptop to get a better view.

"Should the kids be here?" Sile asked Reynolds in an accusatory tone. I wasn't sure if she was genuinely outraged at the girls' presence or if her default mode was caustic and defensive. I was rolling with the latter option, and Reynolds clearly agreed.

"They already know everything anyway," he said in a breezy manner that managed to have a steely undertone. "No point in sending them away now."

"Is that the mound of dirt where you think the femur ought to have been?" Lenny pointed to the screen.

I leaned closer. "Yeah. This is a good shot. Can you zoom in?"

He obliged, and I found myself staring at a partially revealed bony object.

"Could that be it?" Reynolds asked.

"It's the correct shape for a femur," Sile said. "We'd need to blow it up more to know for sure." We all stared at her in surprise. She rolled her eyes. "Don't look so shocked. I take an interest in forensics. I know my way around a skeleton. As soon as the sarge shared his file with me, I brushed up on my old class notes."

"Can you take a closer look at the next photo?" I indicated the thumbnail beside the picture we'd just looked at.

Lenny clicked on the photo and zoomed in on the partially exposed bone. This time, the picture was sharper.

Sile nudged me. "Move it. I want to take a look."

I opened my mouth to deliver a blistering response, and shut it again when I caught Reynolds's warning look. Even if Sile was rude, we needed her on our side.

The young police officer squinted at the screen and pointed. "Can you isolate that section?"

My friend obliged.

Sile muttered under her breath and glared at me. "That looks like a metal implant." Her tone was accusatory, as though we'd committed a crime by making a discovery she hadn't.

I fist-pumped the air. "Go, Lenny. Looks like your hunch was right."

My friend blushed. "Thank Mack. I brainstormed ideas with him."

I took a bite of my steak. It was delicious, but my mind wasn't on my meal. "Where do we go from here?"

"Sile will send the photo file to forensics and see if they can come up with a serial number," Reynolds said.

"Sile will also make a formal request for Richard Carstairs's DNA to be compared to the skeleton's," Sile said in a sarcastic tone. "I know how to do my job, Reynolds. No need to give me paint-by-numbers instructions."

"And no need to call me Reynolds. *Sergeant* Reynolds will do just fine." His tone was mild, but I recognized the dangerous flash in his eyes. Garda Conlan would be wise not to push him too far.

"I want to be a crime scene investigator when I grow up," Hannah piped up, reminding us of the girls' presence. "It sounds so cool."

"I can be a homicide detective," Caoimhe added, "and maybe we'll need to work together to solve cases."

"That's an excellent plan, girls. Speaking of plans —" I turned to the adults, "—want to decide what each of us needs to do next? I can talk to Clodagh Burke."

"No," Reynolds said firmly. "For all we know, she

murdered her husband."

"For all we know, *anyone* involved in the current excavation is a killer. I'll take Lenny with me when I question her. Would that make you feel better?"

Reynolds regarded Lenny. "Frankly, no."

"I'm wounded," my friend responded cheerfully.

"Shouldn't I be the one to talk to Clodagh?" Sile demanded.

"We need to save time," Reynolds pointed out. "You can't do everything. Okay, I'll go with Maggie. We can browse Clodagh's shop. That way, I can act like I have nothing to do with her questions, and I'm present in case of trouble."

I laughed. "Have you seen the size of Clodagh Burke? I could totally take her down."

"Her size is irrelevant if she shoots you. What if —" His sentence was cut short by the shrill peel of the doorbell.

"Are we expecting more guests, Dad?" Hannah asked.

Reynolds frowned. "No. Maybe it's someone from one of the other cottages. I'll go see what they want."

He disappeared into the house, and Caoimhe and Hannah snuck into the kitchen after him. Lenny, Sile, and I remained at the table and ate more of the barbecue food.

A couple of minutes later, Hannah burst into the garden, her eyes brimming with tears. "It's Mum," she squealed, "and she's absolutely furious. She wants to take me home now."

22

A moment later, Robyn Reynolds erupted into the garden, fists clenched and eyes boiling. Like Sile Conlan, her slight build gave her a girlish appearance, and her ferocious expression made me feel sorry for whoever came up against her in court. Robyn had arrived on Whisper Island expecting a fight, and she was determined to get one. My habitual determined self-confidence took a battering under the force of her glare.

She glowered at us each in turn before addressing her daughter. "Come on, Hannah. Pack your bags. We're going home."

The girl's lips trembled. "No, Mum. I want to stay with Dad."

"You can't do this, Robyn." Reynolds's jaw was granite hard. "I have a right to have Hannah stay with me until the end of August. You can't violate the terms of our custody agreement."

She reeled around, nostrils flaring. "Oh, can't I?" She reached into her purse and thrust a piece of paper at him. "According to this, I can. You put our daughter in danger. You're not fit to look after her unsupervised."

As Reynolds read the document, his face grew thunderous. "You want to revoke my custodial rights? This is ridiculous. None of these claims are true. I stopped to see if a man was sick and realized he'd been murdered. The moment my fellow sergeant arrived, he took over the case."

"But *you* called it in. *You* notified forensics."

"As was my duty." He shoved the paper back at her. "You'd have done the same in my place."

Robyn quivered with rage. "I don't go around finding dead bodies."

Lenny slid me a look. "Maybe that's why Reynolds finds you attractive, Maggie," he whispered.

I fought the urge to giggle. Instead, I cleared my throat. "Maybe we should take Hannah and Caoimhe to the games room. Come get us when you're finished tearing each other's hair out."

Robyn rounded on me. "You're not taking my daughter anywhere. Are you this Maggie person Hannah has been complaining about?"

I drew in a breath. The words stung but I wasn't surprised the girl had complained about me to her mother. When I looked at Hannah, she flushed, suddenly finding her shoes fascinating. I jutted my chin and stared her mother down. "Guilty as charged."

Robyn gave me a once-over and wrinkled her nose. "I don't want Hannah exposed to private investigators, or anyone else associated with law enforcement."

"I guess that includes you," I said without hesitation. "You're a lawyer, aren't you?"

The woman drew herself up to her full height, bristling with rage. "That's different."

"Baloney. You're part of the justice system, and so are we. I was with Liam and Hannah when we found the body, as was Caoimhe." I indicated the other girl, who'd retreated to the corner of the garden, presumably to avoid the warring parties. "The girls were never in any danger."

"She's right, Mum," Hannah said in a small voice, casting me a sheepish look. "I might have exaggerated about Maggie. She's not *that* bad."

"Maggie is fab," Caoimhe said, suddenly finding her voice. "I'm sorry you're upset, Mrs. Reynolds, but we've had a smashing time."

A pained expression crossed over Robyn's face. "You must be the girl Hannah mentioned."

Caoimhe nodded. "Can Hannah come to the games room with me to play? She's kind of upset, what with all the yelling."

Robyn had the good grace to blush. "As long as Hannah comes with me the moment I tell her to."

"Caoimhe's supposed to stay the night," her daughter protested. "It's not fair."

"Go to the games room, love," Reynolds said gently. "I'll come and get you soon."

Lenny tugged on his goatee. "I guess we'll leave you guys to it."

"That's a smart idea," I said, seizing his arm. "Coming, Sile?"

"Heck, yeah." She wrinkled her nose. "If I wanted to see a couple tear each other's hair out, I could have spent the weekend with my parents."

With these happy words, Sile marched into the kitchen and through Reynolds's cottage, Lenny and I hot on her heels.

When the police officer stepped outside the front door, she ran straight into Alan Doherty—or rather he ran into her.

The archaeologist leaped back in alarm. "Oh, sorry. I came looking for Maggie. Susie said she'd seen her go to Liam's cottage."

"I'm here," I said, dodging past Sile. "What's up, Alan?"

The young man thrust his hands into his pockets. "I wanted to talk to you, if you have time."

I felt Sile's eyes bore holes in me, but I ignored her. I indicated the bench in front of my cottage. "Want to sit for a while?"

"Sounds good."

Alan took a seat beside me and Lenny hauled the reluctant Sile in the direction of the games room. The police officer snuck curious glances back at us, clearly longing to hear what the archaeologist had to say to me. Sile was no fool. She sensed Alan was here to talk about the case. Perhaps there was hope for Whisper Island's police department after all.

I regarded Alan. He'd acquired bags under his eyes since I'd first met him, and the stress lines around his mouth had deepened. "What's up? You look worried."

"That's because I am." He massaged his temples and took a shuddery intake of breath. "Sergeant O'Shea's looking for me."

"I was under the impression that he was busy with the golf tournament."

Alan shook his head. "That's what people say, but I don't think so. He was skulking around Smuggler's Cove this evening, asking questions."

A bad feeling settled between my shoulder blades. What was the notoriously work-shy sergeant up to? What nugget of information had he ferreted out that had persuaded him to trade golf for work? "Did he speak to you?"

The guy shook his head. "I dodged him and came to talk to you."

I eyed him shrewdly. "Is this about your boat trip on Saturday?"

"Yeah." A look of guilt flashed over his face. "I wasn't entirely honest with you when we talked before."

"I guessed," I said, deadpan. "What parts of the story did you leave out?"

A deep flush reddened Alan's cheeks. "I knew which boat Richard had rented because I followed him to the boat rental place and hung around outside. After he'd left, I waited for a few minutes and went in and rented my boat. I told the man behind the desk I'd arranged to meet Richard at sea, but my phone wasn't working so I couldn't call him to find out the type and name of his boat."

"And the guy gave you the details?"

The young archaeologist grimaced. "Yeah."

I made a mental note to have a word with Nick Sweetman about security at his joint. That was assuming he was still alive after Jennifer had finished with him. "What was the idea? You wanted to follow Richard? Isn't that kind of creepy?"

"I didn't mean it to be creepy. I wanted to confront him about Susie. Find out what really happened."

"Whether or not they'd had a fling?" I prompted.

He nodded.

"Sorry, but that is total stalker behavior."

Sweat beaded on Alan's upper lip. "You don't understand."

"What I understand is that you boarded Richard's yacht. What happened after you went on board?"

"It's before I went on board that you should be concerned about." The man's eyes darted to the side.

"I know it sounds bad, but I swear he was dead when I got on that yacht."

"What time was this?" I asked, thinking of the Richard-lookalike jogger.

"I'd been out on the water for a while. I guess it must have been around eight."

That tied in with the estimated time of death, and ruled out the admittedly slim possibility that Richard —or whatever his name really was—had been alive when I collected Caoimhe.

"Why didn't you call for help?" I demanded. "You must have realized you were looking at a potential crime scene."

"I know I should have called the police." His voice broke and he took a moment to compose himself. "I panicked. Lost my mind. I got back in my boat and sailed as far away from that yacht as I could. I didn't stop to think until I got back to Smuggler's Cove."

"Why didn't you go straight to the cops the moment you docked?"

The man fiddled with his sleeves in a nervous gesture. "I was afraid they'd accuse me of the murder."

"Not if you explained the situation exactly as you've done here. Tell the police the truth and help them to rule you out of their inquiries."

He choked back a laugh. "You don't get it, Maggie. The police would have every reason to suspect me of murdering Richard."

"Because you were jealous of him flirting with Susie?"

"Not just that." He squeezed his eyes shut. "But yeah, it was one of many grievances I had with the man."

"Care to elaborate on that statement?"

He opened his eyes and held my gaze. "Richard Carstairs—the *real* Richard Carstairs—was my father."

23

I sucked air through my teeth. "That's why you fainted when you saw the skeleton. You knew you were looking at your father's remains."

"Yeah. I mean, I'd expected I might come across him, but seeing the skull like that…" Alan shivered in spite of the warm evening.

I glanced in the direction of Reynolds's cottage, but the front door was still firmly shut and the raised voices from the back yard indicated that he and Robyn weren't finished arguing.

I turned my attention to the man sitting beside me. "Alan, I want you to tell me everything, and you need to leave nothing out this time."

His Adam's apple bobbed, but he nodded. "Okay. What do you want to know?"

"You said the man in the pit was your father and that he was the real Richard Carstairs. What makes you so sure?"

He stared at his boots and remained silent.

"Come on, Alan. You must have a reason for suspecting the skeleton is your father."

He looked me straight in the eye. "I more than suspect, Maggie. I *know* he's my father. That's why I wanted a job on this excavation. The opportunity to see Susie again was a bonus, sure, but she wasn't the reason I applied for the position."

"Why were you certain your father was buried on that site?"

His protective shutters slammed down. "I can't tell you that."

"I'm not a fool. I know Clodagh Burke was married to Richard Carstairs, and I'm assuming she's your mother. If you're trying to protect her, it's too late."

The guy flinched, but he didn't deny my supposition. "Yeah, Clodagh's my mother. Doherty was her maiden name, and I started using it after…after my father died."

"Did he die around the time of the 2000 excavation on St. Finbar's Hill?"

"Yeah. Just after they'd finished. That's why sh— why *we*—decided to bury him farther down the hill. With all the machines that had gone up and down the hill during that excavation, the grass was patchy in places. It was easy to make the burial site blend in with the landscape."

"Whoever this 'we' was, I don't think it included

you," I said gently. "You can't be more than twenty-five now."

"I'm almost twenty-six," he said with an air of defiance.

"That would have made you nine at the time of your father's death. I can't see a nine-year-old dragging a body up a hill and digging a grave deep enough to go unnoticed for seventeen years."

He chewed on his lower lip. "It was my fault he died, though."

"How can you think that? You were just a kid."

His laugh was laced with bitterness. "Just a kid who shot his father."

"Accidentally or deliberately?"

He sneered at me. "It was no accident, and I have no regrets."

"A nine-year-old doesn't kill without a reason," I insisted. "What did he do to drive you to kill him?"

"He was a violent, jealous brute." The intensity of his words convinced me he was telling the truth, at least about his father's character. "On the night he died, he accused my mother of cheating on him and beat her up. Ironic considering the number of times he'd left her for other women."

"Did you shoot him to stop him hurting your mother?" I pressed.

"Yeah. He wouldn't stop hitting her." His voice rose a notch. "I thought he was going to kill her."

"So you killed him first?"

"Exactly." He spoke the word with pride.

"What sort of weapon did you use?" I asked, watching his face for his reaction.

A wary expression settled over his features. "I don't know. Some old weapon. My parents were into historical reenactments. One was lying around."

An antique flintlock musket just happened to be lying around the house, locked and loaded? I didn't buy it.

"Okay, so you shot your father and you and your mother buried his body on St. Finbar's Hill. Did anyone help you?"

"We managed it ourselves." The words were defiant, daring me to contradict him.

"What tale did your mother spin to explain Richard's disappearance?"

Alan shrugged. "That he'd left her. He already had a reputation for running off with his latest fling, and his drinking had grown out of control during his sabbatical. His colleagues weren't surprised that he took off, and Mum didn't get the impression they were all that disappointed."

"Your father wasn't popular at the university?"

"He was a brilliant academic, but arrogant and difficult to work with."

"How did archaeologists react when he turned up again, alive and well?"

Alan wrinkled his nose. "The man who stole my father's identity didn't come on the Irish archaeological scene until this excavation. He was careful to take jobs far away from Ireland. Until recently, Mum and I weren't aware he existed."

"It must have come as a nasty shock when you discovered that Professor Frobisher planned to excavate in the area where you'd buried your father's body."

"That's one way of putting it." He snorted. "But finding out a guy calling himself Richard Carstairs and trading on my father's credentials had snagged a prominent position on the excavation team was a far bigger shock."

"You and your mother both made sure to get jobs on the dig in case the body was discovered, right? And to keep an eye on the fake Richard Carstairs?"

He nodded. "Yeah. We figured that if the skeleton was going to be dug up, we'd better be on site to make sure it was never connected to my father."

I digested this information for a moment, and then fired my next question at him. "Alan, did you steal the femur?"

He jerked to attention. "How did you know about that?"

"The skeleton's left thighbone is missing. My assistant and I guessed that it contained some sort of identifying feature such as an orthopedic implant."

He rubbed his temples. "You guys are good. Yeah, my father was in a car accident when he was at university, and ended up needing major surgery on his left leg. Mum knew the skeleton would have some sort of screws or implant and she was worried they could be used to identify it."

"So the fainting incident wasn't just the product of a nervous collapse? You wanted to steal the femur when no one was looking." The words were out of my mouth before I remembered Tommy's photos. If Alan had stolen the femur during his fainting spell, it wouldn't have shown up in those photos.

Sure enough, Alan shook his head. "I wanted to take it then, but I had no opportunity. And then your boyfriend was on patrol and wouldn't let anyone near the pit."

"If you didn't take the femur, who did? Your mother?"

"No. Like me, she couldn't get anywhere near the skeleton once the commotion started."

"Someone stole it," I insisted. "It didn't disappear on its own."

"My guess is the impostor took it." Alan grimaced. "Not long after my mother got home on the night the skeleton was found, she got a letter."

I perked up. "What did this letter say?"

"That if she didn't want the femur handed over to the police and her cover story blown, she needed to pay ten thousand euros."

I whistled. "That's a lot of dough for a craft store owner to come up with."

"Tell me about it. Mum guessed the letter was from the fake Richard. He'd already threatened her at the beginning of the excavation."

"I guess he figured she had more to lose than him if the truth got out."

Alan nodded. "He correctly guessed that my father was dead. Why else would my mother not object to a stranger using Richard Carstairs's identity? If she'd had any sense, she should have gone to the police and pointed out he was an impostor. Then when the body turned up, he'd be the prime suspect."

"But she didn't."

His lips twisted into an ironic smile. "Until he pressed her for money, we were hoping we could all ignore one another until the dig was over."

"Did Fake Richard know you were Clodagh's son?"

"No. As soon as she found out about the impostor, Mum insisted we pretend we didn't know one another, and after he threatened her, she was adamant."

"You've used the word 'threaten' twice now when referring to Fake Richard's initial interaction with your mother," I said. "Did his threats include demands for money?"

"No. The threats didn't come until after the skeleton was discovered."

"And they came in the form of an unsigned letter?"

He nodded. "You know the type: cut out letters from a magazine."

"Didn't it strike you as strange that Fake Richard would send an anonymous letter instead of demanding money in person?"

Alan frowned. "No one else knew the skeleton was my father. Even the impostor just guessed my father was dead and had died an unnatural death. The skeleton turning up confirmed his hunch, and I suppose he decided to make money out of the discovery."

"Did you or Clodagh sneak up to the excavation site the night after the skeleton was discovered?"

"Both of us." Alan sighed. "She'd arranged to meet the blackmailer up there, and I didn't want her to go alone. I hid on the other side of the hill, but even I heard your pal, Lenny, howling the place down. I guess the blackmailer did, too, because we didn't see anyone while we were making a run for it."

"Lenny had a close encounter with nettles," I said. "In a delicate area."

Alan recoiled. "Ugh."

"Exactly." I shifted position on the bench. "To get back to the case: everyone on Whisper Island knows Clodagh. She's lived here for years. Why didn't they realize Fake Richard was an impostor?"

"My parents moved to Whisper Island a few months before the excavation," Alan explained. "My father had a sabbatical from the university, and he knew he'd be working on the excavation during the summer months. He was too much of an academic snob to make friends with the locals. As far as I know, the only semi-sociable activity he participated in was a historical reenactment. Besides, the impostor looked enough like my father to pass inspection if he happened to run into islanders who remembered him."

"But why didn't they recognize you? Didn't you go to school on Whisper Island?"

"No. I went to boarding school in Dublin." His lips twisted into an ironic smile. "And I was a fat kid. I look a lot different these days."

"You never came to the island to visit your mother after your father's death?"

He shuddered. "After what happened to my father, I never wanted to set foot on this island again. The only reason Mum stayed was because she lived in fear that the skeleton would be found. It's an obsession with her. I went to boarding school, willingly, and spent school holidays with my aunt in Dublin."

"Do you have any idea who the man posing as your father really was?"

Alan shook his head. "No clue. He could be anyone."

"Does your mother know?"

He paused for a fraction of a second too long before answering. "She says not."

"Thanks for telling me this, Alan. Would you be willing to talk to Garda Conlan? She's in the games room at the moment. Given your age at the time of your father's death, you have nothing to fear from the law."

A fact that I found extremely convenient—too convenient. I definitely needed to talk to the people at George Fort about loading and firing a Brown Bess.

"I don't know. I mean…" Alan trailed off and gave a defeated half-shrug. "Oh, all right. I guess I'll have to make a formal statement at some point."

"Given that you know the identity of the man in the pit, yes."

I glanced in the direction of the games room. As I'd suspected, Sile was peering out the window, watching me and Alan. I smiled at her and beckoned for her to join us. Quick as a flash, she darted out of the games room and hurried over to my cottage.

When she reached the bench she raised one eyebrow in a sardonic arch. "Do you require my assistance?"

"This is Garda Conlan, Alan." I looked from my companion to the young police officer. "This is Alan Doherty, one of the archaeologists working on the excavation. He just revealed an important piece of information to me regarding the identity of the skeleton. I thought you'd like to hear what he has to say."

Indecision flickered across Sile Conlan's face. For a moment, I feared she was going to insist on conducting the interview on her own, but she nodded and pulled up a chair. "Okay, Alan, what do you know?"

He darted me a look of panic, and I gave him a reassuring smile. "Just tell her what you told me."

His Adam's apple bobbed. "The guy in the pit— the skeleton—was my father."

To her credit, Sile didn't flinch. "What was his name?"

Alan stared at the ground. "Richard Carstairs."

Sile slow-blinked. "Okay. Why don't you start at the beginning."

Alan told his story with more confidence on the second round. Sile asked intelligent questions and scribbled notes. When Alan's tale was finished, she slipped the notepad back into her pocket. "I'll need you to make a formal statement at the station."

"But you believe me?" Alan stared at her wide-eyed.

"It's not my job to believe or disbelieve, just to sift through the evidence."

A clever non-answer. *Bravo, Sile.*

Alan shifted his gaze to me. "And you, Maggie?"

I avoided looking at the police officer when I responded. "I believe you didn't kill Fake Richard."

His shoulders sagged with relief. "Will you come with me to the station?"

"I'm not a lawyer," I protested. "You need a solicitor, not me."

"I'd still like you to be there," he said simply. "I trust you."

I caught Sile's eye. "Do you have an objection to me sitting in?"

Sile Conlan gave me a long look. "If it's what Mr. Doherty wants, fine, but he'd be smart to call a solicitor as well."

"I'm on it." I slipped my phone from my pocket and hit Jennifer's number. "Hey," I said when she answered. "I'm sorry to bother you on your day off."

The lawyer laughed. "Don't tell me. You need me to represent someone until a criminal lawyer can come to the island."

"You got it in one. Are you sure you can do it?"

"No problem. Nick ran off to deal with yet another work crisis, and I'm at a loose end."

I winced. I'd bet the faithless Nick had a rendezvous with Ellen Taylor. "Want to meet us at the station? We'll be there in around thirty minutes."

"Sure. I'll see you there."

I disconnected and strode over to Sile's car, where she was stowing Alan in the back seat. "I'll tell the others I'm going and follow you in my car."

"Okay, but make it quick if you want to sit in on the interview."

"Got it." I sprinted to Reynolds's cottage and banged on the door.

He answered, red-faced and visibly out of sorts. Robyn hovered behind him, and treated me to the full force of her death ray stare.

"Alan Doherty just confessed to murdering Richard Carstairs." I took pleasure at Robyn's intake of breath. "The *real* Richard Carstairs, who just so happened to be Alan's father."

Reynolds slow-blinked. "Can a kid fire a flintlock musket?"

"That's what I want to find out at the military history museum tomorrow."

Reynolds grabbed his wallet from a shelf next to

the door. "I have to go to the station, Robyn. I can't risk having Sergeant O'Shea screw this up."

His ex-wife's lips formed a thin line. "I'd expect nothing else from you, Liam. Your work always comes first."

"For heaven's sake," I snapped. "You guys are worse than the summer camp kids I chaperoned last week. Liam, you don't need to come with me. Sile is escorting Alan to the station, and he went willingly. Robyn, I understand you're concerned for Hannah's safety, but I wasn't lying when I said she was never in danger. If I may make a suggestion, why don't you ask Caoimhe's parents if the girls can move the sleepover to their place? Then you guys can fight until dawn if you feel like it."

Reynolds rubbed his jaw. "That's not a bad idea. Will you keep me up-to-date with what's happening at the station, Maggie?"

"Of course. I'll call you later." I jerked my head in the direction of the games room. "I'll just say goodbye to Lenny."

I nodded to both of them and sprinted over to the games room. I tumbled inside, breathless. "Can you look after the girls for a sec? I need to accompany Sile and Alan Doherty to the police station."

"Dude," Lenny said, awed. "Has he confessed?"

"To the first murder, but something doesn't add up. I'm not convinced he did it."

"Don't leave me hanging, Maggie. What's fishy about his confession?"

I glanced over my shoulder. Sile stood in front of her car, vibrating with impatience. "I'm sorry, but I don't have time to explain. I'll call you from the station."

"He can go with you," Reynolds said from the doorway. "Robyn and I can handle the girls."

Lenny bounced on the spot. "Awesome. Thanks, dude."

Reynolds shot me a grin. "Nothing to thank me for, Lenny. You were doing me a favor."

"Will you let us know what happens?" Caoimhe asked. "We're dying to know the whole story."

Hannah nodded enthusiastically. "We don't want to be kept out of the loop. After all, Caoimhe provided you guys with important information."

I laughed. "You two are unbelievable. Yes, Caoimhe did help the investigation. I'm due to call your dad later, Hannah. I'm sure he'll keep you informed."

BEFORE WE GOT into my car, Lenny insisted on retrieving the bag of brownies from my cottage. After he'd stashed them in the glove compartment, we fastened our seat belts and I started the engine.

"Talk about drama," Lenny said when we were motoring down the coast road. "That ex of Reynolds is a piece of work."

"She's just worried about Hannah's safety. And

she does have a point about Reynolds being obsessed with his job."

My friend stared at me, aghast. "Are you sticking up for her? She's a pain in the behind."

"Oh, she's a witch. I'm not disputing that for an instant." My grip around the steering wheel tightened. "I hope she doesn't give Liam too hard a time while we're at the station."

"Speaking of the station, can you fill me in on what Alan told you? I'm bursting with curiosity."

"Sure."

For the rest of the drive to Smuggler's Cove, I relayed Alan's story in detail and my doubts about its veracity. "He's telling the truth on most points. I'm sure of it. But I'm equally certain that he's protecting Clodagh. The question is, will she let her son take the fall for her?"

"I think we're about to find out," Lenny said as we pulled into the police station's parking lot. "That's her over there."

Sure enough, Clodagh Burke was hurrying toward the station, accompanied by her husband, Tom. I parked the Yaris and Lenny and I jumped out of the car.

In spite of her few minutes head start, Sile had just parked her car in front of the station's entrance. "Sheep," she said dryly in response to my questioning look. "A farmer insisted on herding his sheep across the road just as we came along. Still, no harm done. By the way, I—"

Whatever Sile had been about to say was drowned out by the sound of a vehicle roaring into the parking lot. The police officer and I exchanged matching what-the-heck looks as Sergeant O'Shea screeched to a halt in front of her car.

Reserve Garda Timms tumbled out of the passenger side, while his boss heaved his corpulent carcass out from behind the wheel. Sergeant O'Shea flashed us a triumphant smirk.

I didn't need the sinking sensation in my stomach to clue me in that things were about to get complicated, and the constipated expression on Timms's face confirmed my suspicion.

"Thanks for anticipating my need for Mr. Doherty's presence, Garda Conlan," Sergeant O'Shea said to Sile. "I might even let you sit in on our interview."

"Hey, I'm the one who brought him in," Sile protested.

"And I outrank you."

With this parting shot, Sergeant O'Shea swaggered over to the back door of the car and hauled Alan out from the back seat.

"Hey," the younger man protested. "What's going on?"

The police sergeant's smirk grew wider. "What's going on, Mr. Doherty, is that I'm arresting you for the murder of Jason Castle, alias Richard Carstairs."

24

Alan Doherty opened and closed his mouth, fishlike. "It's not true. I didn't kill that man. I killed my father, but not the other guy."

"What other guy?" Sergeant O'Shea demanded. "How many people have you murdered? Are you telling me we have a serial killer on the island?"

"He's murdered no one." Clodagh Burke hurried over to join our rapidly increasing group, her husband by her side. "My son wouldn't hurt a fly. *I* killed Richard."

"Hush, love," Tom Burke said in a tired voice. "It was me, Sergeant. *I* killed Richard."

Sergeant O'Shea's ruddy face turned purple. "What's going on? You can't all have killed the man."

"There are two murder victims," I reminded him. "The skeleton at the excavation site, and the dead guy on the yacht."

The older police officer glowered at me, and

turned his attention back to Clodagh. "Well, Mrs. Burke, which one are you saying you killed?"

She jutted her chin in defiance. "Both."

Alan looked appalled. "Mum, don't be ridiculous. You—"

"Ignore her. *I* killed both men," Tom Burke insisted. "I swear it."

Sergeant O'Shea held up a hand. "That's enough," he roared. "This is a garda station and I'm officer of the law. I won't have this arrest turned into a farce. I'm bringing Alan Doherty into this station on suspicion of murdering Jason Castle. If he wants to confess to more murders, that's fine by me."

"But it's not fine by me." Jennifer Pearce swept down the station steps, elegant as ever in a coral designer twinset and nude stiletto heels, her dark hair twisted into a chignon. "I've been waiting inside to meet my client, and I overheard the cacophony outside. What sort of establishment are you running, Sergeant O'Shea? Isn't it customary to conduct police interviews inside the station rather than in front of it?"

The man's nostrils flared. "I'm in the process of bringing the suspect into the station."

"Which one?" I asked, failing to keep my amusement under wraps. "You've got quite a collection to choose from."

"You've got to believe me." Alan's voice broke on the last word. "I didn't kill the man pretending to be my father. He was already dead."

"You were on his yacht the day he died," Sergeant

O'Shea snapped. "We found your fingerprints. And this morning, your landlady found a bone in your bedroom—the same bone that was missing from the skeleton. That's reason enough to take you in for questioning."

Alan's mouth gaped. "Mrs. Byrne found the femur in *my* bedroom? No way."

"Yes way." The sergeant's smug smile had me itching to slap him. "How do you plan to wriggle out of that?"

"Not another word until I've spoken to my client," Jennifer snapped. "You are a disgrace to your profession." The lawyer turned to the motley group of would-be killers. "I'd like to have a word with all of you if I may."

"All right," Clodagh said. "I suppose it can't do any harm."

Jennifer cast Sergeant O'Shea an imperious look. "We'll be in Room One if you're looking for us."

The police officer gaped at her and spluttered something unintelligible. Jennifer ignored him and herded Alan, Clodagh, and Tom into the station.

After the door shut behind them, Sile Conlan turned to Sergeant O'Shea. "Dad said I'd learn a lot from observing you work. I take it this was an example of a model arrest?"

Lenny and I snorted with laughter.

The older police officer's jowls wobbled. "Laugh away, Ms. Doyle. I suppose I have you to thank for that solicitor showing up. Well, you can forget your amateur detective work. The police have the matter under control."

"You appear to forget that I was a police officer back in the U.S., and I'm a licensed private investigator here in Ireland. That hardly qualifies my investigative skills as amateur."

"A piece of paper says you can hire yourself out to investigate petty crimes." His sneer sent a jolt of anger through my veins. "It doesn't give you the right to interfere in an ongoing police investigation. I don't want to see either you or your pot smoking friend near anyone associated with this case."

I rolled my eyes. "Dude, I live in the same complex as several of the people involved. How am I supposed to avoid them?"

"Well," he spluttered, "don't interrogate them. If I hear you've tried to interfere again, I'll have you charged."

"With what?" I demanded. "Doing my job?"

"I'm warning you for the last time, Ms. Doyle. Don't cross me."

"Are you threatening me, Sergeant O'Shea? Because it sounds like you are. And I don't take police oppression lightly."

"Oh, please. All I'm doing is telling you to steer clear of my suspects. I'm within my rights to do that."

Unfortunately, he was, and we both knew it. I nodded to Sile. "Bye, Garda Conlan. Thanks for your help today."

"No problem." A grin broke through her prickly

demeanor. "Don't go finding more people who want to unburden their souls. We don't have enough holding cells to accommodate them."

"I'll try not to," I said dryly. "Good luck with those interviews."

After everyone had gone into the police station, I looked at Lenny. "I don't think the police will care if I leave my car here for a while. Want to walk and talk? I could do with fresh air after all that drama."

"Sure," my friend replied. "I want to go over the facts again with you. I feel like tonight was an exercise in smoke and mirrors."

"You and me both."

We strolled out of the parking lot and crossed to the side of the road that faced the sea.

A line appeared between Lenny's brows. "Which one of them do you think did it?"

"I'm not sure. My money's on Clodagh for the skeleton murder, but Alan seems determined to take the fall for that one. Yet his shock about the femur being in his room was the real deal."

"This is the same man who admits he was on Fake Richard's yacht the day the guy died, yet remains adamant that he didn't kill him. Do you believe him?"

"I do, actually. I think the yacht scenario played out exactly as he described. Like his allegations about his father's behavior, Alan has a temper and a jealous streak. I saw both in action the day I spoke to Susie O'Malley at the excavation site. Following Fake Richard out to his yacht is creepy as heck, and I wouldn't be surprised if murder was on Alan's mind. After all, Fake Richard had had the audacity to flirt with the woman Alan was in love with, and blackmail his mother."

"But you don't think he killed him?"

"No. His horror at finding the corpse seemed genuine. As for whether he killed his father, I'm going to do some research about that when I visit George Fort tomorrow. I'm not convinced a nine-year-old could handle a Brown Bess, but I could be wrong."

We'd reached the Smuggler's Cove Harbour, one of the two on Whisper Island. In contrast to Carraig Harbour, the one nearest to my home, Smuggler's Cove Harbour was popular with tourists and hobby sailors. As we passed the office of Nick Sweetman's boat rental business, my stomach clenched.

"Are you going to tell Jennifer about Nick and Ellen?" Lenny asked, correctly interpreting my thoughts.

"Yeah." I sighed. "I'm not looking forward to it."

"I don't blame you. Want to take your mind off it by listing the suspects for each of the murders?"

I burst out laughing. "Yeah. There's nothing like unnatural death to take one's mind off other matters. Okay, we've pretty much covered the suspects in the skeleton case, so let's focus on Fake Richard, or Jason Castle."

"I wonder how O'Shea found out his real name," Lenny mused. "Do you think he had a record?"

"Maybe. If his fingerprints were in a database,

that would do the trick. I'm sure Sile will tell Reynolds."

My friend grinned. "And then he'll tell us."

"Exactly."

"For Castle, we have the skeleton trio—Alan, Clodagh, and Tom," Lenny said.

"And all the people involved in the excavation," I added. "That's assuming they were the only ones with a grudge against the man."

"Good guys don't tend to steal other people's identities."

"True." I shook my head and frowned. "What I'd like to know is if Castle *knew* the real Richard Carstairs was dead, or merely guessed. And if he *knew*, he must have been connected to the original excavation, or lived on the island."

"Who do we have on our list? Ellen Taylor?"

"I considered her when we first found Castle's corpse, but her furtive behavior and disappearing acts can be explained by the affair with Nick."

"Professor Frobisher?" Lenny suggested. "He's a grumpy old dude."

"Yes, but I don't see why he'd want to put the excavation in jeopardy. By all accounts, he fought to get the funding for the project, and he works the team like a slave-driver."

"Speaking of money, there's a point I meant to tell you and Reynolds this evening, but it slipped my mind with all the commotion."

"What is it?"

"I'm not sure it's relevant, but it answers your questions about that Ben guy. Remember you asked me to look into his background after Alan suggested he wasn't on the level?"

I nodded. "You said you didn't find anything."

"I didn't." Lenny grinned. "But while I was looking into Professor Frobisher and the funding for the excavation, I noticed that Ben's father had made a sizeable donation."

I sucked in a breath. "Ben got his dad to pay his way onto the excavation team?"

"Looks like it."

"Why, though?"

"According to emails exchanged between the professor and Ben's father, Ben is interested in kick-starting his career as an archaeologist focusing on the British Isles. I guess he got sick of Egypt."

"It sounds plausible enough," I said, "but I'm not going to strike Ben off the suspect list right away."

"Fair enough." Lenny thought for a moment, then said, "What about Susie O'Malley? You thought she had a fling with Castle."

"Yes, but I didn't get an obsessive vibe from her. If she slept with him, it wasn't serious. She was more concerned about avoiding Alan than spending time with Castle."

"Who else is on our list?"

"Technically, the entire excavation team, but we've already named the main candidates. I had the photographer, Ruth Dede, on the list, but she doesn't seem to have had much to do with Castle."

"To sum up, Clodagh and Alan—and possibly Tom—are still the main suspects for the Castle murder."

"Yeah," I exhaled slowly, "but I don't like it. I can't shake the sensation we've missed something. Can you do some internet research on Jason Castle? My guess is that he has some sort of genuine archaeological background or he wouldn't have been able to pass himself off as an expert. Alan questioned Ben's credentials, but no one suggested Castle didn't know what he was doing."

"I can do that. What's your plan? Apart from visiting the fort?"

"I'll take another look at the list of names of the people involved with the 2000 excavation, and find out about the reenactment put on by the Historical Society around that time."

Lenny glanced at his watch. "Want to head back to the car? I should check in on granddad. He invited a group of pals over for poker night. Those geriatric social events can get pretty wild."

I laughed at the mental image of a bunch of octogenarians partying. "Okay. I'll give you a call tomorrow after I visit the fort."

25

On the day after all the confessions, Jennifer and I arrived at George Fort just before it opened at ten o'clock. We'd opted to take my Yaris instead of Jennifer's sleek Mercedes, and from the expression on her face as we bumped over potholes, I suspected she regretted the choice. I pulled into a free spot in the parking lot and killed the engine.

"Thanks for collecting me," Jennifer said. "Are you sure you don't mind dropping me to the station after lunch? I want to let Alan Doherty and the Burkes stew for a while, and then tackle them about their confessions."

I'd been rehearsing what I'd say to her about Nick and it took me a moment to process her question. "Uh, sure."

"Are you all right, Maggie?" Jennifer asked,

concern in her dark eyes. "You've been quiet the whole drive."

"I'm sorry for being quiet. I have a lot on my mind." *Like how to tell you your fiancé is a cheating bag of cow excrement.*

"Isn't your divorce due to come through soon?" she asked. "You mentioned it a few weeks ago."

I nodded. "At the end of the month."

She cast me a look of sympathy. "Do you have mixed feelings about it?"

"Actually, no," I said honestly. "I'll be relieved when it's final and I can close that chapter of my life."

She frowned. "If the divorce isn't bothering you, what's up? Something's on your mind."

I paused, my hand on the door handle. "I'm trying to figure out when is the best moment to tell you something."

Her eyebrows shot up. "What do you have to tell me?"

I swallowed past the lump in my throat. "It's about Nick."

Jennifer paled under her tan, and her hand flew to her necklace. "I see," she said slowly. "Is it something bad?"

"Yes, I'm afraid it is."

She averted her gaze. "Please tell me, Maggie. It can't be worse than what I already suspect. For weeks, people on the island have been avoiding talking to me. At first, I thought it was my imagination, but at the

Movie Club meeting, islanders I considered friends avoided me."

I took a deep breath. "Lenny and I saw Nick kissing another woman."

A sob escaped her throat, but she nodded. "That's what I thought was up, but I didn't want to believe it. Who is she?"

"Ellen Taylor from the excavation team."

Jennifer fell silent for a tension-filled moment. She fiddled with her engagement ring, eventually wrenching it free from her finger. She stared at the enormous diamond as though mesmerized. "So *that's* who she is. I thought she looked familiar when I saw her in the Movie Theater Café, but it never occurred to me that Nick's ex was connected to the excavation."

My eyebrows shot up. "Ellen is Nick's ex-girlfriend?"

"That's my guess. The woman he went out with before me was called Ellen and she was an archaeologist. I've seen photos of her." Jennifer's voice wobbled. She rooted in her purse for a tissue, but came up empty.

"I keep tissues in the glove compartment," I said.

She opened it, found a tissue, and dabbed at her eyes. "That rat. He swore to me I was being paranoid about him working all the time, but I knew he was lying."

"I'm sorry, Jennifer. I've been there. That's why I filed for divorce."

More tears brimmed in her eyes, but she wore a look of defiance on her pretty face. "Thank you for telling me, Maggie."

"I wasn't sure how you'd take it, but I couldn't stay silent. Not after what I went through with Joe."

Her laugh was brittle. "No, I'm not about to shoot the messenger, or accuse you of lying. Believe me, you're not saying anything I hadn't already suspected."

"But suspecting and knowing are two different beasts," I said gently. "I understand if you want to go home. I'll go with you if you want company. I just didn't want you to be the last to know."

She took a shuddery breath. "No, I want to see the fort. I need the fresh air and the distraction. If I go home now, I'll ceremoniously burn Nick's sailing gear, get arrested, and my next client will be myself."

In spite of the situation, I laughed. "As long as you're sure. If you change your mind at any time, we can go. No questions asked."

But Jennifer proved to be a trooper. She pulled herself together with a grim determination, and listened to our guide with apparent rapt interest for our thirty-minute tour. George Fort was a star fort that had been erected in the late seventeenth century. It had been occupied by the British military until the Irish War of Independence. After the British withdrew from Ireland, the fort had fallen into disrepair. It had been restored during the Nineties and reopened as a museum. In addition to its breathtaking views over the Atlantic, the fort housed a collection of historical uniforms, weapons, and other military para-phernalia. In preparation for this morning's historical weapons display, a wooden viewing arena had been erected in the training yard. If I could persuade Jennifer to join me, I'd like to see the weapons in action.

Once the official tour had concluded, I sidled over to our tour guide, a bubbly redhead in her early twen-ties, and introduced myself. "I'm Maggie Doyle, a private investigator. I'm looking into a couple of cases connected with the excavations on the island and I'd appreciate some expert advice on flintlock muskets."

"Oh, of course." The girl's face lit up. "You're the one who asked Dolly to call me about the cupcakes."

My gaze dropped to her name tag. *D. Kowalski*. "The 'D' stands for Denise," I guessed.

"That's right. I work here twice a week and three days at The Cupcake Café." The girl's expression grew grave. "I heard they arrested a man for murdering that guy."

"Yeah. The police have someone in custody." Several someones, as it happened. Clodagh, Alan, and Tom, were all adamant that they'd killed Real Richard, Fake Richard, or both, and were being detained for further questioning. "You mentioned the guy you sold the cupcakes to had a limp. Can you remember which leg?"

She screwed up her forehead and considered my question. "I'm almost certain it was the right."

"There's no mention of an injury to his leg in the autopsy report," Jennifer interjected. "I read it last night after I took on the case."

Denise glanced at her watch. "I need to get ready for the next tour. Would you like to talk to David Bryant? He's our resident expert on historical weapons."

"That'd be great."

Five minutes later, a rotund little man with enormous glasses ushered Jennifer and me into a room filled with antique weapons. "Here she is," he said with pride. "Our very own Brown Bess."

I examined the firearm carefully. According to the information card on the display case, it had been the basic firearm used by the British infantry from 1740 until the 1830s. The case also contained examples of musket balls similar to the one discovered near Richard Carstairs's skull.

"In your opinion, could a nine-year-old fire a weapon like this?"

Mr. Bryant considered my question for a moment. "It's not impossible, but rather unlikely. The entire length is close to one hundred and sixty centimeters. However, if it was already prepared for firing, I suppose a child of that age could use it. One of our other Brown Besses might be a more likely candidate. The Cavalry Carbine, for example. It's only one hundred and eight centimeters long."

"In addition to the shooting demonstrations here, I understand the Whisper Island Historical Society occasionally stages battle reenactments. Do you supply the firearms for those events?"

"They haven't done a full battle reenactment in a few years," David Bryant said, "but we've allowed them to use several of our weapons for past events."

My heart rate kicked up a notch. "Can you remember if you supplied the weapons for a reenactment in 2000?"

"We did indeed. It was 2000 to celebrate the bicentenary of a rebellion that occurred on Whisper Island." David Bryant's chest puffed out. "I played the role of a British infantryman."

"You wouldn't happen to remember who else participated in that reenactment?"

He frowned. "Now let me see…we had regular members of the Historical Society, and a few visiting members of Fragarach, one of the bigger Irish reenactment societies."

It took me a moment to connect Bryant's pronunciation of Fragarach with the word I'd read recently. "Richard Carstairs was a member of Fragarach," I said excitedly.

"So he was," David Bryant replied with a distinct lack of enthusiasm. "I wasn't overly fond of the man, but I was sorry to hear he died."

"Are you referring to the dead man on the yacht?" Jennifer asked.

"Yes." Bryant looked confused. "Isn't that where he was found?"

"Not exactly, but I can't get into the details." News

of the impostor and the skeleton's true identity hadn't hit the media yet, but it soon would. "Why didn't you like Carstairs?"

A dark expression settled over Bryant's fleshy features. "He didn't treat his wife well. Clodagh's a lovely woman. I was glad when she settled down with Tom Burke."

"I've heard rumors of domestic abuse," I said, watching him carefully.

Bryant looked grim. "I never saw Carstairs hit Clodagh, but it wouldn't surprise me. He was a jealous, controlling man with a terrible temper."

A temper that might have driven his wife to kill him in an act of self-defense… "Could you get me a list of everyone who was involved in that reenactment?"

"I'm not sure that I can provide you with a complete list, but I will be able to tell you who borrowed which weapon. I'll need to check in our admin archives, though. It could take a while." He glanced at his watch. "I'm in the middle of sorting weapons for today's shooting display. Some of the Whisper Island Historical Society's reenactors are showing our visitors how training was conducted at the fort during the eighteenth century."

I perked up instantly at the mention of the display. "I'm interested in attending. Will you include a demonstration of how to prepare and fire a Brown Bess?"

He nodded. "We go through the process step by step."

I slid a look at Jennifer. Despite her pale but poised stance, her eyes told a different story. She was close to her breaking point. I needed to wrap up this interview and focus on my friend. I drew my business card out of my purse and handed it to him. "When you have the info about the weapons borrowed for the 2000 reenactment, please call me on this number."

He took the card but didn't put it into his pocket. "Is the information urgent?"

"I'm not sure," I said, "but it might prove to be very important."

"If you don't mind waiting fifteen or twenty minutes, why don't you get a cup of coffee in our café? I'm due a break and I can use it to dig out that list for you."

My chest swelled, but I looked at Jennifer before agreeing. "How do you feel about hanging out in the café for a while? Or would you prefer to make tracks?"

"Coffee sounds good," Jennifer said. "I could do with a pick-me-up."

"In that case, thanks, Mr. Bryant. If you don't mind digging up that info for me now, I'd appreciate it."

After David Bryant left to look up the list of people who'd borrowed historical weapons for the reenactment, Jennifer and I took a seat in the visitors' café and ordered coffee and scones. Neither were a patch on what we served at the Movie Theater Café, but not even Noreen's delicious berry scones could have tempted Jennifer. She picked at her scone without seeing it, and sipped her coffee black even though I knew she liked it with milk and sweetener.

"How are you holding up?"

Her smile was wan. "I'll be okay. I texted Nick while we were on the tour and told him to move out of my house."

"Whoa." I blinked. "Don't you want to talk to him first?"

She shook her head. "I want him and his stuff out of my house first."

I laid my hand on her arm. "If you don't want to be there when he collects his things, come and stay the night at my place."

She blinked back her tears. "Thanks, Maggie. I'd appreciate that."

A young man wearing a tour guide's uniform ambled into the café and over to our table. "Are you Maggie Doyle?"

"That's me."

He handed me a folded piece of paper. "Mr. Bryant asked me to give this to you. He said he's sorry he couldn't deliver it in person, but he had to take a call."

"Thanks." I took the piece of paper and the tour guide left.

"Well?" Jennifer prompted. "What does it say?"

"Hang on a sec and I'll tell you." I unfolded the

piece of paper and scanned the list. Two names leaped out at me. "Wow. Look at this."

I pointed to two names at the bottom of the list.

"Jay Castle-Conroy and Fergal Castle-Conroy," Jennifer read aloud. "So? Fergal has always been active in the Historical Society."

"First, I had no idea he had a double-barreled name," I said, "and second, doesn't it strike you as odd that Castle is part of it?"

"I suppose," she said slowly, "but the police report only mentions that Interpol supplied the information that a Jason Castle matched the fingerprints of the yacht victim. Sergeant O'Shea is still tracking down more details about the man."

"What if Jason Castle and Jay Castle-Conroy are one and the same?" I suggested. "Jay is a common nickname for Jason."

"True. I can ask Aaron," she said, referring to her boss. "Fergal Castle-Conroy is his client."

"Why didn't I know his surname was Castle-Conroy? Everyone refers to him as Conroy."

"That's because of his grandfather, Donal Conroy," Jennifer said. "He had no sons, and his only daughter, Nuala, was married to a man named Brian Castle. In Donal's will, he left everything he owned to Nuala on the stipulation that she and her children changed their name to Conroy or Castle-Conroy. I guess he didn't want the name to die out."

"According to David Bryant's list, both Fergal and Jay borrowed two different types of a Brown Bess for the 2000 reenactment. Richard Carstairs had some sort of pike, and Tom Burke also had a Brown Bess. All the guys who received firearms were provided with all the necessary gear such as gunpowder and musket balls."

Jennifer sighed. "This doesn't look good for Tom Burke."

"Or Clodagh," I pointed out. "She could have used his weapon, or one of the other firearms used for the reenactment."

"I'll ask Clodagh and Tom about the borrowed weapons when I see them later."

The announcement speaker crackled into life. "George Fort's monthly historical weapons display will begin in ten minutes. All our visitors are welcome to attend. If you'd like to see a recreation of eighteenth century soldiers practicing, please proceed to the training yard."

Jennifer and I drained our coffee cups and stood. "Want to check out the display?" I asked.

The lawyer nodded. "Yes, but I'll call Aaron first. I want to ask him about the Castle-Conroy family. I haven't lived on the island long enough to know all the ins and outs."

"Okay. I'll save you a seat."

I left Jennifer in the café and followed the flow of visitors out to the training yard. The place was packed and I had to fight my way up to a free area on one of the benches. I sat down with relief and spread my legs wide on the bench in an attempt to save space for Jennifer.

"Hey, Maggie," a familiar voice called from behind me.

I whipped around to see Hannah sitting beside Caoimhe and Melanie.

"Hey," I said in surprise. "I didn't expect to see you guys here."

Melanie cast me a look of perplexity. "They begged me to bring them along. I had no idea Caoimhe was interested in historical weapons."

I exchanged a loaded glance with Melanie's daughter. "What brought on this sudden onset interest?" I asked deadpan.

Caoimhe held my gaze. "I wanted to show Hannah some of Whisper Island's history."

"Right," I drawled, noting Hannah's guilty flush. The girls had overheard enough of our conversation at the barbecue to know about the musket. "It's great when kids express an interest in learning about the past."

"I guess." Melanie didn't look convinced. "I was surprised because Paul was supposed to take all the kids to a water park in Clare.

I looked from Hannah to Caoimhe. If the girls were willing to forego a trip to a water park, they had to be engaged in amateur sleuthing. I swallowed a sigh. The last thing I needed was two kids tagging along while I made inquiries.

A moment before the display began, a breathless

Jennifer struggled up the steps and joined me on the bench. She sat down, panting. "Sorry. I ran."

"No problem. Did you get through to Aaron?"

"Yeah. That's why I ran." She lowered her voice and shoved a piece of paper into my hand. "I scribbled down the specifics in case we were overheard."

I unfolded the note and scanned its contents.

Jason Castle-Conroy is Fergal Castle-Conroy's brother. Before Fergal took over the family farm, he got a master's degree in history. His brother went on to get a Ph.D. in archaeology. The Castle-Conroy brothers were both employed at a historical research center in Galway until Jason was accused of embezzling money from a research project he was in charge of managing. In 2002, Jason was convicted of the crime and sentenced to two years in prison. Since then, he hasn't been back to Whisper Island—as far as we know.

"Whoa." A criminal record was a strong motivation for a guy to use other people's identities, especially if he wanted to return to work as an archaeologist.

"Who's Jason Castle-Conroy?" Caoimhe demanded. "Is he related to Bethany from the hair salon?"

I groaned. "You shouldn't read over people's shoulders."

"Sorry," the girl said, not sounding in the least contrite.

"They're an odd family," Melanie said vaguely.

"He loves to jog through our grounds, but he never says hello."

I jerked around so fast I was sure I'd pulled a muscle in my neck. "*He?* Do you mean Fergal Castle-Conroy?"

"Yeah," she said. "He's very fit, in spite of his leg."

I exchanged a glance with Jennifer. By now, she'd have read the files on the skeleton case—both the official one and Reynolds's version—and she'd be aware of the Richard lookalike I'd seen jogging, as well as the limping man who'd collected the cupcakes from Dolly's the day before the murder.

"Do you know how Fergal got his limp?" I asked Melanie.

"A car accident, I believe." She screwed up her forehead. "Or was it a motorbike?"

A vision of the orthopedic device in the skeleton's leg danced before my eyes. "When did the accident happen?"

"I'm not sure, but I know it happened while he was studying in the UK."

I almost shot out of my seat, adrenaline pumping through my veins. "Do you know where he went to university?" I demanded.

Melanie blinked, taken aback by the urgency in my voice. "Oxford, I think. No, Cambridge. Yes, that's it. My mother always used to say it was a shame that he'd had so much education only to end up as a farmer."

My brain was working overtime. The real Richard Carstairs had been at Cambridge, and he'd have been around the same age as Fergal Castle-Conroy. Could they have known one another? And more relevant, could they both have sustained leg injuries in the same accident?

Judging by Jennifer's excited expression, the same thoughts were in her mind. She pulled her phone from her purse. "I'll text Aaron to find out."

"Awesome. When you speak to Clodagh later, ask her if Richard knew Fergal from university."

"Richard Carstairs?" Melanie's interest had been piqued. "The man you found dead on the yacht?"

"Not exactly."

"He had loads of IDs, Mum," said Caoimhe. "We don't know who he really was."

Hannah regarded me with a pensive expression. "I think Maggie knows."

Caoimhe bounced in her seat. "Who was he?"

The ping of an incoming message on Jennifer's phone saved me from answering. "What did Aaron say?"

"That Fergal got his leg injury in a car accident while he was studying for his master's degree at Cambridge. He's not sure of the year, but estimates it must have been in the late Eighties." Jennifer glanced at her watch. "I'd like to know what Clodagh has to say about the cause of her late husband's limp."

I got the hint. "Want to give the display a miss?

We can leave now and head straight to the police station."

"Would you mind? I'd like to speak to Tom and Clodagh sooner rather than later." The wobble in Jennifer's voice indicated that her desire to be alone wasn't motivated solely by the need to speak with her clients.

"No problem." I stood just as the men putting on the historical weapons display trooped into the yard. The six guys participating in the demonstration wore old-fashioned uniforms that were exact replicas of what the soldiers stationed at George Fort would have worn in the eighteenth century.

Caoimhe leaped out of her seat. "Look, Maggie. See the man with the limp?"

I scanned the group of soldiers and my heart thudded. "Is that—?"

"Fergal Castle-Conroy," Melanie finished for me. "I'd forgotten he was involved in these monthly demos, but then I don't pay much attention to the activities of the Historical Society."

Jennifer must have recognized my dilemma from my expression. "Do you want to stay? We can if you want."

"No, you should speak to your clients." I pulled my car key from my purse. "Why don't I stay and you take my car?"

She looked doubtful. "Are you sure? How will you get home?"

"I'll get the bus to Smuggler's Cove and meet you

at the station. My offer for you to stay at my place still stands."

"You can get a lift with us," Caoimhe said. "We're supposed to meet Hannah's dad at the Movie Theater Café for ice cream later."

"Is that okay?" I didn't relish the idea of getting a ride with my erstwhile nemesis, but I wanted to observe Fergal in action.

Melanie pursed her lips but inclined her neck. "No problem."

I turned back to Jennifer. "See? Problem solved."

"If you're sure…"

"I am." I gave her an impulsive hug. "Are you okay to drive?"

Jennifer blinked back tears. "I'll be fine. It'll give me time to pull myself together before I face that odious man."

In spite of the gravity of the situation, I snorted with laughter. "You're well able to handle Sergeant O'Shea. He positively wilted when you got all officious with him yesterday."

A smile broke through the lawyer's pained expression. "That was fun."

"It was, wasn't it?" I stood back. "Good luck. I'll see you later."

After Jennifer had left, I settled down to watch the display. I'd wanted to see it in order to get an idea of how a Brown Bess worked, but I couldn't take my eyes off Fergal Castle-Conroy. The weapon in his hand was shorter than the Brown Bess David Bryant had shown me. From a distance, it was hard to tell, but I guessed Fergal had a Cavalry Carbine.

Before the demonstration began, Fergal saluted someone in the audience. I followed the direction of his gaze. Bethany sat on the other side of the training yard, high up in one of the viewing stands. She grinned and blew her father a kiss. I returned my attention to Fergal and the weapon he held in his right hand. An icy sensation snaked down my spine.

David Bryant, resplendent in his costume, stepped forward and began a wordy discourse on the various weapons that were included in the display. As Bryant's monologue drew to a close, my phone buzzed with an incoming call. It was from Lenny. Ignoring the disapproving looks from the people around me, I hit connect.

"Hey, Lenny. What's up?"

"Where are you?" My friend sounded anxious. "Did you go to the fort as planned?"

"Yes. I'm here now."

"I'm at Granddad's this morning, and I filled him in on yesterday's drama. You'll never guess what. He thinks Jason Castle, a.k.a. Fake Richard, is Fergal Castle-Conroy's brother."

I regarded the dark-haired man who'd saluted Bethany. This was definitely the guy I'd seen jogging on the morning of the yacht murder. He was a darker-haired and clean-shaven version of his brother. "I know," I said to Lenny. "Aaron Nesbitt told Jennifer."

"Did Aaron mention the part about Bethany?"

My eyes immediately swiveled in the direction of the young redhead. She sat composed on her bench, her hands hidden behind a voluminous purse, and her eyes obscured by sunglasses. "What about her?"

"Granddad says Bethany's parents are actually her aunt and uncle. Apparently, Bethany's biological father, Jason, was a single dad. After he went to prison for something—Granddad can't remember what—Fergal and his wife got custody of Bethany. They raised her as their own and she refers to them as Mum and Dad."

"Wow," I breathed. "I didn't expect that."

"Neither did I. And here's the kicker. After Granddad filled me in on the connection between Fergal and the dead dude, I got busy on the internet. It turns out that Fergal and Jason were at the same posh Dublin boarding school as Richard Carstairs."

"Lenny, you are a genius."

"It gets better. Remember the info I dug up about Ben Dunne's father making a sizeable donation to the excavation, presumably to get his son a job on it?

"Yeah. Have you discovered more details?"

"Oh, yeah." His excitement was palpable. "Mark Dunne, Ben's father, also contributed money to the 2000 excavation courtesy of his historical research center."

I sucked in a breath. "The place where the brothers worked?"

"Bingo. So I did some more digging. Turns out

that this Mark Dunne dude also went to the same posh boarding school as Carstairs and the Castle-Conroys, and later to Cambridge. And one of Dunne's classmates at Cambridge was Tom Burke. Dunne has a conviction for drunk driving and causing a crash while under the influence."

"I can guess who was in the car with him at the time," I said, barely able to contain my excitement.

"Your guess would be correct. Burke, Carstairs, and Fergal Castle-Conroy. Tom Burke and Mark Dunne emerged from the wreck unscathed, but both Fergal and Richard sustained serious leg injuries."

Mindful of the curious ears around me, I stood and moved gingerly through the crowd gathered on the benches and down the steps. I chose a position at the edge of the standing spectators that was far enough away from people who could overhear my conversation, but close enough to keep my eye on Fergal Castle-Conroy. "Your details about the accident explain Fergal's limp and the need to make the skeleton's femur perform a disappearing act."

"Yeah. We now have a solid link between all of them, including Ben," Lenny concluded, "but we still don't know which one killed the real Richard in 2000."

"I'd imagine they were all involved," I said. "Either in the murder or in the cover-up."

"Then why did Jason decide to pretend to be Richard? He had to have known someone would recognize him?"

"But would they? With the beard and the gray ponytail, he'd changed a lot since his youth. Depending on his motives, he may not have cared about being recognized. We know he threatened Clodagh, so what was to stop him from having threatened Fergal, too?"

"True. Here's the funny thing about his conviction for embezzlement. He was adamant that his brother set him up and that their boss was in on it."

"He claimed Mark and Fergal framed him?" I frowned. "But why?"

"I don't know. Granddad said Jason had a rep for being a hard drinker. Maybe they thought he was a loose cannon and wanted to discredit anything he said. Even if they hadn't killed Richard, any involvement in covering up the crime would make them liable."

"Lenny, I need you to do me a favor. Can you call Reynolds and Sile Conlan? Tell them I need backup."

Lenny groaned. "Promise me you're not going to do anything stupid, Maggie. At least wait until I get to the fort before the fun starts."

I choked back a laugh. "You're unbelievable. I'm watching a man holding a lethal weapon who—" I broke off, sensing I was under observation, and glanced to my side. Sure enough, Hannah, Caoimhe, and Melanie stared back at me with matching expressions of fascination. "Never mind," I said to Lenny. "Just get me backup, please."

When I disconnected, Melanie said, "Should I get the girls out of here?"

"I don't want to cause any unnecessary panic," I replied, keeping my voice low. "By the time the police get here, the display will be over."

And Fergal Castle-Conroy would no longer be in possession of a firearm.

"I know that look," Melanie insisted. "You know who killed the man on the boat. That's why you want backup."

"Aw, Mum," Caoimhe protested. "You can't make us go now. Things are just starting to get interesting."

"Yeah," Hannah agreed. "We don't want to miss out on the fun."

"I'm taking you home this instant." Melanie took a firm grip on each girl and marched them out of the training yard, ignoring their accusations of ill usage.

After they'd left, I noticed that Jennifer had tried to call me while I'd been speaking to Lenny. I hit her number and checked on the progress of the display. Fergal was still within my line of vision. "Hey, Jennifer," I said when she answered. "What's up?"

"Sergeant O'Shea and Sile Conlan are on their way to the fort. When I pressed her, Clodagh crumbled. She claims she killed her husband in self-defense and Tom and his friends buried the body."

"The friends being Jason and Fergal Castle-Conroy?"

"Exactly. And here's the kicker: the whole thing went down at Richard's thirty-ninth birthday party.

Do you think that ties in with the thirty-nine cupcakes?"

I frowned. "Yes, but wouldn't it have made more sense if Jason bought the cupcakes to freak out Tom and Clodagh? Why would his killer buy them?"

"That's just it," Jennifer said. "I think Jason did buy the cupcakes with the intention of upsetting Clodagh and Tom. Apparently, they'd intended to go out to Dolphin Island that day for a picnic. I suspect Jason intended to show up with the box, or drop off the box to scare them."

"But what about the limp Denise noticed?" I demanded. "They can't all have leg issues."

"According to Alan, Richard tripped over a shovel at the excavation site on Thursday and sprained his ankle. My guess is that that's why he was favoring one leg over the other."

"Did Tom and Clodagh ever confront Jason about him stealing Richard's identity?" I asked.

"Yes," the lawyer said, "but he just laughed in their faces and said they had more to lose than him if his ruse was exposed."

"And then he tried to blackmail them," I guessed.

"Correct. Clodagh and Tom suspect he did the same to Fergal."

"Thus giving Fergal a motive to kill him."

"Yeah. Garda Conlan was quick to accept this version of events, but Sergeant O'Shea was not thrilled to find his detective work turned on its head."

I laughed. "I'll deal with him when he gets here."

"Well, your aunt's brownies might help," Jennifer said. "I hope you don't mind, but I found them in your glove compartment and took them into the station to have as a snack."

"Brownies?" I squeaked. "Please say you didn't eat them."

"Unfortunately, no." The lawyer sounded irritated. "O'Shea scoffed the lot while I was telling him what Clodagh and Tom had said."

"The lot? You mean he ate them *all*?" I recalled the sandwich bag. There had to have been at least six brownies in it.

"Yeah." Jennifer sighed. "I needed a sugar shock to help me through the day after the Nick news. I hope O'Shea gets indigestion."

If the older policeman had eaten six hash brownies, he'd have a more dramatic reaction than mere indigestion. A bubble of laughter surged through me and I struggled to keep my cool. "Uh, okay. I guess I'll see him and Garda Conlan when they get here."

"Don't do anything foolish, Maggie," Jennifer said. "Wait for the police."

"Unless I need to, I won't move a muscle until they arrive."

I disconnected and slipped the phone into my purse. The weapons display came to an end, and the participants bowed to the audience. One by one, they filed out of the yard and through a door to my left. My hand was in my purse in an instant, searching for the floor plan in the visitors' brochure Jennifer and I had received when I'd bought our tickets. According to the map, the door led to the soldiers' sleeping quarters and was now used as the museum's offices.

I darted through the crowd at speed, retracing my steps back to the main entrance of the building. Although I had no intention of confronting Fergal on my own, I didn't want to risk him slipping away. I didn't know why I felt so strongly about keeping the man under surveillance. It wasn't as if he was aware the police were on their way to question him over his brother's murder. All the same, I couldn't not keep an eye on him, especially in a place filled with people and potentially lethal weapons.

Following the map, I snuck through a door marked "Staff Only" and into a dark, stone passageway. Male laughter floated out from a room at the end of the corridor. The reenactors, I guessed. I sidled along the wall and maneuvered myself into an alcove just beyond the slightly ajar wooden door. I'd barely had time to catch my breath when a voice sounded in my ear.

"Hello, Maggie. I thought you'd show up." The cold steel of a gun pressed against my back.

26

"Bethany," I whispered, the final pieces of the puzzle falling into place.

She pressed the gun harder into my back. "Don't even think about screaming. I'll shoot you before anyone has a chance to reach you."

Sweat beaded on my forehead. "Can't we talk about this? If you let me go, I'll try to help you."

"I don't want your help. Why did you have to interfere?" the girl snarled, keeping her voice low. "Everything would have been fine if you hadn't meddled. When I saw you at the shooting display today, I knew you were here to cause trouble."

"I'm not here to cause trouble." I needed to keep her talking and buy myself time until Sile Conlan showed up. "I found Jason's body. Of course I wanted to know who he was and why someone murdered him."

"I like you, Maggie. I hate having to kill someone

I like." The girl's voice held a high-pitched quality that verged on hysteria. In spite of her words, I had the sense she was putting on an act and trying to scare me. I still had a chance of getting through to her.

"Then don't kill me," I said. "Did Jason try to hurt you? Is that why you knifed him?"

"He was threatening to destroy my life all over again." She jammed the gun into me, making me wince. "I wasn't prepared to let him hurt me and my parents."

"Jason was your biological father," I said softly. "Didn't that mean anything to you?"

Her laugh was laced with bitterness. "It meant about as much to me as it did to him. After my mother died, he dumped me with my aunt and uncle while he swanned off on his archaeological digs. And after he got out of prison, he disappeared without a trace. No birthday cards, no Christmas presents, no interest in how I was. I couldn't let him destroy my life again."

"I can understand your anger," I began, but she cut me off.

"How can you? Did your parents abandon you?"

"No," I admitted, "but—"

"But nothing. You have no idea what it's like to mean so little to your own father that he'd just waltz out of your life and never look back."

"You must have been furious when you found out he was back on Whisper Island."

"Furious?" Her laugh rang hollow. "Fool that I

was, I actually thought he'd get in touch with me. But as the weeks went by and he showed no signs of caring whether I was alive or dead, I gave up hope."

"Did your dad—Fergal, I mean—keep you up to date?"

Bethany snorted. "Oh, no. He wanted to protect me from the whole situation. Dad was livid when Ben showed up on the excavation."

A memory from our conversation at the hair salon danced through my mind. "Ben is your boyfriend," I said. "The one with the rich father who got him a summer job on Whisper Island."

"Yes. We've known each other for years, but we didn't click until I got a job working in Egypt last summer."

The pressure on my back had waned. Whatever had occurred on the yacht with Jason, I didn't think Bethany was a natural killer. However, I'd had enough experience with murderers in the past to know that desperate people take desperate actions, and someone who's killed finds it easier to kill the second time. A rivulet of sweat ran down my back. Through the door, I heard sounds of the reenactors getting ready to leave. I just needed to keep her talking for a while longer. "I can help you, Bethany, but you have to trust me. Put away the gun and let's talk."

She jammed the weapon into my back with force. "Shut up. They're coming out. Keep your mouth shut or I'll shoot you."

One by one, the men filed out of the room, now

dressed in street clothes. The last one to leave was Fergal Castle-Conroy, still clutching his musket. Instead of following the others, he hovered in the doorway until the last of his fellow "soldiers" had disappeared from sight.

"We're over here," Bethany said, bursting my bubble of hope that Fergal might rescue me.

The man whirled around and stared into the dark alcove. Bethany pushed me forward, the weapon still pressed against my back. An expression of ill-disguised fury convulsed Fergal's face. He grabbed my arm and hauled me into the makeshift changing room that was actually an office. I immediately scanned the room for a phone, or an alarm of some kind, but came up empty.

"Sit," he snarled, and shoved me onto a chair.

I slid a look at Bethany and shuddered at the sight of the Glock in her right hand. I'd hoped I was dealing with a less-reliable historical weapon.

Fergal pulled my purse out of my grasp and rifled through it until he'd located my phone. My stomach sank as he smashed the phone against the oak desk, rendering it useless.

"What are we going to do with her, Dad?" Bethany asked. "We can't keep her here for long. Everyone will come back after lunch."

Fergal's jaw tightened. "We'll sneak her out the back entrance and bring her to the farm."

Somehow, I didn't think my trip to the Conroy farm would include a friendly cup of tea and a tour of the premises. I recalled the squeals of pigs I'd heard on the night of the stakeout and shivered.

Out in the corridor, a door squeaked. Bethany jumped, and her grip on the gun wobbled. Fergal's eyes darted to the side. "Can you handle her for a sec? I want to check if anyone's out there."

Bethany's grip on the pistol tightened. "I've got this, Dad."

Fergal slipped out the door, leaving me alone with his daughter. I took a deep breath and assessed my situation. In spite of the gun in her hand and her threatening words, Bethany was no pro. If I could distract her long enough to close the space between us, I could take her down.

I fixed my attention on a spot next to a bookcase, took a long breath, and let out a high-pitched scream. "Look," I wailed, pointing at the wall. "There's a mouse."

"What?" Bethany shrieked and shifted her attention to my imaginary mouse.

I wasted no time. The instant she took her eyes off me, I leaped out of my chair and whacked her right arm. She yowled in pain and dropped the gun. I kicked it out of her reach and punched her in the face.

Bethany's eyes rolled back in her head and she collapsed onto the floor. I grabbed the letter opener I'd spotted on the desk earlier and hacked a piece of fabric from the curtains. I shredded it and used the material to bind Bethany's hands and feet. From the passageway, I heard the sound of running feet. Fergal was on his way back.

He burst into the room, musket at the ready. I grabbed the Glock from the floor and aimed it at his heart. "Drop your weapon."

"I don't think so." He glared at me when he registered Bethany tied up on the floor.

"Come on, Fergal. We both know the Glock I'm holding is more reliable than that old musket."

To my surprise, he smirked, sending a chill down the nape of my neck. "It would be if the Glosh were loaded."

My stomach lurched. I shifted the Glock to the left, aimed at the wall, and pulled the trigger. Nothing happened. I swallowed past the lump in my throat and looked at Fergal.

He laughed. "Not so clever now, are you, Ms. Private Investigator? A Glock with no ammo won't get you far."

"No," said a voice from the hallway, "but this will."

The door swung open to reveal Hannah and Caoimhe, each brandishing a Brown Bess. The full horror of having the girls near a homicidal maniac hit me like a ton of bricks, but the sight of the weapon soaring through the air distracted me from fully processing my fears.

"Catch, Maggie," Caoimhe yelled.

I leaped for the musket, catching it in one hand and swinging it into place. I aimed it at Fergal.

His shock at being ambushed by two kids was wearing off. "You can't be serious. It's not loaded. We always make sure the weapons are empty and cleaned after a display."

"Yours is loaded," I pointed out. "Why shouldn't this one be?"

My words held more bravado than I felt. To my amateur eye, the firearm looked ready to shoot, but Fergal was the expert.

"I watched the guys clean their muskets before they left. It's empty. Mine is the only one ready for firing." He gestured for the girls to come into the room. "I don't want to hurt you, kids. Get in here, sit down, and you'll be okay."

I didn't believe this for one second, and judging by Hannah and Caoimhe's expressions, they weren't falling for Fergal's story. Hannah hoisted her weapon higher on her shoulder. "No way. If you don't drop your gun, I'll shoot you."

Fergal's laugh grated on my nerves. "Come on, kid, it's not loaded."

He took a step toward Hannah and I pulled the trigger. There was a loud bang and the force of the recoil jerked me backward. Fergal yowled with pain and collapsed onto the floor. I staggered but kept my balance, coughing through the cloud of gunpowder smoke.

The girls darted away from Fergal, but not before Hannah kicked his weapon out of reach. Smart kid. I dropped my Brown Bess and made a grab for Fergal's weapon. Muskets were only good for one shot before they required reloading, and I had no idea where to find gunpowder and the other accouterments required to prepare a flintlock musket for firing. If I needed to shoot Fergal again, I had to grab hold of his weapon.

My opponent was quicker than I'd anticipated. He threw himself on top of the musket, and hauled himself to his feet, clinging to the weapon and aiming it weapon at me. "Stay back or I'll shoot."

The loud clang of the fire alarm made us all jump. The people in the visitor's center must have heard the gunshot and decided to evacuate the building.

Fergal looked around the room in panic. Bethany was still unconscious, and we blocked his way to get to her. With a roar of fury, Fergal turned and galloped out the door.

I followed him at a sprint. I'd have caught him with ease had the rat not decided to knock over a filing cabinet in the corridor and block my way. "Do either of you have a phone?" I yelled as I clambered over the wreckage of the filing cabinet.

"I do." Hannah pulled one from her jeans pocket.

"Call your dad. Tell him Fergal is armed and dangerous."

"He has two bad legs," Caoimhe said sagely. "He won't get far."

"Maybe not, but he might shoot someone before he's caught. Speaking of firearms, what are you two doing here? Where did you find those weapons, and why in the heck was the one you threw me primed for firing?"

The girls shifted uneasily. "We didn't want to miss the excitement," Caoimhe said.

"So we snuck after you," Hannah continued. "When we saw Bethany shove you into the office with a gun to your back, we grabbed two of the guns that we'd seen the reenactors put it another room."

"And we figured out how to work a Brown Bess from YouTube," Caoimhe added. "The reenactors had all the stuff laid out in their prep room."

"YouTube," I said dryly. "Of course."

I'd be having a word with David Bryant about firearm safety before and after his monthly displays.

Caoimhe, Hannah, and I climbed over the filing cabinet and raced for the door. Out in the visitors' center, we were greeted with a scene of utter pandemonium. People screamed and parents shielded their children with their bodies. Fergal waved his weapon about, threatening everyone, and trailing blood from his leg wound. When a security guard attempted to tackle him, Fergal shot the guy in the arm and took off at a pace I hadn't expected him to be capable of with his injury.

He sped into the training yard, and I followed. Now that he'd fired his shot, he'd need to stop and reload the weapon with a cartridge containing a lead ball and gunpowder before he could fire another. I didn't intend to give him that chance.

I'd considered the scene in the visitors' center mayhem, but nothing could have prepared me for the shenanigans at play in the training yard. Even Fergal paused his mad dash to gawp. Sergeant O'Shea stood at the center of the yard performing a mad dance that appeared to be a mix between a jig and the cancan.

"The brownies," I said aloud and groaned.

"Ms. Doyle," he shouted when he saw me. "Come over here and dance with me."

"Thanks, but I'll pass." I jerked a thumb at Fergal. "I have a crazed lunatic to catch."

Sergeant O'Shea appeared unfazed by my rejection, or the reason behind it. "Ah, well. Another time."

He went back to his frenzied hijinks, kicking his legs up high and singing an old Irish tune off key.

"Wow," Hannah said from behind me. "Is he high?"

"He's trying to Irish dance," Caoimhe said. "Impressive. He's even worse than I am."

"Go back inside," I yelled at them. "And find Melanie."

Fergal regained his composure at around the same time I did, and took off in the direction of a gate on the other side of the yard. I sprinted after him—no easy feat on cobblestones. To my horror, Sergeant O'Shea decided to join in, running faster than I suspected was healthy for a man of his shape and level of physical fitness. His run soon turned into a jig and he paused to strip off his uniform shirt, eliciting a chorus of horrified squeals from the girls. Where was Sile Conlan? Or Reynolds? Even Lenny would be more help in apprehending a dangerous criminal than this fool.

Meanwhile, Fergal had reached the wooden gate. He yanked it open and ran outside. I picked up the pace and took off after him. The gate opened onto the crowded parking lot. I scanned my surroundings, but the only sign of Fergal was a trail of blood. *Aw, heck.*

And then I spied him between two rows of cars. With a burst of adrenaline, I sprang after him, running hard, and ignoring the horrified stares of the people around me. I'd almost caught up with my quarry when Sergeant O'Shea bounced into sight. He jigged over to me, now down to his socks, utility belt, and underpants—tighty-whities, no less. Good to know my gag reflex was in full working order.

"Oh, gross," said the girls in unison. Clearly, they'd ignored my instructions to go inside and find Melanie.

"Eew," Hannah said, sounding horrified. "Are those skid marks?"

"Probably," I said without mercy. "Just be glad he's still wearing underpants."

While Fergal and I played chase between the cars, the police officer danced and sang and jumped up and down from behind a car like a jack-in-the-box. Man, I needed a pay raise after these shenanigans. My current P.I. rate wasn't sufficient compensation for the sight of a nearly naked Sergeant O'Shea.

"Get behind a car," I shouted at the girls. "And stay down."

To my relief, they obeyed, but Sergeant O'Shea chose this moment to leapfrog over a car and tackle Fergal. Instead of apprehending the man, the police officer squealed in delight and pinched Fergal's cheeks. "Will I arrest him?"

"That might be a smart move," I said, trying not to laugh.

"Okay," he said cheerfully, and proceeded to handcuff himself. He stared at his bound wrists with apparent fascination. "These things are great."

Fantastic. I was attempting to take down a mad guy with a musket ball in his leg accompanied by a stoned police officer. Reynolds would bust a gut laughing over my latest predicament.

"Come on, Fergal. Give yourself up."

He glared at me and lurched forward, shoving Sergeant O'Shea into my path.

"Ooh," said the older man. "Will you give me a kiss?"

"Not even if the survival of the human race depended on it."

I sprang after Fergal, and I'd almost reached him when Lenny's purple van pulled into the parking lot. Fergal, who was checking to see how far behind him I was, stepped in front of the van just as Lenny was turning. The van sideswiped Fergal, and the impact sent him flying onto the hood of a nearby car, moaning and swearing in equal measure.

Lenny, oblivious to the chaos he'd caused, parked and climbed out of the van with a cheerful smile on his face. "Yo, Maggie. Did I miss anything?"

27

"So Fergal and Bethany followed Jason's yacht and confronted him." I took another sip of my Gin Basil Smash. "Did I get that right?"

It was the day after Fergal and Bethany's arrests and I was in Reynolds's backyard to eat the leftovers from the barbecue and get an unabridged update on everything that had happened after Fergal and Bethany's arrests.

"Yeah." Reynolds refilled Hannah's lemonade glass and handed it to her. "Fergal intended to make sure Jason left them in peace, but I don't think murder was on his mind. We haven't established what, exactly, was said, but it looks like Bethany lost her temper and grabbed a knife from the kitchen."

"And provided Jason with the fatal stab wound he was sporting when we found him."

"Exactly."

"What about the femur that Sergeant O'Shea

discovered in Alan Doherty's room?" I asked. "Who put it there."

"Ben Dunne. He'd stolen it on the day Tommy found the skeleton, having been forewarned to do so by Fergal. When Jason, a.k.a. Richard, wound up dead, Ben panicked and wanted to go to the police."

"Let me guess," Hannah said. "Bethany persuaded him not to."

Her father inclined his head. "Yeah. She convinced him that Tom and Clodagh were guilty of both murders and would try to incriminate Fergal. They'd already guessed that Alan was Clodagh's son, and his room at the bed and breakfast was more easily accessible than breaking into Tom and Clodagh's house. Ben was foolish enough to let Bethany manipulate him into committing theft and intimidation, but I don't believe he was involved in the murder."

"Did Jason steal the money from the research institute, or was he framed?" I asked.

"Hard to say," Reynolds said. "It could have gone either way. Neither of the Castle-Conroy brothers was the trustworthy type. If Jason was framed, it gave him a strong motive for wanting to hurt his brother, but it doesn't explain why he threatened Clodagh and Tom."

"It took some guts to come back to Whisper Island and hope no one apart from Fergal and the Burkes recognized him," I said. "Even Dolly O'Brien didn't make the connection and she dated him for a while."

"Don't forget that Jason Castle-Conroy never spent much time on the island. He went to boarding school in Dublin, and then studied abroad. Apart from the excavation in 2000 and the one this summer, he hasn't been on Whisper Island as an adult."

"That's true. And people often see what they expect to see." I raised my glass. "Well done to all of us. With Clodagh and Tom admitting they killed Richard, and Bethany and Fergal in custody, we've wrapped up both murder investigations."

"So we've wrapped up two murder investigations in how many days?" Hannah asked. "I'm just checking so that I can get my story straight for my school friends."

I looked at Hannah and smiled. "Nine, including today."

The girl nodded with satisfaction. "Not bad for my first time as a detective. Caoimhe's thrilled by our progress."

I snorted with laughter. Reynolds rolled his eyes. "Don't let the amateur detective work become a habit," he warned. "I'm still recovering from the shock of finding out you two handled gunpowder."

"But you must admit their YouTube trick was genius," I said. "Hannah and Caoimhe make a good team."

Reynolds groaned. "Don't encourage them, please. I found a gray hair this morning. I'm convinced it's after yesterday."

"Don't worry, Dad. I'll leave out the gunpowder

part when I tell everyone what happened. Sergeant O'Shea's skid marks will be enough to amuse them."

"How is he this morning?" I asked once the laughter had subsided. "Still stoned?"

Reynolds grinned. "He's determined to pretend he has no memory of yesterday. Sile says he proposed to her in the squad car on the way to the station, and then passed out in one of the interview rooms. She left him to sleep it off and took care of all the interviews and paperwork herself."

"That girl will go far."

"At the rate you find dead bodies, we need good police officers on this island," he said wryly.

"No more corpses. I want my next case to be a boring petty theft."

Reynolds threw back his head and laughed. "No way. You're a magnet for drama."

"Maybe Maggie will find a dead body at her Irish class," Hannah said with a gleeful expression.

"Oh, no. My cousin would kill me if I disrupted her lessons. Besides, I need a break from murder and mayhem."

"It's so exciting being around you," Hannah said over the rim of her lemonade glass. "I'm glad Mum let me stay."

Reynolds and I exchanged a loaded look. We hadn't had the chance to talk at length since yesterday's events, but I'd gathered that Robyn had taken a room at the Whisper Island Hotel for a few days, ostensibly to assure herself that Whisper Island was a safe environment for her daughter to spend her summer vacation. Meanwhile, Hannah was back with her dad. Since her heroics yesterday, a new understanding had developed between us, and I hoped this heralded the start of a less rocky relationship with the kid.

Hannah shifted her gaze from me to her father, and back again. With a smirk, she stood, still holding her lemonade. "I'm going to read for a while. Leave you two lovebirds to do the smoochy thing in peace."

I laughed but my cheeks grew warm under Reynolds's steady gaze. "I got mail," I said. "Of the official kind." I drew my official divorce decree out of its envelope and showed it to him.

He regarded me with hooded eyes. "How do you feel about it?"

"Relieved," I said bluntly. "I'm free of Joe for good, and I have enough money in my bank account to pay for Lenny's training. I want to make him my official assistant at Movie Reel Investigations."

Reynolds raised his glass to me. "Congratulations."

"Thank you." We clinked glasses but didn't move away from one another. I stared into his deep blue eyes. We were close enough for me to smell his aftershave and the subtle scent of basil on his warm breath.

"Your birthday is coming up," Reynolds said. "The big 3-0."

"I've been trying not to think about it."

"I have a present for you, but I kind of have to tell you about it in advance." He took a deep breath. "If I kept it a surprise…well, you might feel uncomfortable about it."

I leaned forward, making us nose to nose. "I'm intrigued."

"How would you feel about a weekend away with me once Hannah goes back to school? Just the two of us." He pulled an envelope out of his pocket. "I have reservations for Dromoland Castle."

My heart skipped a beat. Dromoland Castle was one of Ireland's premier five-star hotels. "I'd love that, Liam."

The tension in his shoulders eased visibly. "So it's not an unwelcome gift?"

"On the contrary. I'd love to spend the weekend with you." I brushed my lips over his jaw.

He took my hands in his and kissed them. "Just promise me one thing, Maggie."

I raised an eyebrow. "Yes?"

"No dead bodies in the hotel pool."

I sat back in my seat and laughed. "I'll try my best."

THE END

A NOTE FROM ZARA

• Thanks for reading **The 39 Cupcakes**. I hope you enjoyed Maggie's fourth adventure on Whisper Island! If you liked the sound of the Gin Basil Smash cocktails Maggie made in the story, turn the page for the recipe!

• Maggie and her friends will be back this holiday season for some fatal festivities in **Rebel Without a Claus.** In the meantime, I'm publishing a mailing list exclusive serial called **To Hatch a Thief**, featuring an adventure that occurs between **Dial P For Poison** and **The Postman Always Dies Twice**. Sign up for my mailing list to access the episodes.

Happy Reading!
Zara xx

Join my mailing list and get news, giveaways, and a FREE Movie Club Mystery serial! Join Maggie and her friends as they solve the mystery in *To Hatch a Thief*. http://zarakeane.com/newsletter2

•I also have **an active reader group**, **The Ballybeg Belles**, where I chat, share snippets of upcoming stories, and host members only giveaways. I hope to join you for a virtual pint very soon!

Would you like to try Maggie's recipe for the Gin Basil Smash cocktails that she served in ***The 39 Cupcakes***? Here's the recipe!

GIN BASIL SMASH

- 2 oz (60ml) gin
- ¾ oz (20ml) freshly-squeezed lime juice
- ¾ oz. sugar syrup
- a bunch of fresh basil

1. Put the basil, lime juice, and sugar syrup in a cocktail shaker.
2. Muddle the basil in the shaker (i.e.: press with a muddle stick or a pestle) and shake vigorously.
3. Double strain into a cocktail glass filled with ice cubes.

Maggie's tip: Many recipes for this cocktail suggest the use of Hendrick's Gin, but Maggie's personal favorite is Generous Gin.

Bodyguard by Day, Ex-Husband by Night

The Navy SEAL's Accidental Wife

DUBLIN MAFIA—Romantic Suspense

Final Target

Kiss Shot

Bullet Point (2018)

ABOUT ZARA KEANE

USA Today bestselling author Zara Keane grew up in Dublin, Ireland, but spent her summers in a small town very similar to the fictitious Whisper Island and Ballybeg.

She currently lives in Switzerland with her family. When she's not writing or wrestling small people, she drinks far too much coffee, and tries—with occasional success—to resist the siren call of Swiss chocolate.

Zara has an active reader group, **The Ballybeg Belles**, where she chats, shares snippets of upcoming stories, and hosts members-only giveaways. She hopes to join you for a virtual pint very soon!

zarakeane.com

THE 39 CUPCAKES

EBOOK ISBN: 978-3-906245-53-9

PRINT ISBN: 978-3-906245-54-6

59549109R00208

Made in the USA
Middletown, DE
21 December 2017